Appalachian Intrigue

Appalachian Intrigue

ARCHIE MEYERS

iUniverse, Inc.
Bloomington

Appalachian Intrigue

iUniverse books may be ordered through booksellers or by contacting:

iUniverse
1663 Liberty Drive
Bloomington, IN 47403
www.iuniverse.com
1-800-Authors (1-800-288-4677)

Because of the dynamic nature of the Internet, any web addresses or links contained in this book may have changed since publication and may no longer be valid. The views expressed in this work are solely those of the author and do not necessarily reflect the views of the publisher, and the publisher hereby disclaims any responsibility for them.

Any people depicted in stock imagery provided by Thinkstock are models, and such images are being used for illustrative purposes only.
Certain stock imagery © Thinkstock.

ISBN: 978-1-4759-3573-8 (sc)
ISBN: 978-1-4759-3575-2 (hc)
ISBN: 978-1-4759-3574-5 (ebk)

Library of Congress Control Number: 2012912198

Printed in the United States of America

iUniverse rev. date: 07/23/2012

To those who love the magnificent mountains of southeast Tennessee

Prologue

A gunshot shattered the early evening calm, and a body tumbled awkwardly onto the grimy sidewalk. The intermingled echoes of the muzzle blast and bloodcurdling scream were still ping-ponging between the buildings as the shooter's car quickly careened around a corner and disappeared.

The ambush in River City, Tennessee, was the continuation of a series of violent acts that had taken place in recent months in the picturesque community snuggled between the mountains and the river. Everyone living there was familiar with the stories of nefarious characters who supposedly roam the surrounding mountains at night. It is often difficult to separate fact from myth; even if the stories are more myth than fact, they are frightening enough to keep rational adults away after dark. The only ones not deterred by the stories are the city's hormone-driven teenagers. The mountain's long-abandoned logging roads are the first stop for each successive generation of teenage lovers with newly minted driver's licenses.

One of the paradoxical things about nature is that what is beautiful one day may be lethal the next. A serene tropical island can become a hurricane-ravaged coast. A spectacular snow-capped peak can suddenly erupt and bury a village in molten lava. And in the breathtakingly beautiful southern Appalachians, nightfall can create perfect cover for a deadly assault.

However, even those who fear the mountains at night celebrate their beauty when dawn lifts the menacing veil and erases the shadows. Every morning, throngs of visitors pour into the city to enjoy the splendor of the heavily wooded mountains, florally resplendent valley, and wide, navigable river. When nature merges so much beauty into a single panoramic landscape, it is a magnet for tourists, and River City is nature's beneficiary.

The city enjoys a thriving tourist industry across three of the four seasons of the year; not many show up in winter. They start flooding the city in early spring when flowers emerge in the valley and mountain laurel and rhododendron first bloom on the mountain. They continue coming in summer to enjoy hiking in the mountains and boating on the river. While each season is characterized by its own beauty and uniqueness, the absolute pinnacle of River City's tourist season occurs in the fall. It is the time when the mountain's multicolored foliage briefly flaunts its autumn brilliance just before surrendering to the drab, lifeless color of winter.

Dex and Marie had recently become the most recognizable couple in River City. It wasn't a distinction they had coveted; they would prefer to have it bestowed on others. It had come with too high a price in agony and heartbreak. But tonight, they were putting all of that behind them and taking a risk by going to dinner at a downtown restaurant.

It would be the first time they had ventured out in public together since her recent release from the hospital following a brutal assault. Her assailant still had not been apprehended, and the police had warned them about the possibility of a subsequent attack. But their desperate need to be together trumped the warning and their fear.

Although the first frost foretelling the coming of winter to the southern Appalachians was still several weeks away, there was a noticeable nip in the air. It was a beautiful fall afternoon during the peak of the tourist season. When Dex and Marie arrived at the restaurant, the day-trip tourists were clogging the streets and had taken every nearby parking space. Dex and Marie choose to forego the restaurant's valet service, and the first parking space they found was on a back street several blocks away. Dex squeezed into the space, and they walked back to the restaurant.

As twilight blanketed the valley, they were enjoying a leisurely alfresco dinner on the restaurant's deck suspended above the river. They were oblivious of other diners as they enjoyed the flounder à la Parisienne, a house specialty.

After finishing their meal they continued to linger over an excellent California chardonnay as they held hands and watched the sun slip behind the mountain. The glorious sunset, the bouquet and flavor of the wine, and the soft music playing in the background created a romantic ambiance on an evening where merely being together was the only catalyst needed for their romance.

The lights that flickered on at dusk sent ever-changing patterns dancing over the river's surface. Across the river, a mountain soared like the vertical façade of a Manhattan skyscraper. High above the glow of valley lights, the newly risen harvest moon painted ominous shadows across its face.

When they left the restaurant, most of the day-trip tourists had already left the valley. The few who were staying overnight were either still dining at the local restaurants or already closeted inside their hotels. As Dex and Marie walked toward their car, the moon provided the only illumination of the almost deserted streets.

During the busy tourist season, evening is always a welcome respite from the daytime turmoil. The retail establishments begin closing as soon as the crowds start to drift away, and serenity actually reigns for a few hours before the torrent of tourists begins anew at first light. The back street where Dex and Marie had left their car had been parked bumper to bumper when they arrived, but very few other cars remained when they returned.

Words are often superfluous between lovers, and Dex and Marie were silent as they enjoyed the crisp Tennessee evening while slowly strolling hand-in-hand toward their car. Dex was preoccupied with a romantic reverie in which passion had been too long deferred, but his daydreams were quickly extinguished when without any warning a man leaned out of the window of a parked car, pointed a pistol in their direction, and pulled the trigger.

Chapter 1

The ambush in downtown River City was just the latest in a series of tragedies that had besieged Dex. The first time he ever thought of his own mortality was the day he became a target. He was eighteen years old and a couple of months shy of high-school graduation. Dex and his friend Hoagie had been on the mountain spying on a moonshine operation when they were surprised by a sniper who was providing security for the operation.

Despite the tragedy of losing both parents at an early age, Dex had in many ways lived a charmed life as a handsome, affable teenager with superb athletic skills. He grew up in the foothills of the mountains surrounding River City, and together with his two closest friends, Marie and Hoagie, he had been exploring the mountains since early childhood.

None of their classmates could understand the relationship between Dexter "Dex" Martin, the handsome, charismatic quarterback of the football team, and the shy, studious Tom "Hoagie" Hogan. They were polar opposites in looks, personality, and about every other way, but they had been best friends since the fourth grade.

Dex was six foot four with broad shoulders and a narrow waist, and he moved with the supple grace of a natural athlete. His close-cropped blond hair, perpetually bronzed skin, and mischievous smile made his lifeguard stand at the country club pool a natural gathering place for the club members' teenage daughters.

His friend Hoagie was short, pudgy, and anything but agile. His face was liberally sprinkled with freckles, and even his unruly tangle of red hair couldn't conceal ears that protruded like the open doors of a New York taxi. He studied a lot, played the tuba in the high-school marching band, and was somewhat introverted. The few dates he had were arranged by girls who wanted to go out with Dex so much that they would talk a friend into a double date with Hoagie.

When he wasn't with Dex, Hoagie spent his time in the band room or the school library. He had no desire to waste time with the clueless, would-be jocks who hung around Dex. Most people thought of Hoagie as a nerd, and he would have no doubt been an easy mark for the school bullies; however, his friendship with Dex kept him in protective custody. No one dared mess with Hoagie.

Ever since the boys' elementary school days, the wooded slopes, streams, and cliffs of the mountains had been the friends' backyard playground. Until she moved away, Marie was usually with them on their regular trips to the mountain. They scaled the rock cliffs, swung from trees on ropelike vines, and when Marie wasn't along, they hiked to Mystic Lake to swim nude in the pool below the waterfall. And although they would have been grounded for life if they had ever been caught, they also surreptitiously explored several of the mountain's numerous uncharted caves.

When they were younger, the three friends played cowboys and Indians in the foothills, but as they grew older, the mountain became the venue of far more interesting activities. At the annual Baptist church outing on the mountain, thirteen-year-old Dex stole his first kiss from perky Bunny Fountain. At least, he thought it was stolen. He didn't know that Bunny, with the encouragement of her girlfriends, had carefully orchestrated his initiation to romance.

Over the years, several neighborhood kids were abandoned on the mountain in one of Dex and Hoagie's elaborately planned hunts for the nonexistent snipe, a bird that has never been seen in the mountains of Tennessee. The victims didn't realize it was a hoax until they found themselves stranded and had to stumble down the mountain alone after dark. And in what clearly delineated a rite of passage, three days after getting his driver's license, Dex and Laura Dean Adams steamed up the windows of his grandmother's Chevrolet while parked on one of the mountain's abandoned logging roads.

Although they knew the mountain's fabled history, Dex and Hoagie staked out each trail and cliff as if they were the first to discover them. The entire mountain range had been violently disgorged from the earth's core by a great prehistoric earthquake, and over the years nomadic tribes, European-born settlers on their western migration, and Cherokees trudging along on the Trail of Tears had all passed through the mountains. But the mountains that towered over River City were perhaps best known for having been a blood-soaked battleground in a war where brother fought brother to determine the fate of a still-struggling nation. Throughout recorded history, the foothills of the southern Appalachians had at various times been the setting for stunning victories, devastating losses, great joys, and mournful sorrows.

If he had been asked, Dex couldn't have explained why he and Hoagie continued their Saturday morning expeditions. It was just that the mountains were there, and they always climbed them. They knew where the wild muscadine vines grew and when the high-ridge persimmons ripened from dreadfully bitter to saccharine sweetness. They could easily locate several raccoons' den trees and groves of hickory nut trees where the squirrels congregated to feed. They had discovered these things when they were in elementary school, and even now as high-school seniors they still returned to the mountains almost every weekend.

As Dex raced toward adulthood, the mountains surrounding River City were omnipresent in his life. They were where he went with friends for recreation, but they were also his sanctuary when he wanted to spend time alone.

Chapter 2

An unusually cold winter ended, the spring rains were behind them, and the days were getting longer and warmer as summertime gradually drew near. Dex and Hoagie started their climb up the mountain just after dawn, and by midmorning, they were standing on the escarpment overlooking their valley neighborhood.

In the past century, the valley had evolved from pastoral to mostly urban, but the mountains had changed very little. In the fall of 1863, Confederate soldiers stood on the escarpment near where Dex now stood and looked down at the garrison of Union forces that foretold the looming battle to control the high ground.

From his vantage point at the crest of the mountain, Dex looked down and saw a spiral of smoke lazily curling skyward through a canopy of hardwoods. The smoke was a sure indication that the area's ubiquitous mountain men had fired up another still and were cooking a batch of what was variously known as white lightning, corn liquor, or moonshine.

Most people were sensible enough to avoid the moonshine operations; Dex and Hoagie not only didn't try to avoid them, but they actively sought them out. When they spotted the smoke on that particular morning, it was as if their adventure for the day had been preordained. They couldn't resist the temptation of getting up close and personal.

Dex said, "Okay, Hoagie, now we get some excitement."

Hoagie smiled. "And I thought this was just going to be another day in paradise."

Everything Dex knew about moonshine he had learned from overhearing adult conversations, since he had never tasted it or any other alcoholic drink. He had been told that the popularity of the sweet-smelling booze was related more to cost than taste, since it was distilled from cheap, readily available ingredients and was not encumbered by taxes or regulatory oversight. It was also far more potent than legal liquor, and that made it the mountain man's ideal answer for a cheap Saturday night drunk.

Dex had heard that helicopter surveillance had significantly reduced the production of moonshine in Tennessee, but he had stumbled across enough of the clandestine operations over the years to know that they had not completely disappeared. The process hadn't changed in a hundred years. It was still surreptitiously produced in crudely designed stills, and bootleggers still delivered it to the distribution points. The vehicles they used had been improved, but they still preferred older, nondescript cars equipped with oversized engines that allowed them to beat the deputy sheriffs in high speed chases to the county line.

Dex and Hoagie climbed down from the escarpment and traversed the face of the mountain until they were close enough to detect the sweet smell of the "recipe."

At that point, Dex grabbed Hoagie's arm and whispered, "Okay, Hoagie, no more talking. Stay behind me, and don't make any noise."

Hoagie nodded a response, and they resorted to hand signals as they slowly crept into position behind an outhouse-sized boulder. Peeking around it, they could clearly see the moonshine operation nestled under a canopy of century-old hardwoods. The trees most likely protected it from helicopter surveillance. A small spring bubbled up beside the still and supplied the water needed in the process. A mountain laurel thicket concealed the still from a nearby trail. From ground level, it was essentially undetectable, but when it was in operation, the smell of fermenting corn was a dead giveaway.

The boys saw sacks of cornmeal, sugar, and yeast stacked beside a cord of firewood and watched as the wood fire under the cooking pot heated the fermented corn mash. Heat created a gaseous vapor that was drawn into one end of a copper tube and intoxicating liquor dripped out the other end. The moonshine was hand-carried in gallon jugs from the still to the bootleggers' cars and would eventually be sold in one-quart fruit jars through the back doors of roadhouses.

Dex and Hoagie had seen this type of still in the past, but some were even cruder. Several years earlier, three deaths had been linked to poisoning from consumption of moonshine that was being distilled in an automobile radiator. That may have slowed down consumption, but it certainly had not stopped it.

The soft gurgling of the spring and the crackling of the fire were the only sounds as three overall-clad mountain men sat silently waiting for the jug under the tube to fill up. Dex and Hoagie's youthful boldness, together with a mistaken belief that they were obscured from view, allowed them to calmly observe the whiskey-making process. The three men at the still hadn't seen the teenagers crawling into place behind the boulder, but the fourth man—a lookout sitting thirty feet up in a large sweet gum tree—did see them. The mountain's early morning silence was shattered by the sharp crack of a rifle, and debris exploded from the rock the teenagers were using for cover. Their boldness quickly disappeared, and Dex yelled, "Run, Hoagie, run!"

Hoagie didn't need the encouragement. In a heartbeat they were in an athletic sprint, careening recklessly down the mountain. Hoagie, although not nearly as athletic as Dex, stayed surprisingly close on Dex's heels for the first few minutes, but when Dex looked back over his shoulder, he saw that Hoagie was starting to lag behind. He knew that if they stayed on the main trail, whoever was after them would probably catch Hoagie.

Dex yelled back, "Hoagie, get off the trail. Go straight down the mountain."

They both veered off the familiar, well-worn path and sought the concealment of thick underbrush. When Dex realized that the shooter was just scaring them away and had never been following them, he stopped to allow Hoagie to catch up. While he was waiting, Dex thought back several years to when there was always three of them involved in their mountain adventures. Marie Murphy had been the third member of the teenage trio, and even she could outrun Hoagie, but then Marie could also outrun most of the boys in the neighborhood.

Dex and Marie had been inseparable as they grew up next door to each other, but when they were freshmen in high school, she moved to Atlanta with her parents. Dex hadn't seen her since. He was glad Marie wasn't on the mountain with them that day.

Marie had been like a sister, although she looked and acted more like a brother. It wasn't that she was unattractive; it was just that her athletic ability, androgynous appearance, and complete disinterest in making herself look more feminine made him not think the same way about her as he did about other girls.

Marie could throw a baseball as well as any of the boys in the neighborhood and was a much better all-around athlete than Hoagie. Although he had always thought of her as just one of the boys, Dex knew that the tall, skinny tomboy with pigtails was, despite her boyish appearance, a girl, and he didn't think girls should have to dodge bullets. He smiled when he thought about how highly she would have resented him trying to protect her just because she was a girl.

A few months before Marie moved to Atlanta with her parents, Dex noticed that the pigtails disappeared and curves that hadn't been there before began to develop. He still didn't think of her as a girl, not a real girl anyway, but he did notice that some of the boys at school were beginning to pay a lot more attention to her.

Dex had a hard time believing it had been over three years since Marie last joined them on one of their mountain treks. Thinking about her while he was waiting on Hoagie to catch up was the first time she had crossed his mind in a while. He hadn't forgotten her; he had just moved on in his life and been totally consumed by high school and, particularly, athletics.

Dex had always been the de facto leader of the threesome, and even though none of the three would have had any idea what de facto meant, they depended on Dex, and he felt responsible for them when they were on the mountain. While he was waiting on Hoagie to catch up, he had time to replay the scene in his head. Since the shot had come from behind them and their backs were clearly exposed, he knew they would have been fairly easy targets if the shooter had really wanted to hit them.

He was smiling and casually leaning against a tall oak tree when Hoagie finally caught up and sprawled on the ground at his feet. Hoagie was breathing heavily, sweating profusely, and his voice was raspy from the exertion. The initial shock of the gunshot and the long scramble down the mountain had taken a toll on him.

"Dex, I don't know why you're smiling; there's nothing funny about almost getting killed. That wasn't a toy gun; the bullet ricocheted off the rock right beside my head."

Dex rolled his eyes. "Hoagie, those hillbillies could hit the eye of a squirrel at a hundred yards. If they'd really wanted to kill you, your fat butt would already be in a hole up there and they'd be shoveling dirt on top of you. They just don't want people snooping around when they're making moonshine."

Dex had no way of knowing then, but the next time he was exposed to gunfire it wouldn't be just to scare him.

The boys walked the rest of the way down the mountain since they no longer felt threatened. Just before reaching the valley, Dex suddenly stopped and said, "It was Snake."

Hoagie jumped and looked all around him, "Where's the snake?"

"No, dummy, there's no snake here. I'm talking about up on the mountain. Did you get a good look at the guy at the still wearing that shabby red baseball cap? It was Snake Wilson, I'm sure of it."

"I thought he was still locked up somewhere in a juvenile detention place. You couldn't have seen him."

"That was three years ago. We were freshmen when he was arrested and sent away for having a gun at school. He's obviously out now. I'm sure that was him sitting on that wood pile."

"Dex, everyone thought he brought the gun to shoot you. You'd just kicked his butt in that fight at the bus stop, but I still don't know what the fight was about."

"I didn't tell anyone but the principal why we were fighting, because I had promised not to tell. But that was a long time ago. If you swear to never repeat the story, I'll tell you what the fight was about."

"Dex, have I ever repeated something when you asked me not to say anything? I am not going to tell anyone. I'm just curious because I had never even seen you talk to him before you beat the crap out of him in front of half the student body."

"The day before the fight, he followed Marie home and attacked her at her house. She hit him in the head with an empty flower pot, and while he was dazed, she ran next door and told me. I went after him, but he was already gone when I got there, and I couldn't find him."

"So that's why you pounded him so bad he had to go to the hospital?"

"Marie was upset and embarrassed. She said she could never go to school again because he might attack her again, and she was afraid all her friends would find out about it. I told her I would make sure Snake never harmed her again and that no one would ever know what happened. I caught him in front of school the next day and unloaded on him. Unfortunately, a lot of our classmates were there waiting on the school bus and saw the fight. They all wanted to know why we were fighting, so I just said that he had done something I didn't like.

"I know that he swore to several people that he would get even with me. Several people told me he brought the pistol to school to shoot me, but after he was arrested, I never saw him again until a few minutes ago. If you remember, Marie moved to Atlanta a few weeks later. There wasn't any reason for people to know what started the fight."

Chapter 3

The day Dex became an orphan, his parents had left him with his grandmother while they went boating. They were filling the boat with gas at a marina dock when something ignited the fumes. The resulting explosion and fireball engulfed them and sank their boat, along with several others that were docked in close proximity.

Dex's only surviving relative was his father's widowed mother, Gwendolyn Martin, whom he knew as Gigi. She took the five-year-old child into her home and raised him as if he were her own. Gigi's husband had died a couple of years before Dex was born, and she was living on social security and a little income from in-home clothing alterations she made for neighbors. Fortunately Dex's father had a twenty-five-thousand-dollar life insurance policy with a double indemnity benefit for accidental death. The fifty thousand dollars was helpful, but it was still a financial struggle for Gigi.

When he was older, Dex helped financially by mowing the neighbor's lawns, delivering morning newspapers, and performing other odd jobs. The resolute determination, which was later so evident in athletics, was first noticed by the customers on his paper route. He ignored the cold, damp winter mornings, picked up the papers before daylight, and pedaled his bicycle up and down the neighborhood hills to make sure his customers received their papers before breakfast.

Dex was the best athlete in the neighborhood long before his size caught up to his ability. He and his friends played sandlot baseball during the hot summer afternoons, and in the fall they poured the sand out of the tow-sack bases and converted the vacant lot for football. After Christmas each year, they moved to a friend's backyard, where a makeshift basket was nailed to an old oak tree. The basket was originally placed low enough for the pint-sized players to reach it with the ball, but each year it was nailed a little higher on the tree.

When Dex was finally old enough to ride his bike to the neighborhood recreation center, he could still barely get the ball to the regulation height basket, but he spent countless hours practicing. At first he had to beg the older boys to let him join their game, but as he grew taller, he was one of the first ones chosen when pickup teams were selected.

Through hard work and innate athletic ability, Dex developed into a very good basketball player. However, by the time he reached high school, he had decided that football was his first love. He enjoyed the physical contact and even thrived on the preseason, two-a-day practices that most players dreaded.

Bob Delaney, the head coach, called him aside after the first couple of weeks of practice.

"Dex, I'm impressed with your ability and courage, but you're only fourteen and some of the seniors outweigh you by over fifty pounds. I don't want you to give up, but it's probably going to be next year before you get any playing time. We've got three upperclassmen fighting for the quarterback position, and you told me you were dead set on being a quarterback."

"Coach, don't give up on me. I'll try harder. I want to play."

Dex worked harder than he had ever worked in his life over the next few weeks, and a few days before the season opened, the coach talked to him after practice. "Dex, you've surprised me and all the other coaches. We've never had a freshman start a football game here, but you have earned the chance. You are going to start at quarterback Friday night."

Dex weighed only 145 pounds and was still a couple of inches shy of six feet, but he made up in desire and ability what he lacked in size. That night he impressed everyone with his courage. He stayed in the pocket until the last minute before releasing the ball, even when he knew he was going to get clobbered. In that first game he completed ten of fifteen passes, and one was a forty-five-yard bullet for the touchdown that won the game. He immediately became the most recognized member of his freshman class.

During his four years in high school, Dex grew six inches taller and gained over fifty pounds. He started attracting college scouts when he was just a sophomore. Meanwhile he and Hoagie remained best friends. Hoagie carried his tuba in the marching band as proudly as Dex carried a football.

They were both talented in their own way, but Hoagie couldn't throw a football and Dex was tone deaf; they shared friendship, not talent.

Dex's first steady job was as a lifeguard at the River City Country Club in the summer between his sophomore and junior years in high school. The members' daughters congregated around his lifeguard stand in their skimpy bikinis, but he secretly despised the snobbish prep school debutantes. He would have rather kissed Hoagie than date one of them. Their parents were not very subtle in their condescending attitude to all the club's employees and were particularly tactless in letting Dex know that their daughters were off limits to the club's "hired help." Dex ached to tell the members and their daughters just what he thought about all of them, but he endured the indignity without comment because he needed the job.

In his senior year, the River City Wildcats lost only one game. When the season was over, Dex held several personal school records and was honored with a number of regional athletic awards. The colleges that had been recruiting him for three years stepped up the pressure. He received scholarship offers from over ten colleges, but after discussing it with Coach Delaney and others, Dex narrowed the potential choices to three Southeastern Conference schools: Auburn, Alabama, and Georgia. He understood how fortunate he was to have options, but they made it difficult to decide on a single school. After visiting several schools, Dex finally chose Georgia because he liked the campus, coach, and program. There was an added incentive in his selection: Hoagie had already accepted a band scholarship to Georgia.

Dex's commitment was the lead story on the local sports page, and newspapers all over the state of Georgia picked up the story. It was the first time the Bulldog fans saw a name in print that would later become very familiar to them.

Marie hadn't seen Dex since moving to Atlanta, but when she saw the article in the Atlanta *Journal Constitution*, she cut it out and saved it. Over the next few years, she saved an extensive collection of articles about her former neighbor's football career, for reasons she didn't even try to understand.

Even though Dex had decided on a college, he still had to get through the remaining months in high school. In the whirl of activities before graduation, the incident at the moonshine still became just another event that hurtled past, along with the senior prom, May Day, baccalaureate, and graduation.

That summer Dex returned as a lifeguard at the country club, to the delight of the members' daughters. In the first week, he met Marcy Bennett, a new waitress who had also just graduated from high school and was working to earn money for college. She told him she was getting the same "You're not one of us" treatment from the club members. The shared experience of having to deal with the members' rude arrogance created a common bond between them.

Dex and Marcy spent their lunch breaks together laughing at the snobbish, egocentric members who strutted around the club trying to impress each other in their cutesy golf and tennis clothes. Marcy and Dex dated throughout the summer, and although they enjoyed each other's company, what they enjoyed most was that their relationship irritated the hell out of the debutantes.

Chapter 4

On a Saturday in late November, two days after Thanksgiving, the distinctive aroma of barbeque was drifting throughout the crowd that had gathered for the final game of the season. Georgia's tailgate parties were legendary, and the noise created by hundreds of fans at the various pregame parties had been intensifying since midmorning. About an hour before game time, the crowd—now thoroughly sated with barbeque and booze—started putting away the tailgate paraphernalia and moving toward the entrance gates of Sanford Stadium. By kickoff, the pandemonium inside the stadium had intensified to a deafening roar as almost one hundred thousand "Dawg" fans filled every seat from the field to the highest tier.

It was the last game that Dex Martin would ever play between Sanford's fabled hedges. Over the previous four years, the strong-armed quarterback had demonstrated unparalleled athletic and leadership abilities in an offense that was well-fortified at every position. A combination of talent and confidence in his own ability had made him a four-year starter and endeared him to the fans. It was a foregone conclusion that he would be an NFL first-round draft choice, and it seemed inevitable that after today's game he would simply have to wait for the draft to become the game's next twenty-two-year-old millionaire.

Georgia was undefeated, ranked third in the national polls, and heavily favored to win the day's game with in-state rival Georgia Tech. Tech was unranked and not in the same conference, so the game had little significance outside the state. But national polls and athletic conferences had little to do with the excitement surrounding this annual game. It was all about pride and bragging rights in the state of Georgia.

Just before game time, Georgia's mascot, a snow-white bulldog with an acronym for a name and a face that only a Georgia fan could love, waddled onto the field dressed in his red game sweater. When Uga first appeared, everyone knew the kickoff was imminent, and a deafening roar erupted from the crowd.

While the teams huddled on the sidelines, the captains met in the center of the field for the coin toss. Georgia won the toss and elected to receive. As Dex trotted to the sideline, he pointed to the stands where the band was seated. The tuba player stood up and pointed back. This had become a ritualistic pregame salute between the Georgia quarterback and his best friend Hoagie Hogan.

The kickoff went deep into the end zone and was not returned. Georgia started from the twenty with a draw play that was stopped at the line of scrimmage. A sweep around the left side lost five yards when someone missed an assignment. On third down, Dex scanned the defense; the Dawgs needed fifteen yards. He expected Tech to be pinning back their ears and coming for him, and he noticed the weak side cornerback inching toward the line. He stood up and shouted, "Martin, stay in and watch thirty-four." He didn't wait for the fullback to respond, he simply barked out the rest of the count.

When Dex took the snap, he immediately realized that more than the corner was coming in the blitz. Out of the corner of his eye, he saw the middle linebacker shoot the gap, and he knew he was in trouble. He rolled from the pocket to buy time. His primary receiver was covered, so he checked downfield for an alternate. Burl White, his wideout, had managed to get a step of separation from the strong safety and was streaking down the right sideline. Dex had to stop his scramble and firmly plant his right foot to gain the leverage he would need to make the long pass. He snapped his arm back and whipped it forward in the fluid motion that had made him so good at throwing the long ball. But before the ball cleared his hand, he felt a jarring impact. All his weight was on the right foot he had planted so solidly in the turf, and it didn't move with the impact. He felt his leg snap with a sickening crack as pain washed over him.

Dex collapsed. He was unaware that the ball had bounced on the turf only a few yards from where he was sprawled on the field. He fleetingly saw the shock on the face of Don Mason, his right guard. The pain kept pulsing in waves as he tried to reach for his leg. Rolling on his back in agony, the entire contents of his stomach exploded onto the turf and the unseasonably warm fall day seemed to suddenly turn cold as he shivered uncontrollably. Before he passed out, Dex looked down and saw the jagged end of a bone protruding from his leg between his knee and ankle.

Dr. Jerome Adams, the team physician, was quickly on the field. One look at Dex's leg and he instinctively knew that as the jagged end of the bone tore through the flesh, it had probably caused extensive collateral damage. He also knew that any fracture that created an open wound, particularly one exposed to the grunge of a football field, presented the risk of serious infection. He immediately removed his belt and used it as a tourniquet to stop the profuse bleeding.

He stood up and yelled to the sideline, "Get the gurney out here right now, and have the ambulance stand by."

As soon as they had Dex loaded in the ambulance, Dr. Adams climbed in beside him.

"Don't stop at the local hospital. Let's get him to Munson in Atlanta as soon as possible."

A hush had fallen over Sanford Stadium as the siren screamed from the speeding ambulance. The outcome of the game had suddenly become less important to the thousands of Georgia fans packed in the stadium. Many hardened football fans were seen with their heads bowed.

Dr. Adams was not just the team physician, he was also an avid Bulldog fan, and he was going to make sure Dex was seen by the most skilled orthopedist available. His preferred surgeon worked at Munson Orthopedic Hospital in Atlanta, and that was where he directed the ambulance driver.

Dex was conscious now but in such intense pain that he would later remember only snippets of the conversation with Dr. Adams during the trip that seemed to last forever. He overheard the cell phone conversation the doctor had with the Atlanta hospital.

When the call was over he asked, "Will they be able to fix my leg?"

"Dex, I know this doctor well, and in my opinion he's the best around. Let us worry about your leg and you just try to stay positive."

Even in his condition, Dex realized that Dr. Adams had not actually answered his question, but he wasn't in any state to follow up.

The orthopedic surgeon met them in the emergency room, evaluated Dex, and rushed him directly to surgery. After the surgery was completed, Dex spent another hour in recovery before he was transferred to a private room.

Dex's head was still foggy from the heavy sedation, and although he realized he was in a hospital room and vaguely remembered the ambulance trip, he had no concept of elapsed time. He was having difficulty keeping his eyes open and focused as he slowly recovered from the anesthesia, but he sensed that someone was in the room with him. He thought he was hallucinating when he saw a beautiful woman standing beside his bed. But then the mirage said, "Hello, Dex," and he realized it was not his imagination. The voice was strangely familiar and seemed to be coming from somewhere far away. He was struggling to overcome the anesthesia, and his eyelids were still fluttering as she leaned over the bed and held his hand between hers.

"I was watching the game on TV, and when they announced where they were taking you, I beat the ambulance here. I've been in the waiting room with Dr. Adams, waiting for them to move you into a room."

Even before he could focus his eyes enough to see her clearly, her unique, husky voice triggered his recognition.

"Marie, Marie Murphy, where . . . come from?" He was still having difficulty enunciating words, and his throat was so dry it felt like he had been eating sand. Although he was still not fully awake and was mumbling, she seemed to understand him because she smiled, squeezed his hand, and nodded.

"Marie, haven't seen . . . how long? Thanks. Still remember me." He knew what he wanted to say but the words weren't coming out right, and she couldn't help but chuckle at his rambling speech.

"Oh, come on, Dex, everybody in Georgia knows you, but I'm glad to see that celebrity hasn't caused you to lose your modesty."

Recovery from the effects of the anesthesia wasn't Dex's only problem. He was also having difficulty reconciling his memory of Marie, the next-door tomboy, with the stunningly beautiful young woman standing beside his bed. A cloudlike mane of curls had replaced the familiar pigtails in her raven hair. Before tumbling onto her broad shoulders, the dark tresses caressed a face with coal-black eyes, full sensual lips, and a straight aristocratic nose. Her high cheekbones and jet-black hair pointed like a genealogical signpost to her distant Cherokee ancestors. These Native American features were still clinging for recognition even after the infusion of European DNA from several intervening generations.

Since he was flat on his back, it was hard to estimate height, but Dex thought she must be almost six feet tall. He also noticed that the jeans and turtleneck sweater clearly indicated her once-skinny frame had filled out remarkably well. She would never again be mistaken for one of the boys.

When Marie sat on the side of the bed, the movement caused Dex to grimace with pain. She noticed his reaction and walked around to the foot of the bed. He had a quizzical expression when he noticed her subconsciously adjusting the apparatus elevating his leg without even looking at the controls.

Marie laughed and said, "Don't worry, Dex. I'm a nurse, and I worked at this hospital for several months after I finished nursing school."

Dex was now fully awake, and they had been talking for about twenty minutes when Hoagie burst through the door. He had changed out of his band uniform into an old sweatshirt and ragged jeans that looked like Goodwill discards. Hoagie always perspired, even walking from the dorm to his classes, but his concern for Dex and the agitation of Atlanta traffic had caused his sweatshirt to become completely drenched. Sweat had also darkened his fiery red hair and caused it to lose any semblance of order as it flopped around his flushed face.

Hoagie was focused on Dex and the equipment elevating his leg and didn't even notice someone else was in the room. "Are you okay? What'd they say? How long you gonna be here? What'd they do to you?" The questions breathlessly tumbled out and all ran together.

Dex managed a grin. "Hoagie, for God's sake, calm down." His efforts to calm his excitable friend had never worked before, and that day was no exception. Hoagie had run all the way from the parking lot, and when he started looking around the room for a place to sit, he saw Marie for the first time. He said hello but clearly didn't recognize her.

Marie smiled and said, "Hello, Hoagie."

The use of his name caused him to have a perplexed look as he glanced back and forth between Dex and Marie. They both smiled and enjoyed his confusion.

"Hoagie, surely I haven't changed that much since the last time I beat you arm wrestling."

"Marie, where the hell did you come from?" He grabbed her in a bear hug and, despite being three inches shorter, lifted her completely off the floor.

Chapter 5

Moving to Atlanta when she was fifteen years old was a traumatic experience for Marie. She had lived in the same mountainside neighborhood her entire life, gone to school with the same friends since the first grade, and grown up with Dex, her best friend, living next door. Suddenly she was uprooted and found herself in a new city, neighborhood, and school where she didn't know a single person.

For weeks Marie sulked in school, staying to herself, and at home she made sure her parents didn't forget how upset she was about the move. She was miserable the first few weeks, but eventually she met new friends and her outgoing personality returned.

In high school, Marie played on the basketball team, wrote for the school paper, excelled academically, and made the National Honor Society. In the summer before her senior year, a friend talked her into volunteering at a hospital, and she soon began to explore the idea of becoming a nurse.

As a volunteer, Marie was a gofer for the nurses, but while they were using her to do their grunt work, she probed them for information about their careers. Her questions were seemingly endless. "Why did you decide on nursing? How long did you have to go to school? What did you study? Would you do it again?"

By the time she returned to school that fall, Marie had already made her career choice. She entered nursing school immediately after graduating from high school and completed her associate degree in two years. She finished second in her class, passed the national licensing exam, and was immediately hired as a registered nurse by Munson Hospital. Although she originally planned to attend night classes to also get a baccalaureate degree, fortuitous circumstances soon altered those plans. She had only been working in the hospital for about six months when a nursing friend, who was preparing to start a maternity leave, approached her about filling in for her on a private-duty assignment outside the hospital.

"Marie, I'm going to have to have to take about a month before the baby is born and probably two months after that. I'm sitting with and caring for a lovely elderly lady whose only family lives several hundred miles away. Her son is paying me much more per hour than I'm making at the hospital, and I wish you would take over for me until I get through my maternity leave."

"It sounds interesting, but I need more details about what I would have to do."

Her friend explained the job and assured Marie that it would not interfere with her work at the hospital. She took over during her friend's maternity leave and discovered that she enjoyed the freedom of working as a private-duty nurse more than she did in the hospital's structured clinical setting. Over the next few months, Marie did a lot of research, asked a lot of questions, and discovered there was an immense demand for private-duty nurses. This was partially because of a shortage of qualified nurses, and also because a lot of nurses were not comfortable working in an unsupervised environment.

Marie was both self-confident and self-motivated, and this seemed like a perfect opportunity to her. Her father, who was a CPA, helped her prepare a business plan for a start-up company to provide private-duty nurses to the public. The pro-forma outlined a plan for her to provide part-time nursing assistance for homebound elderly individuals who did not require full nursing home care. Her idea was that if a nurse regularly checked on elderly or disabled patients, it would allow these individuals to remain in their homes for years, in some instances, before they would have to transition to a nursing home.

Marie envisioned making regular rounds at the patients' homes to check vital signs, make sure prescriptions were filled and being taken properly, and make sure the patients were eating nutritionally. In some cases, a physician might require other services that she would be able to perform.

Marie clearly wasn't a pioneer in this field, but she planned to differentiate her company from the proliferation of run-of-the-mill home healthcare agencies by delivering specialized services that a client could choose from a menu of reasonably priced options. The services included scheduling medical appointments as well as providing nonmedical assistance like traveling with or for the patient on shopping trips to a pharmacy or supermarket.

Marie's plan was to promote the services to physicians rather than directly to the patients. The attending physician could determine what services were needed and check them off on the menu of services forms that she would provide to them. She could then approach the patients or their adult children and reach an agreement to provide the service prescribed by the physician. Her basic premise was that in an increasingly mobile society, children often didn't live in the same city as their elderly parents and providing for their parents' care was a heart-wrenching problem. Marie wanted to provide a dependable and affordable solution for this long-distance elder care dilemma.

Marie's father got her an appointment with a friend, who was in the commercial loan department at Proudland Bank & Trust Co. in Atlanta. The loan officer was impressed with Marie's presentation and the originality of the plan she had developed and agreed to provide a start-up loan, which her father cosigned. Within a few weeks RN4U, Inc. was operational. Her letterhead spelled out "Registered Nurses for You" on the second line, in case someone failed to grasp the acronym she had cleverly selected for her new business.

The business prospered almost immediately, and within a few months, Marie had to hire another nurse because she already had more patients than she could possibly handle alone. As she had correctly anticipated, the shortage of nurses in general, and particularly those who could function without constant supervision, created an ideal market for RN4U. Marie's newly discovered entrepreneurial acumen also contributed to her rapid expansion. In less than a year, she had eight full-time nurses on her staff. The burgeoning business had forced her to give up her own hands-on nursing activities, and she was now devoting herself full time to the marketing, sales, and administration of RN4U. Direct referrals were coming from a growing number of physicians, and Marie was even beginning to furnish nurses on an hourly basis to several small clinics in the area.

Marie's sudden success left little time for her personal life. She didn't date very often, and on the rare occasions when she did accept an invitation for a night out, it was usually with a doctor who referred patients to her. She thought of these as business meetings, although the doctors may not have thought of them that way.

In the time she was at Munson Hospital, Dr. Bill Bishop, a young resident, was the only one she dated more than a couple of times. She went out with him fairly regularly for three tumultuous months and then broke it off because Bishop's behavior had grown more and more bizarre.

She had made no promises to him, but he started crowding her and acted as if they had some type of lifetime commitment. He wanted to be with her every hour when they were not on duty at the hospital. When he was on night duty, he would often call and wake her up after midnight. The calls were ostensibly to just talk, but it soon became obvious that he was checking up to see if she was dating someone else.

Marie ended the casual relationship with Bishop the night he confronted her in front of her apartment and demanded to know where she had been. She had received a call from an old high-school friend who was in town for a meeting, and she met him for dinner at a downtown restaurant. They had both written for the high-school paper and were good friends, but they never dated. Marie enjoyed seeing her old friend again, and they sat and talked for several hours. When she got home, Bishop was sitting in his car in front of her apartment. He grabbed her arm as soon as she got out of her car and started to interrogate her.

"Where the hell have you been all night?"

She was shocked by the question and his apparent attitude. "It's none of your business, but I had dinner with an old friend."

"You didn't eat until midnight. You've been out with some old lover, and I'm not going to stand by and let you get away with it."

"Wait just a minute. What I do with my time is none of your business. I don't owe you an explanation for anything I do."

"As long as we're together you're not going to go out with other men, so you can tell whoever he is that he better stay away from now on."

"I don't know where you got the idea that we are together. We have been to dinner a few times. From now on, you're the one who is going to stay away. This ends right here. I don't want to see you again, and if you keep calling to check up on me, I'm going to get a restraining order. Now get out of here."

Marie turned and walked up the steps to her front door, but Bishop was still yelling at her when she went in the apartment and locked the door. Within an hour he called to apologize.

"Marie, I'm sorry. I just care so much for you that I go crazy thinking about you dating other men. I won't do anything like that again, but please accept my apology. I want to continue seeing you."

"If it makes you feel any better, I'll accept your apology, but I'm not going out with you again, and if you harass me at work, I'll report it to the hospital administrator." She hung up before he could reply.

They both knew that she couldn't help but see him daily because they worked in the same area at the hospital. But after that, Marie avoided all of Bishop's attempts to engage her in a conversation. She saw his car following her on a couple of occasions, but he never again showed up at her apartment.

Although Marie didn't find out until later, she was not the only one who was having trouble with Bishop's erratic behavior. He was being argumentative with the other physicians, and several nurses had accused him of being verbally abusive. After repeated warnings, he was placed on probation by the administration, ordered to undergo an examination by the staff psychiatrist, and told that any further problems would result in his termination.

Marie's nursing supervisor approached her and asked her about Bishop. "Marie, I don't know if you are aware of it, but Dr. Bishop has got some problems with the hospital administrator, and he has been telling people that he is involved in a very serious relationship with you. Is that true?"

"It was never anywhere near serious from my standpoint. We had a bizarre confrontation in front of my apartment recently, and I've already told him that I don't want to see him again. He is the last person in the world I would be serious about."

"Okay, I just wanted to make sure you were aware of his problems and to warn you to be careful. A lot of young physicians have difficulty with the stress of the long hours and constant pressure of a metropolitan hospital."

Marie found out just how serious his problems had become when she was asked to meet with the staff psychiatrist.

"Marie, the normal doctor-patient relationship would keep me from discussing one of my patients with you, but there are circumstances that take precedence over that relationship. One such situation arose during my recent interview with Dr. Bill Bishop."

"What did he say?"

"During the session, he became highly agitated and blamed you for some problems he's having at the hospital."

The psychiatrist was referring to his notes, and Marie started to say something, but he held up his hand to stop her.

"He said he was involved in an intimate relationship with you, and that you were planning to be married before he caught you running around on him. He went on to say that he couldn't concentrate on his work for worrying about what you were doing when you weren't with him."

Marie was incredulous and was speechlessly shaking her head when the doctor said, "Wait a minute, that's not all. Near the end of the session he was almost crying and said he should have killed you. He said some other things and called you some words that weren't very nice, but that was the crux of the threat."

When Marie regained her composure, she said, "Doctor, I think he's gone off the deep end. We dated casually for a few months, marriage was never mentioned, and we certainly didn't have an intimate relationship. Furthermore, he would be the last person I would want to marry. I made no commitments to him, and what he caught me doing was having dinner at a restaurant with an old high-school friend. I've already told him I wouldn't ever go out with him again because of his bizarre behavior. I think he's nuts, but do you think his threat might be credible?"

"Well, 'nuts' probably wouldn't be my clinical diagnosis, but it may be more descriptive than what I will ultimately put in my report. Marie, there really isn't any way to determine if he might try to carry through on a threat like this; however, you need to be very careful, and I strongly suggest that you have absolutely no further contact with him."

Bishop's erratic behavior continued at the hospital, and he was finally terminated. Marie moved on to start RN4U and had not seen him since. She did later hear from a friend at the hospital that he was working in a public health clinic in Birmingham. Although she could never be sure, there had been several times when she felt someone might be following her.

Since leaving the hospital, Marie's social life had definitely taken a backseat to her new business. When she could get away from the office, she spent her time selling the services of RN4U by calling on potential clients. That did sometimes involve having dinner with a potential client or referral source, but she never considered those meetings as dates.

Chapter 6

The hospital room of a trauma victim is an unusual venue for a party, but one was in full swing in Dex's room. He had substantially recovered from the effects of the anesthesia, and medication was controlling the pain in his leg. The last one to join the impromptu party was Gigi, who had driven down from River City. She was relieved to see Dex wave and smile at her when she walked in the room and then she stopped abruptly when she saw Marie. Hoagie may have had trouble recognizing Marie, but Gigi immediately knew that this was the grown-up version of the girl who had been like a second grandchild to her.

"Oh, Marie, just look at you, all tall and beautiful, but I'll bet you still like peanut butter and jelly sandwiches."

When Marie was growing up next door, she ate almost as many meals at Gigi's house as she did at home, and Gigi remembered that had been her favorite snack.

Marie laughed as she hugged Gigi, and said, "You're right, and no one has ever made them better than you."

Marie's move to Atlanta had left a void in Gigi's life. She had been the daughter and granddaughter she always wanted but never had, and after Marie moved, Gigi had missed her almost as much as Dex.

After a few minutes, Hoagie said, "I hate to rush off, but it looks like the quarterback is going to live, and I've got a paper to research and write before class on Monday."

Marie stayed a little longer but wanted to give Gigi and Dex some time alone. She said, "I was doing some paperwork while watching the game. I left it piled on my kitchen table when I left for the hospital. I need to get back and finish it, but I will come back in the morning."

"Marie, I've got to leave tonight because I have to take care of the nursery at church tomorrow morning. Will you check on Dex while he's in the hospital and let me know if I need to come back?"

"Gigi, I'll check on him every day, and I'll keep you posted. I know most of the staff at the hospital, and I will make sure they take good care of him."

As soon as Marie walked out the door, Gigi turned to Dex with an expression that wordlessly asked the question he was expecting.

"I swear, Gigi, until about an hour ago I hadn't seen or talked to her since she left River City." Then he added with a grin, "But today may change that."

Although Marie enjoyed seeing her old friends, the afternoon had also been very unsettling for her. She didn't even remember driving to her apartment until she was pulling into the parking lot. She originally went to the hospital to simply check on an old friend, and her reaction after seeing him was entirely unexpected. It wasn't the seriousness of his injury; as a nurse she had regularly seen much more serious trauma. It was the strong emotional reaction that was so disconcerting.

Marie had many cherished childhood memories of Dex and all the good times they had, but after leaving River City, she got caught up in her new life and didn't often think about him until she started seeing his name in the Atlanta newspaper after he signed with Georgia. After that, it would have been difficult not to follow his career. For the past four years, his name had been in the sports section of the Atlanta *Journal Constitution* almost daily.

During the four years Dex was at Georgia, Marie thought about calling him many times. She had watched him play in several televised games and even sat in the stadium one time when he was playing at Grant Field in Atlanta. But she convinced herself that with the media exposure he was receiving, he probably wouldn't be interested in hearing from the former girl next door. She never made the call.

Marie was shaken by her reaction to seeing Dex, and she was trying to rationalize how she was feeling. She had always thought of herself as a sensible person. She didn't fall in and out of love with the guys she dated and never had much of an emotional connection with any of them. She had seen friends shattered by failed romances and didn't think she would ever be weak enough to let it happen to her. But now the possibility that she might have such strong feelings for her childhood friend terrified her. Suddenly she wasn't quite so sure about her ability to maintain her common sense in this situation.

Marie kept telling herself to slow down. Her thoughts were racing far ahead of reality. If Dex had not been injured, she probably would have never seen him again. But he did get injured, she had seen him, and as crazy it seemed, she sensed that in some unforeseen way the events of this day were going to have a dramatic impact on her life.

She had always thought it was amusing when her girlfriends talked about falling for someone when they first met; it certainly never happened to her. But seeing Dex after seven years was almost like a first meeting, and from the way he kept staring at her, she didn't think her reaction was unilateral. Something emotional definitely happened between them at the hospital, but she didn't know how to categorize it. Romantic reactions were far outside her realm of experience, but she knew what she was feeling wasn't the reaction one would expect from merely seeing an old friend.

The rational side of Marie's brain kept reminding her that this was Dex, her former buddy, her next-door neighbor; she had known him all of her life, and she had never felt romantically attracted to him. But a sixth sense was waging war on rationality.

After she gave up on the office paper work that she planned to do, Marie took a drawer out of her dresser and turned it upside down on her bed. It was the repository for all the clippings from Dex's football career at Georgia. She would be humiliated if anyone, especially Dex, ever discovered that she had a drawer in her dresser that was level full of photos and articles chronicling his career. She didn't even know why she had collected them. Was it just idle interest because she knew him? Could she have had a premonition that there would be a reunion some day?

Marie had recently seen him in a television interview, dressed in street clothes, and remembered thinking, probably for the first time, that Dex was a good looking guy. In retrospect, she supposed he always was, but she had never thought about him in that way. With all the adulation he had received from fans, he could have easily become arrogant, but at the hospital he appeared to have been completely unaffected by his celebrity.

Marie looked at the collection of newspaper photos for a long time before sliding them back in the drawer. She was still perplexed about her bizarre reaction to seeing him, but she had to admit that it wasn't friendship that was messing with her mind.

Marie had no intention of pursuing him like a groupie, but she did regret that she had never called him. She went to bed and tried to sleep, but as soon as she closed her eyes, her mind went into overdrive, replaying everything that had happened in the hospital room. She tossed and turned throughout the night and was wide awake long before the irritating buzz of the bedside alarm clock.

While she was getting dressed the next morning, Marie turned on the television; the first thing she saw was footage of Dex being loaded into the ambulance. That was followed by a brief interview in the hospital waiting room with Dr. Adams. She had been sitting in the room when that video was made.

The reporter started the interview by saying, "We are at Munson Orthopedic talking to the Georgia team physician about the injury in today's game to quarterback Dex Martin. Dr. Adams, can you describe Dex's injury?"

"About all I can tell you is that he suffered a broken leg, is currently undergoing surgery to repair the fracture, and will probably be confined to the hospital for several days."

Marie turned off the television and continued dressing. It was Sunday; she didn't have to go to the office, so she dressed casually and left for the hospital. As she drove, her mind wandered, and she couldn't escape the thought that somehow the events that were occurring now were going to change her life.

Dex was propped up in bed reading the morning paper when Marie walked into his room, and his leg was no longer elevated.

"Hey, Marie, you just missed the surgeon. By the way, he says he knows you."

"Yeah, we worked together here in the hospital. I see he decided to no longer elevate your leg."

"I told him it was uncomfortable and he said it wasn't necessary anymore. What is it with this diet of cream of wheat and canned fruit? It's the worst junk I've ever tried to eat."

He had pushed the tray away from his bed, and since he was grumbling about the food, Marie knew he was feeling better.

"Dex, how would you like to take a little tour of the hospital?"

"Is that your idea of a cruel joke?"

She didn't answer but smiled and walked out of the room. She returned a few minutes later pushing a wheelchair.

"All right, let's get moving. A few laps around the hospital may help your grumpy disposition. Let's get out of the room for a little while."

"Are you sure this is okay? I thought I was going to have to stay flat on my back until they let me out of her."

"If you stay flat on your back, you'll never get out of here. I'm not going to hurt you, so just be quiet and let the nurse handle this."

Marie helped Dex into the chair, adjusted the support under his leg, and rolled him into the hall. At the nurse's station, she paused to introduce him to a nurse with whom she had worked.

"Judy, this is an old friend, Dex Martin. He's in room 503, so if you get a chance, check on him from time to time, but don't believe anything he tells you about growing up next door to me."

"Hey, that sounds interesting. I'll drop by to see you, Dex."

The tour wound through several floors of the hospital and eventually stopped on an outside patio where they sat and talked for a long time. They discussed old friends, former schoolmates, and the old neighborhood.

"Tell me how you got into nursing?'

"I interned one summer as a nurse's aide while I was in high school, and I just fell in love with the whole concept. I went directly from high school to nursing school, finished in two years, and got my license as an RN."

"What about this nursing business you mentioned yesterday?"

"With all the drugs you had yesterday, I'm surprised you even remember me mentioning that I had my own business. I really got into it by accident. I filled in for a friend on a private-duty assignment and discovered that I liked working for myself."

Marie went on to tell Dex all about how she started RN4U. He was still having difficulty adjusting to the fact that this beguiling young woman was not only his former tomboy buddy but was also now a full-fledged entrepreneur. After she answered all his questions about RN4U, he reluctantly talked a little about his career at Georgia and his plans to play professional football. Marie had some experience with his type of injury and suspected that the residual effects of the injury might alter his plans. She wisely did not share her thoughts with him because she knew that was a discussion he should have with his doctor.

The discussion with the doctor came two days later, and by happenstance, Marie was there when it took place. To save time, she normally ate lunch at her desk, but on this day she went by the hospital at noon and took Dex a large chocolate milk shake. He was drinking the shake and they were talking when Dr. Adams, Dex's coach, and the orthopedic surgeon walked into the room at the same time. Marie already knew the two doctors, and Dex introduced her to his coach.

The surgeon said, "Marie, would you mind waiting outside for a few minutes?"

She started toward the door, but Dex said, "Marie, wait a minute." He seemed to sense what was coming and said, "Since all three of you came together I don't think you're going to be giving me any good news today. Marie is a nurse and a very good friend, and I want her to stay and hear what you have to say."

Dr. Adams nodded at the surgeon, and they all looked at Dex as the surgeon cleared his throat and spoke. "Mr. Martin, you're right. We don't have good news for you, but it's not as bad as I was afraid it might be when I first examined you. By recognizing the extent of your injury and getting you here quickly, Dr. Adams probably kept you from being permanently crippled, if not worse. You had an open fracture of the tibia and fibula with vascular impairment. I took a lot of time with the debridement of the wound, but there can be no assurance that all of the contaminants from the playing field were successfully eliminated. You will have to be closely monitored for any evidence of subsequent infection at the wound site. While you were still anesthetized I had to manipulate the severely misplaced bones back into alignment. The bones were then stabilized with screws and an external fixator and—"

Everyone else in the room was nodding as if they understood everything the doctor was explaining, but Dex's head was spinning. "Wait a minute, Dr. Adams. Slow down and let me make sure I understand what you're telling me."

"Okay, sometimes we get a little carried away with the medical jargon. An open fracture is when a broken bone penetrates the skin. This creates an enhanced risk of severe infection. What I did was clean the wound as well as I could and then pulled the bones back into alignment. I placed a screw through the skin into the bone above and below the fracture site. Then I anchored the long rod you can see on your leg between the two screws to hold the bones into place until they can knit.

"However, before I even addressed the fractures we had to have a vascular surgeon restore full blood flow to your leg below the fracture site. There are some major arteries and veins in that area that were damaged when the broken bone tore through the surrounding flesh. That was all repaired before I stabilized the fractures. It should all heal, and when it does we will remove the screws and rod."

Dex smiled for the first time and said, "So then I will be cleared to play again. I need to get cleared well before the NFL draft next spring."

"I can appreciate how much this means to you, but we've all discussed it, and it is our opinion that due to the severe nature of the injury, you would risk being permanently crippled if you were to suffer another trauma to your leg. If it was my decision, with that possibility, I could never clear you for any type of contact sport."

His coach spoke up and said, "Dex, you know how I feel about you, but we have always been honest with each other. Every pro scout in the country is going to know about the severity of your injury, and there isn't going to be any team that would be willing to take that chance, even if you were willing to do so."

The football dreams of Dex Martin, perhaps the most gifted athlete to ever come out of River City, Tennessee, ended that afternoon. Gone were the dreams of instant riches from an NFL contract.

When everyone else left the room, Dex and Marie stared at each other for a long time before he finally spoke. "Well, I guess I have to start planning my life all over again. Playing professional football is the only thing I've thought about for years, but now that's out the window. Marie, I'm going to graduate from college in about six months, and I don't have a clue what I'll do with the rest of my life."

Dex was somehow maintaining his composure, but Marie wanted to cry because she knew how disappointed he was. Instead, she smiled, held his hand, and said, "Dex, you've always been a fighter. I don't know what you'll decide to do, but you don't need football to be a success. You can't be as close to someone as we were as kids without knowing what they are made of. You'll be successful no matter what you do; you just need to decide what you want to do and start working toward that goal."

In the past when people talked about Dex and success, it was always linked to athletics. His worth as an individual had always been related to his ability to throw a football, and until now it never occurred to him that this was a rather shallow way for an individual to be defined. Marie had just told him that she was confident he could be successful in something other than athletics; her belief and support couldn't have come at a more opportune time.

Dex's career-ending injury proved to be an epiphany in his life. Whatever he might ultimately decide to do, providence had just forced an irreversible detour that completely changed his focus. He had to concentrate on academics, as he should have at the beginning of his college career. Unfortunately, he now only had about six months to prepare for whatever goal he was going to pursue. He had a 2.5 grade-point average, but ever since he had been in elementary school, his teachers had said that his scholastic ability far exceeded his actual achievement in the classroom. That had to change immediately, and he vowed while still in the hospital that he would start applying himself in ways he had never done before.

The physical rehabilitation from his injury and increased emphasis on academics occupied most of Dex's time in the next few months. The developing relationship with Marie was a major motivating factor to work hard on his rehab and academics. They talked by phone at least twice a week, but when the screws and external fixator were finally removed and he could once again drive, he made the trip to Atlanta every Friday after his last class. He spent Friday and Saturday nights on the sofa in her one-bedroom apartment. The sofa was definitely not his idea.

Chapter 7

Dex and Marie spent so much time together that friends started posing questions like, "What's really going on between you two?"

Their typical response was to just laugh and say, "Oh, we're just good friends."

But they weren't fooling themselves or anyone else; they were rushing headlong into something a lot more intimate than mere friendship. Dex had never been particularly timid or reticent around other girls, but so far he was with Marie. The baggage of their childhood friendship presented a barricade that he had not yet figured out how to breech. He even wondered if it would feel incestuous to kiss his former buddy. They enjoyed and treasured every minute they could spend together, but so far they both shied away from talking about the changing nature of their relationship.

To further complicate the situation, Dex was intimidated because Marie was already a successful entrepreneur running a profitable business. He was embarrassed by his financial situation. Instead of wine and dinner in nice restaurants, they drank beer and ate pizza and take-out Chinese in her apartment.

One night after eating another cardboard-tasting pizza, Dex finally spoke up. "Marie, I know before I started dominating your weekends that you dated some doctors who took you to fine restaurants, and I'm embarrassed that I can't afford to entertain you that way."

"Don't be ridiculous, Dex. I know you're still in school, but if you really want to go somewhere, I'll be happy to pay for it."

"That isn't going to happen. You may think I'm chauvinistic, but I'm not going to start letting you pick up the tabs."

"Well, your birthday is in two weeks, so at least let me take you to dinner to celebrate that."

Dex didn't even like that idea, but he reluctantly agreed, and Marie made a reservation at Southern Nights, one of Atlanta's new upscale restaurants. When they left the apartment the night of the date, Dex was wearing the only suit he owned and the new tie Marie had bought him for his birthday. Marie was stunning in a simple, black, off-the-shoulder dress, adorned only with the pearl earrings and necklace she had borrowed from her mother for the evening.

At the restaurant, heads turned as the couple was led to their table. Dex was accustomed to being recognized, even to being hounded for his autograph, but this was entirely different. The people weren't watching him; all eyes, including his, were on Marie. She ignored the stares with the grace of a woman who knows she's attractive but is not very impressed with it. It occurred to Dex for the first time that few things were more appealing than a lovely woman who doesn't define herself by her appearance.

If Dex had ever had any doubt about his feelings for Marie, they disappeared when she smiled at him across the candlelit table. He had fallen completely in love with her. He still had no idea how to broach the relationship subject with her, but he vowed to himself that before the night was over he would finally muster the courage to tell her how he felt.

As the elevator descended from the rooftop restaurant after dinner, Marie said, "Do you realize that we have never danced together? There's a little jazz club near the apartment, and I think we should drop by there tonight."

"You do remember that you're talking to the guy with a gimpy leg, right?"

"Oh, come on, you're not going to use that as an excuse. Your limp is almost completely gone."

Dex soon forgot about the lingering twinge in his leg as he held her close, shuffled his feet, and slowly moved on the dance floor. After the first few minutes, Marie abandoned the traditional waltz hold and locked her hands behind his neck. He followed her lead, putting both arms around her slim waist and pulling her closer.

Marie whispered, "The music has stopped."

Dex continued to sway with the music in his head and asked, "What music? I kind of like this." He thought to himself, or maybe he even whispered in her ear, "I'd be happy if we could dance like this all night."

They were both silent in the drive back to her apartment. Dex was thinking about how to broach the subject that he had vowed to himself he would address tonight, but he had no idea what she might be thinking. He could tell that she was worried about something because worry always put a deep crease in her otherwise flawless forehead, and one had been there since they left the club.

When they walked into the apartment, Marie led Dex directly to the sofa and asked him to sit down. She backed off a few feet and said, "Dex, just sit there for a minute. Something has been bothering me for weeks and I need to talk about it, so please let me finish before you say anything. If I don't get this out now, I may never again have the courage. It's embarrassing, but I'd rather talk about it now than try to explain it if things get more complicated."

She closed her eyes and paused for a moment before saying, "I'm falling in love with you. Maybe I've always been in love with you and was just too pigheaded or afraid to admit it, even to myself. I don't know how you feel about me, or if you have ever even thought about how you feel."

She paused again, but when he didn't say anything, she continued. "No matter what you think, you damn well better not laugh at what I'm about to tell you. The point is I'm twenty-two years old, I have very little experience dealing with relationships, and I'm a complete sexual neophyte."

Dex smiled and started to get up, but she wasn't through pouring out her heart.

"Look Dex, don't start getting any ideas; I'm not ready to jump into bed with you. I don't even know where we're headed, but wherever it is, I know I've never been there before. I'm confused, and I'm unsure about how you feel about our relationship, or whatever you call what we have going here."

Dex started to respond, but she held up her hand and stopped him.

"Dex, if the time ever comes when I'm ready to make the commitment, which I've never made before, I don't want the decision to be made in the heat of passion. I want it to be made because I love and trust you, and because I think we have a future together."

She stopped abruptly, but when he still didn't say anything, she continued. "Okay, I'm through embarrassing myself. Now you can laugh, leave, or do whatever you think is appropriate, because this may be completely one-sided and never have crossed your mind."

When Dex stood, Marie melted into his arms as he whispered, "Marie, I've been in love with you for a long time, and yeah, consummating that love has crossed my mind every minute for the past three hours."

Dex was a little surprised that kissing his "buddy" didn't feel weird, but he wasn't surprised that he once again found himself sleeping on the sofa. It would take more than a declaration of love to overcome that barrier. He was at least glad that she had mustered the courage to say what he had wanted to say. They had finally defined their relationship, and he no longer had to conceal his true feelings for her.

Chapter 8

The following Saturday night Dex and Marie returned from a movie and parked on the street in front of her apartment. They were laughing and talking as they got out of the car, but Marie suddenly stopped laughing, and Dex saw that she was staring at a man walking toward them from the other side of the street.

"What's going on, Marie?"

"Let's get inside, Dex; you don't want to talk to this guy."

"Who is this? Do you know him?"

She didn't answer, but the man said, "Well, Marie, you sure don't waste any time."

"Bill, what are you doing here? I told you to stay away from me. If you start any trouble, I'm going to call the police." She took the cell phone out of her purse and dialed the first two digits of a 9-1-1 call.

Dex was looking back and forth between the two of them. It was obvious that they knew each other and that Marie was very upset, but he had no idea what it was all about.

"Why shouldn't I start trouble? Are you afraid junior here will find out what kind of harlot he's going out with?"

At that point Dex had heard enough. He grabbed the arm of the man she had called Bill and said, "I don't know who you are, but you better back off before you get your butt kicked back across the street."

Bill turned and took a round-house swing at Dex, who easily deflected it with his left shoulder. Dex's uppercut started somewhere near his waist and snapped Bill's head back when it connected with his chin. He went down like a bowling pin and didn't make a move to get back on his feet. Marie was pulling on Dex's arm, and when he turned toward her, the man managed to get up on his knees and lunged at him. His shoulder hit the injured leg, and Dex cried out in pain, stumbled backward, lost his balance, and fell on his back. Bill scrambled up on top of him, grasped Dex's head in his hands, and was trying to smash it against the pavement. Even though his leg was throbbing with pain, Dex managed to flip Bill over on his back and ended up sitting astride him. He pulverized his face and head with both fists until the man stopped trying to fight back and was just trying to cover up.

Dex's rage replaced all reason. Marie was screaming for him to stop, but he continued to viciously batter Bill's face until she finally grabbed his arm. Bill was bleeding profusely from his nose and had two ugly facial lacerations. One was a three-inch-long gash under his chin that was a result of the initial uppercut. Marie knew it was going to require a number of sutures.

When she helped Dex to his feet, his leg was in so much pain that he was only able to hobble to the apartment steps before he had to sit down.

"Who is this jerk, Marie?"

"His name is Bill Bishop. He's a doctor that I worked with and dated a few times, but he's also an obsessive lunatic. I told him a long time ago to stay away from me, but he can't seem to understand that I don't want to have anything to do with him. I'll fill you in later, but I'm going to call an ambulance now."

Bishop had partially regained his senses and was trying to sit up. Blood was streaming down the front of his sports jacket and white dress shirt. "I don't need a damn ambulance, but you better tell your lover that he has just made a serious mistake. He's going to regret getting involved in this."

Dex tried to get up off the steps, but the intense pain in his leg forced him to sit down again. Bishop took the opportunity to get to his feet and make it across the street to his car. Before speeding away he yelled, "You haven't heard the last of this, you bitch, and your lover is never going to see me coming when I pay him back."

After she helped Dex upstairs, Marie told him the story about how Bishop's bizarre behavior led to his dismissal from the hospital staff and how he blamed her for his problems and threatened to kill her during his session with the staff psychiatrist.

"Why haven't you reported this to the police? The guy threatened to kill you?"

"I don't want to go through that whole process of going to court and testifying. He's working in Birmingham now, and after the beating you just gave him, I doubt if he will ever come around again."

Chapter 9

Dex graduated in May with a bachelor's degree in business administration. He still hadn't even had a job interview. The only prospect he had was from a small high school outside Savannah that was interested in hiring him as a head coach. The school hadn't had a winning season in years, and he didn't want to coach anyway, so he simply told them he wasn't interested.

Gigi's house in River City was in a declining neighborhood and needed a lot of repairs that she couldn't afford. Dex had not told her, but he had planned to buy her a new house with the signing bonus he expected to get from the NFL. Now that wasn't going to happen, and he felt that he had to move back to River City to take care of her. Gigi was still in pretty good health, but she was getting to the age where health would become more of a concern, and he was her only living relative.

Fate had slapped Dex in the face and now he had to swallow his pride, forget what might have been, and move back in with his grandmother. On his first night back in River City, he climbed into the same bed he had slept in most of his life, and he knew that this time it wasn't just for summer vacation. He had come full circle. He was twenty-two years old and once again dependent on Gigi for room and board, just as he had been when he was a five-year-old orphan. He thought that when he graduated their roles would be reversed, but until he got a job, he couldn't even support himself.

Dex stayed awake for hours staring at the plaques and trophies on the bookshelf in his old bedroom. He remembered how proud he was when he received each one, but he now realized how meaningless this entire childhood memorabilia was to an adult. If he had not known that Gigi treasured all of his awards, he probably would have thrown them all away.

If Dex had any marketable skills, he wasn't aware of them. He didn't have any idea what he might be qualified to do. His prior job experience consisted of being a paperboy, lifeguard, and laborer. There was nothing there to enhance a résumé, and the ability to hit a receiver on a deep fly pattern wouldn't impress many personnel managers. Of course, he did have a degree in business administration, but without some practical experience, his degree wouldn't differentiate him from all the other business graduates who would be applying for the same jobs. Dex had always had an unpretentious self-confidence, but now he was anything but confident about his future.

As he lay in bed that night, Dex thought back over the few meaningless jobs he had had. He enjoyed his paper route, and the lifeguard job was fun for a couple of summers. The worst job he ever had was working at a factory loading twenty-five-pound boxes of bottles in a boxcar. At the beginning of each shift, the boxes were pretty light, but eight hours later each box felt like it weighed a hundred pounds. The only pleasant memories he had about that summer job was the time he spent with Doris Jean Lewis. She worked inside the factory packing the boxes that Dex later stacked. She was far too intelligent to be spending her life at the end of a conveyor belt, but Doris Jean, who he quickly nicknamed DJ, had been infected at birth with what Eugene O'Neill called "the most deadly and prevalent of all diseases." But if poverty was her diagnosis then hope was her elixir.

DJ's father deserted the family, and she had to drop out of high school in her senior year to help support them. The factory was the only job she could get, but she had hoped that it would be for only a short time. She had dreams back then of getting her GED and going on to college.

Intelligence is a God-given gift for most people, but in her case it was a curse. She was smart enough to understood her dilemma but unable to do anything to change it. Even though she was attractive, bright, energetic, and personable, poverty had crushed her dreams, and she had finally accepted her fate.

DJ was nineteen when she met Dex and was already three years into the mind-numbing job of packing bottles in cardboard boxes. Before she met him, she rarely dated and actually preferred to spend her free time in the public library. Her library card was a passport to a world she would not otherwise have known. The literary giants of past generations were her best friends.

Dex first noticed her sitting in the area of the plant set aside for brown-bagging.

"Hi, I'm Dex. Do you mind if I sit here?"

"No, that's what all the chairs are for. I'm Doris Jean. Have a seat. I haven't seen you here before. You must be new."

"Yeah, I just started last week. How long have you been here?"

"Long enough to know I'd rather be anywhere other than here. I just passed my third anniversary."

"Does it get any easier to deal with the heat and noise?"

"I guess it must because I don't pay much attention to it anymore."

They continued to chat until their lunch break was over and started meeting each day for lunch. They started dating a week later. DJ was a world apart from the spoiled sorority debutantes that Dex frequently dated on campus. If she was envious of those who had more, she never talked about it. Despite her situation, she was basically a cheerful person, and she made Dex happy when he was with her. Before either of them realized it was happening, their casual dating evolved into a blazing summer romance.

In retrospect, they probably weren't fooling themselves into thinking long term, but Dex adored DJ and enjoyed being with her more than anyone he had ever dated. They never talked about anything beyond that summer. DJ knew Dex was returning to college, and he knew that she would continue working in the factory after he was gone.

That summer Dex practically abandoned Hoagie and his other friends because he preferred DJ's company to hanging out with the guys. They spent time between shifts swimming at the mountain lake where he and Hoagie swam when they were in high school. Often they would just sit on the shore and talk for hours.

By the end of the summer, Dex was convinced that he was in love with DJ, and even now, years later, he still refused to categorize it in his mind as just a typical summer romance.

They drifted apart after he returned to school that fall, and the following spring she married a soldier and moved to Germany. Dex sincerely hoped DJ was happy and that her soldier appreciated the diamond in the rough he married. If he ever knew anyone who truly deserved a good break in life, it was Doris Jean Lewis.

Chapter 10

Everyone had warned Dex about the dismal job prospects in River City, and their warnings proved to be prophetic. He could not even get an interview. Employers were holding applications on file from well-qualified prospects for months. It was an employer's market. When a job became available, the employer simply went to the file cabinet and plucked out an application. There was no need for additional interviews or applications.

Dex did everything but hand out résumés on a downtown street corner. He made dozens of phone calls and mailed countless résumés, but he wasn't able to get in the front door of a potential employer.

The recession that ravaged the country had officially ended almost a year before, but River City still had lingering economic problems. The city had suffered what the mayor called a "double whammy." They not only had to contend with the countrywide recession, but they lost a lot of well-paying manufacturing jobs when a large metal fabricator moved their operations to Mexico. Several smaller employers fell prey to the recession and simply closed their doors forever.

Hoagie found a job almost immediately as a music teacher and band director at the county high school. Dex was happy for his friend, but it made him feel even more like a failure. His best friend and girlfriend both had careers, and he couldn't even get an interview.

Having self-doubt and feeling like a loser was a new experience for Dex. Athletics had allowed him to live a charmed life. He had never been egotistical, but he had always had a well-adjusted feeling of self-confidence. Now for the first time in his life, he was beginning to feel like a real loser. He wondered how Marie felt about being stuck with someone who was apparently chronically unemployed. It was certainly embarrassing to him.

To loosen up his stiff leg, Dex jogged each morning on the high-school track before the students arrived. One morning he noticed Bob Delaney, his high-school coach, watching him from the bleachers. Delaney had been like a surrogate father to his star athlete; however, Dex had been purposely avoiding him since he had been home. Delaney had told him a year before that he was looking forward to one of his athletes making it in the NFL. That wasn't going to happen now, and Dex hated to see the coach disappointed.

"Coach, what're you doing sitting up there watching an ex-jock trying to relive his youth?"

"Son, you may be an ex-jock, but you're still young; you just run like an old man. How's the leg?"

"It's still a little stiff. I run every morning to loosen up, but it also takes my mind off the fact that I can't get a job. I've discovered that River City isn't a hotbed for employment. You don't happen to know anyone looking for a green kid with a new business degree, do you?"

Delaney was watching on television when Dex suffered his career-ending injury. "Dex, I know how hard this has been on you. It's been hard on me too. When I saw you leaving the field on that stretcher, I felt like I'd been kicked in the stomach."

"I appreciated you calling me while I was in the hospital. I've been planning to come see you, but I have been spending all my time looking for a job."

"Dex, it isn't your fault. The economy in this area is still pretty slow. In fact, it has been so bad that most of our kids aren't coming back home after graduating from college."

"I felt like I needed to be here to take care of my grandmother, but as it's turned out, she is still taking care of me financially. It's getting rather embarrassing."

"Dex, if we can just find some way to exploit it, you may have an advantage here. Everyone still remembers you because you brought a lot of favorable attention to our school and the entire town while you were playing here. There ought to be some way to parlay your name recognition into an opportunity. Let me talk to some people and see if I can help. Why don't you come over to our house for dinner tomorrow night? Betty would love to see you."

"I'd love to, but my girlfriend is going to be in town. Could I bring Marie? I'd love for you and Mrs. Delaney to meet her."

As soon as he asked the question, Dex suddenly remembered his last conversation with Marie. He would have to do some serious fence-mending before he took her to meet anyone. Their argument the previous weekend had been rather heated and was still not resolved. When he last talked to her, she was still coming on the weekend, but it was obvious she was still mad about what he had said.

Dex had already been planning to apologize, grovel, or do whatever was necessary to try to smooth over their first real argument. The argument was a result of his grumpy disposition over his employment situation. Marie had merely said she was happy that Hoagie found a job, but her comment struck Dex as a criticism of his own unemployment, and he reacted angrily.

"Look, I've done everything possible to find something. Don't blame me because I can't toot a tuba."

"Dex, I'm not criticizing you. I'm sure you're going to find a job soon."

For weeks, she had been overly optimistic, and her constant encouragement and unbridled confidence had begun to irritate him. She kept telling him that everything would work out if he would just keep a positive attitude. He should have been grateful for her support and encouragement, but instead it finally frustrated him to the point to where he took it out on her.

"Damn it, Marie, everyone is not as lucky as you. It doesn't happen that fast for everyone."

Luck was not a word he should have used with Marie, who had worked twelve-hour days and taken on huge financial risks to build her business. She responded with fire blazing in her eyes.

"You don't know what you're talking about. Being successful in a business venture has very little to do with luck and a whole lot to do with working your butt off. Luck is when a cornerback falls down and one of your limp-arm, off-target passes gets caught for a touchdown."

The argument that ensued was pretty ugly. Dex learned a lot that day about her pride and steely resolve. When challenged, she could become hard as nails in a heartbeat and hold her own in a confrontation with anyone.

Dex quickly decided that retreat was the wisest course of action. During the two-hour drive back to River City, he tried to reconstruct the argument but kept coming up with the same conclusion: he had acted like a jerk. She was just being supportive, and his bruised self-image had caused him to take his frustrations out on her.

It was a retrospective thought, but Dex now knew that individuals in love have an increased capacity to hurt each other. He also now knew one of Marie's "hot buttons," and he would never touch that one again. He called to apologize as soon as he got home, but she remained pretty frosty even after his apology.

After the invitation from Coach Delaney, Dex called Marie's apartment, got her answering machine, and left a message asking her to get there a couple of hours early because they were going to have dinner with some friends. He needed the extra time to try to calm her down before they showed up at the Delaneys' house.

Dex watched through the window as Marie parked her car and started up the walk to the front porch. He could tell by the purposeful stride and stern facial expression that she was probably prepared to renew the argument. He needed to do something quick to defuse the conflict or he was going to be in for a miserable evening.

He opened the door before she reached it and literally pulled her inside the house. Before she had a chance to deliver the speech she had probably been rehearsing all the way from Atlanta, he said, "Marie, I love you. I'm sorry I acted like a jerk and took my frustration out on you."

Dex had learned a valuable lesson about admitting responsibility and being truly penitent. She shook her head and then wrapped her arms around him.

"You're right. You really were a jerk, but I still love you; so let's not talk about it anymore."

When Delaney and his wife met them at the door, Dex introduced Marie and then noticed there was another couple sitting in the living room. Delaney introduced them to Jim and Andrea Mitchell.

"Dex, Jim and Andrea have only been in River City for a few months. Jim is vice president and national sales manager for Argon Pharmaceuticals. We play golf together, and he takes all my money."

Dex said, "Jim, I've lived here my entire life, and Argon has been here since before I was born. I know they have something to do with drugs, but I never have really understood exactly what they do."

"We manufacture and distribute a wide array of over-the-counter medications. Supermarkets and others distribute some of our products, but most are sold at pharmacies just like prescription drugs. You've probably used a lot of them and just had no reason to know they were manufactured by Argon."

They talked for a while about how the company had expanded over the years, and then Betty Delaney announced dinner was ready. While they were eating, Mitchell said, "Dex, before moving here we lived in Columbia, South Carolina, and I saw you play once against the Gamecocks in Columbia."

Delaney started to tell a story about Dex's high-school career, but Dex stopped him by saying, "Jim, I love the coach, but if you let him get started talking about football, we will still be sitting here in the morning."

Dex knew where this conversation was headed, and he was trying to steer it to another subject. There was a time when he had enjoyed talking about the game and his career, but lately he tried to move on from that time in his life. It would always be difficult in River City for people to think of him as anything but an athlete, but he was trying to change the perception.

Dex said, "Marie and I grew up next door to each other, but she moved to Atlanta when we were in high school. It was seven years before we saw each other again. We spend a lot of time together now, but I don't pull pigtails like I used to do."

They all laughed and then Andrea asked, "What do you do in Atlanta, Marie?"

"I'm a nurse, and I own my own business providing in-home care for elderly patients."

"Do you work by yourself?"

"No, I have a staff of several nurses. My company is named RN4U, and I've been in business for a little less than two years."

Andrea said, "That's fascinating. I'm a nurse too, but I haven't practiced in several years."

The women continued to carry on their conversation, and Delaney suggested the men move out onto the patio where he could smoke. His wife had created a no-smoking zone in the house. Dex still remembered his foul-smelling cigars and could appreciate her position.

After they were settled on the patio, Mitchell said, "Delaney tells me you're looking for a job."

"Yes, I am, but it's a pretty tough job market in River City. I haven't had any luck so far. My business degree doesn't seem to impress anyone, and there aren't many jobs available."

"When we were on the golf course this morning, Delaney told me a lot about you. I've got an idea that I'd like to discuss with you. Argon has a new product that we're about ready to bring to market. We've been putting together a marketing plan while we look for an experienced pharmaceutical salesman to lead the sales in our test market area. We haven't looked at anyone without sales experience, but if you have any interest, I've got an idea I would like to get together and discuss with you."

"I'd love to talk to you, but I don't have any sales experience. I also don't know anything about drugs, unless you want to count the love affair I had with pain pills after my injury. I ate them like candy for a couple of months."

Mitchell laughed and said, "Why don't you come by my office at ten o'clock Monday morning and we'll discuss it? I want to introduce you to our CEO and some of the other executives. I can't make you any promises because they may not agree with what I have in mind, but I think it's worth a shot."

Chapter 11

Dex and Marie were both happy when they left the party. The interview was the first encouraging news he had received. Marie had created a bond with Andrea because of their nursing connection, and she had enjoyed herself. There was nothing Marie would rather talk about than RN4U, and Andrea's curiosity had given her an opportunity to talk about her favorite subject. As they were leaving, Andrea whispered to Dex, "That's some girl you've got there. Don't let her get away."

Marie returned to Atlanta Sunday afternoon, and Dex and Hoagie went out for their favorite weekend meal. Hoagie's mother had been pumping him full of vegetables since he had been home, so he was ready for pizza. Over a large pizza, Dex told him all about his scheduled interview at Argon

On the way home, Hoagie drove. Dex's car was parked on the street in front of Gigi's house. When they turned onto their street, they saw a man kneeling beside his car. The man saw them slowing down and quickly sprinted between two neighbor's houses. They didn't even try to chase him. Dex's injured leg prevented him from running faster than anyone other than maybe Hoagie.

When they walked around to the curb side of the car, they saw that the valve stem was cut on both right tires, which were completely flat. The vandal used red spray paint to scrawl a message on the car's white door: "Next it be you face, purty boy."

Dex called the police, but they were unable to give the investigating officer any type of helpful description. They told him that the man was fairly tall and wearing dark pants and a dark shirt. Dex knew that with that nondescript information there wasn't a chance of apprehending him.

The cop looked at Dex's car. "Slashing your tires could have been just a sick prank."

Dex was aggravated that he was too easily dismissing the vandalism, and he said, "Is the message on the door a prank too?"

The cop scratched his chin. "If it is, it's a pretty sick one. You got any enemies?"

Dex laughed. "How about a million Vols fans?"

The cop obviously wasn't a football fan. He just stared blankly.

"We beat Tennessee three years in a row, and I don't think I'm one of their favorite people. I've had a few angry phone calls and letters, but no one has ever done anything like this."

"You got any of those letters?"

"The university athletic department turned them over to the Athens police department; they may still have them. Actually, some of them were pretty funny. They used the same good grammar as the guy who just painted my car."

"Well, I guess it's a place to start," the cop said with little enthusiasm.

The message on the door may have been illiterate, but it foretold more trouble ahead. This wasn't likely to be the last thing Dex would hear from this unknown villain.

When Dex arrived at Argon the next morning, the receptionist called upstairs to announce his arrival and told him to take the elevator to the third floor. When he exited the elevator on the executive level, Mitchell's secretary was waiting for him.

"Mr. Martin, if you could have a seat for a minute, Mr. Mitchell and the others will meet you in the boardroom."

She returned a few minutes later and ushered him into the ornately adorned boardroom. Mitchell was there with six or seven other people sitting around a walnut conference table that could seat at least twenty people. They all rose as Dex walked in, and Mitchell introduced him. All the people in the room were senior officers, including the chairman and CEO Robert Stonecipher.

After the introductions, everyone sat at the table and, apparently in deference to his position, waited for Stonecipher to start the conversation. "I hope you don't mind if I call you Dex." He continued without waiting for an answer to his rhetorical question. "I feel like I know you because I've followed your career at Georgia with some interest. Actually, with the sports-dominated newspaper in this town, I didn't have much choice. Your name recognition is one of the reasons Mitchell wanted us to meet you. I'm sure you realize that we don't usually convene an executive meeting to interview an applicant, but this is a different situation, and you are not the usual applicant. But more than that, the position we want to discuss involves a concept we have never tried before. We've been meeting this morning to discuss an idea that Mitchell has proposed—one that may be mutually beneficial to you and Argon."

Stonecipher continued. "Frankly, I've never had a lot of confidence in celebrity product endorsements, but Mitchell has made an interesting proposal, and that's the reason for this meeting. To be fair, your sports popularity does not qualify you for what we want to do, but it could be beneficial in this particular situation if you have the other attributes we need."

Stonecipher was a pacer, and he was walking back and forth behind the conference table across from Dex as he talked. "We are bringing to market a new product and will initially test market it in the Southeast. Of course, this is the precise region where your name recognition is the highest. Let me hasten to point out, however, that we are not just looking for an endorsement. We could buy a celebrity endorsement. What we need is a full-time employee with the personality and ability to actually sell our product to physicians and pharmacies."

Stonecipher cleared his throat and continued. "We've had a search firm looking for an experienced pharmaceutical salesman to head up a product-specific sales effort, but Mitchell has proposed an alternate approach. The name recognition aspect is not lost on us, but we are only willing to consider the possibility of hiring someone without experience if we believe that individual has the potential to be trained to sell in our rather specialized market. Jim Mitchell speaks very highly of you and believes that you might have that potential. He will discuss the details with you later, but we wanted to get everyone together this morning so you could meet our team and we could get to know you."

The CEO buzzed his assistant, and she brought in a tray of sweet rolls, which were apparently already prepared for the meeting. In the next few minutes Dex had an opportunity to informally speak with each of the executives as they stood around the room. He surprised himself with the ease he had in communicating with them. Perhaps all those after-game interviews would prove to be useful.

When Stonecipher said he had to leave, all of his subordinates knew it was time to go to work, and the room quickly emptied. Dex followed Mitchell back to his private office.

"Dex, I hope we didn't overwhelm you with all those people, but I thought it was important for them to get to know you since the position we're talking about creating is something we've never done before. I had to sell the idea to the old man, and I didn't need to have any of the other executives oppose me. I've found that the best way to eliminate opposition is to make everyone feel like they participated in the decision. I know you were nervous, but you handled it well. I made a point of talking to Stonecipher and each of the others while you were circulating among them. They were all impressed. But before I get too far into this, I need to know if you are even interested in a position with Argon."

"Mr. Mitchell, I'm definitely interested. I appreciate what you've done and look forward to the opportunity."

Mitchell said, "Okay, but call me Jim. We'll have to line you up for an interview with the shrink that evaluates all new sales employees. Then we'll have our agency run a background check to make sure you haven't robbed any banks. You'll also have to go up to human resources, fill out about ten pounds of forms, interview with the director, and pass a standard employment physical."

Although he carefully concealed any outward sign of discomfort, knowing that some agency would be running a background check terrified Dex. This had been his greatest fear when he started his job search. He worried about what would happen if a potential employer found out about the Florida incident.

Mitchell pulled a large manila folder from a drawer. "I saved for last the very thing you probably wanted to discuss first. The compensation package is multi-tiered and would combine a base salary of seventy thousand dollars, a bonus based on sales, and our standard benefits package. If you are as successful in sales, as I think you could be, you could approach six figures in your first year. Personnel can explain the whole package to you later. We'll furnish you a company car, and after the first year, you'll be eligible for the company's incentive stock option program. I'll explain the option program later, but all you need to know now is that if the company does well financially, you can make a lot of money in options."

As he drove home, Dex's head was spinning. He didn't understand all the details, but he did understand that he was offered a job, contingent on passing a psychological test, physical exam, and background check. He also knew that if the Florida incident was discovered in the background check, he would probably be disqualified; however, it had been three years, so maybe they wouldn't find out about it.

The compensation offered by Argon wasn't what he had been expecting from the NFL, but it was a lot more than he ever thought he could get without throwing a football. He couldn't wait to share the news with Marie. If this job worked out, he would be able to have his own apartment. Maybe Marie could sleep on his sofa for a change.

Dex was scheduled to meet with the shrink on Wednesday morning. When he arrived at the doctor's downtown office, he discovered from the sign on the door that the guy was actually an industrial psychologist, not a psychiatrist. The distinction was insignificant to Dex.

Dex enjoyed their conversation and talked openly about his family, teenage years, and college experiences. He left the office feeling very good about the meeting, but then the realization of what happened suddenly struck him. The psychologist had very effectively lulled him into a comfort zone to get inside his head. He had to admit that the guy was very good. For the next hour, he replayed the conversation over and over, trying to remember just what he'd said and how he'd said it.

That same afternoon Dex was scheduled to be back at the corporate headquarters to meet with Ralph Bell, the vice president of human resources. At his office, an administrative assistant said, "Mr. Martin, before meeting with Mr. Bell, you will have to fill out our standard employment application." The assistant then led Dex to a small room and said, "Here are the application forms. Please complete the front and back of all three pages. When you finish, bring them to me and I will notify Mr. Bell."

She closed the door and left him alone. Dex was about halfway through the employment application when he came to the question he'd been dreading: "Have you ever been convicted of any offense other than a minor traffic violation?" Now Dex was faced with the first ethical question that he had to confront in the business world. Should he lie and hope that the truth was never discovered, or should he tell the truth and risk not even being given an opportunity to explain?

He put the pencil on the table, leaned back in the chair, closed his eyes, and considered his course of action. This could turn out to be a life-altering decision. He could tell the truth and risk not getting the job, or take the easy way out and just say no on the application. If he didn't tell them, the arrest in Florida would probably never be discovered. While he was sitting with his eyes closed, Dex's mind raced back to the summer when he was thirteen years old.

Chapter 12

Dex had just finished the seventh grade. The day after his last day of school, he went fishing at his favorite pond, and it turned out to be one of the most memorable days in his life. An old man was sitting in the exact spot where Dex usually fished. He was under a canopy of trees and concentrating on the end of the cane pole he had anchored in his grasp.

Dex stopped to watch when he saw him catch a fat bluegill and bait his hook with a white gob of something that Dex couldn't identify. He watched the man pull one bluegill after another from the pond's murky water before his curiosity overpowered him.

"Hey, mister, what is that white stuff you're using for bait?"

"Son, dat be crawdad tails. Sit yourself down here and let old Geechee show you how to do some fishing."

Dex watched as the elderly black man broke the tail off of a live crawfish, peeled the shell back, and baited his hook with the white meat of the tail. Dex sat beside him until the man had about fifteen fish on his homemade stringer and decided to quit for the day.

That was the first of many days they fished together that summer. Until he met Geechee, Dex had never had a close relationship with an adult other than his grandmother. He was so young when his parents died that all he knew about them came from stories Gigi told him. There was an old photograph on her mantel of him standing between them, but Dex had spent so many hours staring at the photograph that he was no longer sure whether he actually remembered them or he just remembered the images in the photograph.

Dex's meeting with Geechee couldn't have come at a more opportune time. He had just had his thirteenth birthday, and like all children entering their teens, he was passing through an emotionally awkward stage where the idealism of youth bumps up against the realities of life. Puberty and the emergence of hormones contribute to the confusion, and the lessons learned during this impressionable time stay with teens as they struggle into adulthood and beyond. Geechee helped bridge the gap between where Dex had been and where he was headed, and he discovered that he could safely share his innermost thoughts with his new friend.

Geechee must have been about seventy when they met, and he was the first black man with whom Dex ever had a conversation. No one Dex met since had a greater influence on his life. He still believed Geechee was probably the smartest man he ever encountered, even though he essentially had no formal education. He was certainly the most unforgettable person he ever met.

Although Dex didn't discover it until years later, "Gullah-Geechee" is a culture and a dialect spoken by descendants of African-American slaves who live on coastal islands and in communities along the Georgia and South Carolina coasts. Their dialect is a lilting, English-based Creole that has been preserved by their relative isolation.

Geechee, the only name by which Dex ever knew him, had left his home near Charleston at an early age and worked at several jobs before he was old enough to work on the railroad. He was a railroad porter for years before a back injury forced him into early retirement.

Although he was basically illiterate, Geechee seemed to instinctively understand what was important in life. Even now after Dex had graduated from college, he still thought that Geechee probably had a better understanding of the purpose of life than anyone he had ever met.

Geechee's lifestyle didn't require many creature comforts, and he didn't have many of them. He lived on the edge of the city garbage dump in a one-room shack beside the unmanned facility where the city sewage was processed. The city apparently tolerated his presence there because his shack was a deterrent to any vandal who could endure the stench of the waste treatment facility and garbage dump long enough to get into mischief on the property. The creek that flowed past the garbage dump was the most severely polluted waterway Dex had ever seen. Even Geechee, who was known to eat things that would repulse other men, refused to eat the fish from that creek. There was a fabric-dying facility several miles upstream, and the water in the creek changed colors daily in accordance with what dye was being used on a particular day.

He told Dex over and over, "Don't you be eating no fish come outta dat crick."

There was no electricity or running water in Geechee's shack. His meals were either roasted over an open fire spit or boiled in a large iron pot. Dex had seen pioneer women wash clothes in pots like that in Western movies. His water for drinking and cooking was captured in a barrel strategically placed to catch the rain as it ran off the shack's tin roof.

In retrospect, Dex now thought his relationship with Geechee probably had something to do with his lack of a father figure, but a mutual love of the outdoors was the direct link that connected two individuals from different generations, cultures, and races. Geechee was a mentor and a friend to the impressionable teenager. While he was teaching Dex to fish and trap wild animals, their long conversations were also teaching him the difference between right and wrong and how he should treat others. He learned more about how to live his life sitting outside Geechee's shack than he ever learned inside a classroom.

They talked for hours outside the shack while sitting on the truck seats Geechee salvaged from the dump. Geechee would often grill a rabbit or boil an opossum while they talked. Dex caught many of the old man's meals in the homemade traps Geechee taught him to make.

The group of five ponds where they fished several days each week during that long summer were shallow craters in the earth that remained after clay had been excavated a century earlier to mold the red-tile pipe that was common in that era. It was about a mile from Geechee's shack to the ponds, and they would usually follow the railroad tracks to get there. Geechee encouraged Dex's unsuccessful attempts to travel the entire distance balancing on one track.

"Fore summa be gone, you gwine to do it to da fishin' hole."

When they didn't follow the railroad tracks, they took a path that followed a buried gas pipeline through an otherwise impassable swamp. The path paralleled the polluted creek that either drained or filled the swamp, depending on the amount of rainfall in the area. The only fishing equipment that each of them owned was a cane pole they had cut in the swamp. The swamp was also where they collected the crawfish they used for bait.

Geechee told Dex, "When I's on the tracks, I seen dem folks in Nawlins boil dem crawdads til they be red as clay. Den dey's eat 'em up and suck on da heads."

As Dex pondered his dilemma over the arrest question on the application, he thought back to that summer. In his mind's eye, he could still see Geechee sitting at his favorite fishing hole. He would know how to answer this question. Dex's association with Geechee taught him that character and integrity were the most important traits an individual could possess and human dignity has nothing to do with education or money. He also learned that there was very little difference between a thirteen-year-old child and a seventy-year-old child, except for a few wrinkles. Dex had heard racial slurs at school, but he now knew that the only difference in the races was the color of the skin, and the only important difference between the rich and poor was attitude.

When Dex started the eighth grade that fall, he was gradually lured away from Geechee by athletics and a sudden interest in girls. Later that year, he read in the newspaper that the charred remains of an unidentified man were discovered in the rubble of a shack that had burned to the ground next to the city dump.

If measured financially, Geechee's net worth was zero, and he was buried in a pauper's grave with no marble tombstone marking his final resting place. But Geechee had riches and self-dignity and wisdom beyond what most men ever knew. His economic status caused most people to consider him a failure, but Dex knew that no man who was a failure could have ever had such a positive influence on the life of a teenage boy.

And now, from his unmarked grave, Geechee provided the answer to the question that was plaguing him. Dex picked up the pencil and wrote, "Yes."

Chapter 13

Dex nervously handed the application to the administrative assistant, who asked him to have a seat and wait. She delivered it to Bell in his office, and the ten-minute wait seemed like an eternity. When she finally returned and ushered Dex into the office, she left him standing in front of the desk. Bell was looking at the application and simply motioned for Dex to have a seat.

Dex held his breath as the executive finally laid the application on his desk, took off his glasses, and looked at him.

"Well, Mr. Martin, do you want to talk about it?" There was no need to explain what he meant.

Dex cleared his throat and said, "Yes, sir. I appreciate you giving me an opportunity to explain what happened. Several people advised me not to answer the question truthfully on an application, but as badly as I need this job, I can't start my career by lying on an application. They said that an employer would probably never discover it because it happened in Florida, and they are probably right, but I just couldn't do that."

He took a deep breath and continued. "It happened on spring break in Florida during my freshman year in college. I'm not going to make an excuse, because I was guilty as charged. You can call it youthful indiscretion or simple stupidity, but whatever label you put on it, I was wrong."

Bell frowned as he nodded and then leaned back in his chair and folded his arms across his chest.

"I was eighteen years old. I had been involved in athletics all my life, and I had never even had a beer in high school. We just finished spring football practice, and the spring break from classes started. We had a week before we had to be back in school, and I went to Daytona Beach with several of my teammates."

Dex nervously cleared his throat and said, "There were about a hundred kids at a hotel pool party, and some guys from Auburn started trash-talking about Georgia. My friends and I had been drinking, and I don't think they had any more experience with alcohol than I had. A fight started, and we threw several of the Auburn guys in the pool and then threw the pool furniture in after them. The next thing I knew the police were there, and we were arrested and charged with drunk and disorderly conduct and destruction of property. We had already spent what little money we had, so we had to spend the night in jail. The next day we pleaded guilty to the charges, and the judge fined us and ordered us to pay restitution to the hotel for the damaged furniture. My grandmother wired me the money, and I worked that summer to repay her. That's the whole story. I've been worried about this coming back to haunt me for three years, but I had to tell the truth."

Bell stood and walked over to stare out the window. Dex was sure that he had just blown a job opportunity, but when Bell turned around he was smiling. "Dex, when we get to know each other better, I'll tell you about some of the dumb-ass things I did in college." The rest of the interview went well, and Bell told his assistant to schedule an appointment for him to take the employment physical.

Dex passed the physical exam on Thursday and was told to report to work the following Monday. He would be reporting directly to Jim Mitchell in sales, but Dex's work would also be coordinated with the corporate marketing department. Mitchell would be responsible for his sales training, and the marketing department would work with him to build a campaign using his name recognition as an athlete.

Dex didn't want to become the poster boy because it would again reinforce his image as the quintessential jock. He talked to the marketing personnel, and they said they understood his concern and promised that the campaign would be handled stylishly. They also invited him to participate by sharing his thoughts throughout the process.

Dex spent several weeks working with marketing, and by the time the campaign began to take focus, he was comfortable with the professional way it was being presented. The plan was for Dex to make some television and radio spots while the graphic arts department designed some attractive magazine ads featuring him in his uniform. He had asked, and they had agreed, that in the advertisements he would be identified as a full-time employee of the company and not just another jock being paid to read a script.

While he was meeting with marketing, Dex was also working several hours each day with Mitchell for sales training. Mitchell was planning a joint sales trip through the targeted states to introduce Dex to physicians and pharmacies, deliver samples, and discuss the new product. The trip was planned to coincide with the initial release of the marketing campaign on radio and television.

The night before he was supposed to leave on the trip, Dex was at home watching TV with Gigi. They were waiting on Hoagie, who was coming over to play cards with them. Suddenly Dex heard Hoagie yelling in the front yard and then pounding on the front door. When he opened the door, a very agitated Hoagie grabbed him by the arm and said, "You gotta come see this."

"Slow down, Hoagie, come see what? What're you talking about?"

"Dex, just get out here and look at what's hanging on that maple tree." Gigi followed them out on the porch, and as soon as she saw what Hoagie was pointing at, she ran back in the house and called the police. Within a few minutes, two police cars with flashing blue lights pulled up in front of the house, and a group of neighbors, attracted by the yelling, gathered in the yard.

There was a dead opossum with an ice pick stuck through its head, pinning it to the maple tree in the front yard. Its obscene, hairless tail was hanging straight down the tree trunk, pointing to a note that was nailed to the tree.

The note, on a sheet of plain paper, contained only three typed words that had obviously been cut from a magazine or some type of printed material. Dex read the poignant note aloud, "You be next."

The same officer who had investigated his slashed tires looked at the note, scratched his head, and said, "What does that mean?"

"I guess it means he wants to stick an ice pick in me. How do I know?"

"You got any enemies?"

"Officer, you already asked me that one time. Most people have enemies, and I must have picked one up somewhere, but I don't know who it is or what his beef is with me."

After the cop photographed the dead animal and collected the note, he asked, "What are you going to do with that thing?" It was obvious that he didn't want to touch anything close to it.

Dex shook his head in disgust, held the opossum by his tail, and jerked the ice pick out of the tree. He saw the squeamish cop's reaction, so when he walked by him he purposely let it slip out his hand and fall near the cop's foot. The cop jumped about three feet.

"I'm sorry; it slipped out of my hand." Dex picked it up again, walked to the backyard, and put it in the trash can.

After the police left and the crowd dispersed, Hoagie said, "Dex, you've got to have some idea who's doing this. What have you done to make someone this mad?"

"Hoagie, I haven't got a clue what this is about, but as far as I am concerned it has gone way beyond a practical joke. Somebody has now threatened to slash me with a knife and stab me with an ice pick. I can take care of myself, but I am worried about Gigi since both of these incidents have happened here at the house."

The next morning Dex and Mitchell left on the long-planned sales trip. They started by driving to Nashville and then they doubled back to Knoxville, where they spent the first night. The second day they made calls in Asheville before finishing the day in Charlotte. Mitchell had carefully planned the trip to introduce Dex to physicians that were already recommending Argon products and might be more inclined to suggest a new product to their patients.

Mitchell had always thought the worst part of the job was sitting in a physician's office waiting for him to finish with his patients. He had warned Dex about being impatient, but on this trip, he noticed that when he and Dex were jointly announced, they were quickly worked in between patients. He soon realized this was because Dex's name was being recognized. He knew this would bode well for the planned marketing blitz, so he started having Dex approach the office manager and use his business card to announce their arrival.

After a two-day swing through Columbia, Charleston, and Savannah, Dex and Mitchell spent Friday morning making calls in Atlanta. Mitchell invited Dex to call Marie and see if she could meet them for lunch. Although he talked to her by phone every night, phone calls didn't do much to nourish their budding romance. Lunch with a third party present wasn't much better, but at least he got to see her.

When Mitchell left the table to set up another appointment, Dex said, "Marie, this pace isn't going to go on forever. I hope you understand that it's very important for me to spend a lot of time on the job while I'm trying to establish myself."

She held his hand and said, "Hey, I started a business from scratch. I know what it's like. We've got a lifetime to be together." Dex wasn't sure how to respond since it was the first time either of them had suggested anything resembling spending a lifetime together. He was relieved when he saw Mitchell returning.

Chapter 14

Marie was concerned. The message on her answering machine asked her to contact Proudland Trust at her earliest opportunity to set up an appointment. She had no idea why they wanted to see her. Curiosity was quickly replaced by terror. Could they call the promissory note prematurely? She wasn't behind on the payments; she made them each month several days before they were due. Her business was doing well, but she wasn't in a position to pay off the loan. The note didn't mature for another year. She hesitantly called the bank to inquire about the nature of the meeting.

"Good afternoon. This is Marie Murphy, and you left a message for me to call this number to set up an appointment."

"Yes, Mr. Sloan asked me set up a meeting with you and the head of our trust department. Mr. Sloan will also be joining you. Would tomorrow morning at ten be convenient for your?"

"Yes, I can make it then, but can you tell me the reason for the meeting?"

"I'm sorry, but Mr. Sloan just asked me to set up the meeting, and he is not in the office now."

Marie was still puzzled. Her contract didn't have anything to do with the trust department. She didn't even fully understand the function of a bank's trust department.

When Marie arrived the next morning, she was ushered into the conference room where two men were waiting for her.

Sloan said, "Good morning, Marie. I'd like you to meet Harvey Blake, the vice president of our trust department."

Blake said, "Marie, I'm glad to finally meet you. I've heard so much about you and your business recently. Please have a seat."

She sat across the long walnut conference table from them and declined the offer of coffee because she didn't trust her shaking hands to hold a hot cup. While the two men were getting their coffee, Marie had an opportunity to look around the spacious conference room. The formal décor of the paneled room did nothing to dispel her anxiety. The walls were lined with black-and-white photographs of dour-faced old men, whom she assumed were members of the board. There was a projection screen protruding from a slot in the ceiling at one end of the room, and speakers and telephones were set up, apparently for conference calls, on either end of the long conference table.

Blake, who was obviously senior to Sloan, smiled at her and started the conversation. "Ms. Murphy, I asked for this meeting because I wanted to get to know you. I'm somewhat familiar with the nursing business you started and your start-up loan from Proudland."

Marie nodded but didn't say anything. She was worried that this was where he was going to drop the bomb that would destroy everything she had worked so hard to build.

Blake continued. "Congratulations on your success. I understand your business is doing very well and performing well ahead of your original projections. We may be in a position to help you grow even faster."

Marie was relieved but still confused. How was the trust department going to help her business grow? She smiled but kept her perspiring hands folded in her lap below the table. She was determined not to let them see that she was intimidated. Then she realized they were waiting for a response from her.

"That sounds interesting, and I'm always interested in expanding my business, but what does nursing have to do with the trust department?"

"That gets right to the heart of this meeting. We have contractual agreements to manage the trust accounts for a lot of our wealthiest customers."

Marie nodded as if she was familiar with that phase of banking, although she had never really thought about it.

"Frequently the department is also responsible for providing long-term care if the customer's physical or mental health deteriorates to a point where they are no longer able to function independently. Unfortunately we are handicapped in providing this service because we have no expertise in caring for the aged or infirmed."

Although she still didn't know where he was headed, Marie was beginning to understand why she was in the meeting. Maybe he wanted her opinion on health care for the elderly. This was certainly within her range of experience.

Blake paused until Marie nodded to indicate she was following him.

"Frankly, we don't have the expertise to determine when full-time nursing care is required, and we don't fully understand the alternatives. We know there are intermediate steps between independent living and nursing home care, but we need help in identifying those steps."

Now Marie understood how RN4U could help the trust department, but she let Blake continue uninterrupted.

"We would be providing a far greater service to our clients if we could offer professional assistance in making those decisions. These are the areas where we think your company might be able to assist us. What are your thoughts about this so far?"

Marie was glad to finally have an opportunity to contribute to the conversation.

"I understand the problem, and our company regularly assists our clients and their families with these decisions, but the process doesn't simply involve relocation."

Blake said, "That's exactly right, we want to make sure we have considered all the alternatives before recommending full-time care. But even if they are placed in a full-service nursing home, our responsibility doesn't end with just relocating them. We also want to continue monitoring the care of our clients even after they are in a full-care facility." Blake sat back and waited for Marie to respond.

"Mr. Blake, let me say first that this is definitely something we would be interested in doing and something for which my staff is well qualified. But you've caught me completely off guard, so help me understand what you're proposing. I assume we would be working directly for the bank, and that the bank would pay our service bills. I also assume we would enter into some type of contract with you. Is that correct?"

Blake simply nodded, and Marie continued. "Your idea on how it should be done perfectly coincides with our business model. It not only demonstrates a humanitarian approach to a problem that is only getting worse as our population ages, but I suspect that it is also an excellent competitive move by Proudland. I'm not aware of any other institution whose thinking has progressed this far. I'm impressed by your plan."

Blake said, "Thank you, Ms. Murphy; we do care very much about providing for the people who entrust us with their money and their lives. Your comment about competition is also insightful. We would indeed be the first trust department to offer a comprehensive program like this. I'm beginning to understand why Sloan was so impressed with your business acumen and why RN4U is prospering."

Blake continued, "We also have an ongoing situation we need to discuss, but we must insist that you keep this aspect confidential. We are in final negotiations to buy Heritage Bank & Trust Co. of River City, Tennessee, and we will want to extend this same service to the people who are being served by that bank's trust department. Have you considered expanding outside of Atlanta?"

"To tell you the truth, I've been so busy getting the legs under this business that I haven't had much time to think about geographical expansion. But yes, when I wrote the first business plan I included a section on expansion but took it out before I submitted it to the bank. I was afraid Mr. Slone would think it was too much pie in the sky from someone who had never even been in business. Actually River City would be a natural expansion for me, because it's my hometown and I still have a number of connections there." Talking about connections in River City was a stretch, but she thought it sounded good.

"Marie we will have our legal department prepare the contract, and you can have your attorney approve it. Expansion will increase your expenses, and I will be happy to approve an increase in your loan and an extension on the term of the loan."

"Thank you. I will need to increase the loan, but it's difficult to determine the how much until I know the number of patients, exactly what services we would provide, and what reports the bank will require."

"You're the health-care professional, and we would be interested in what you think would be an appropriate level of service under various medical scenarios. Could you prepare a plan on what you would recommend?"

"If you will furnish me the information on patients, I can have a plan ready for you within a few days."

After she left the meeting, Marie was euphoric. She couldn't believe her good fortune and couldn't wait to tell Dex that she was going to be opening an office in River City. For the rest of the day, her head was in a cloud. She thought of a thousand questions she should have asked. She would have to find and hire additional nurses for each location, but everything would hinge on the number of patients they would have to evaluate.

Chapter 15

Marie's phone was ringing as she unlocked the door to her apartment, and she hurried to answer it.

Dex said, "Hey, babe, I've been trying to call you all afternoon."

"Hi, sweetheart, I was just getting ready to call you. I've got some great news."

He listened as she excitedly told him about her meeting at the bank and the plans to open an office in River City. She expected him to be thrilled, but her news elicited nothing but dead silence.

After a protracted delay, Dex finally said, "Marie, I'm happy for you, but there are some things happening here that we need to discuss, and we can't do it over the phone. I'll drive down tomorrow, and we can have dinner. Don't worry, this is something we can deal with, but we need to talk it through."

Telling her not to worry was ridiculous. She was already worried because she could hear the concern in his voice. She wanted to push him for more information, but he obviously didn't want to talk about it now.

"Dex, why don't you just stay over here tomorrow night? It will give us some time together before things begin to get crazy with your new job and my expansion."

"Okay, I'll see you after work tomorrow night."

Dex didn't want to spoil the moment for her, but he had to forewarn her about the danger. He hadn't told her about the slashed tires or dead opossum because he didn't want her to worry, but if she was going to be spending time in River City, he had to tell her that someone was threatening him. His fear was that whoever was threatening him might transfer their aggressiveness to her.

Marie met Dex at the door of her apartment the next evening with the familiar worried expression on her face. They embraced, and she led him into the kitchen where she had some snacks.

"Marie, I hope you don't mind if we just order in some Chinese tonight. I need to explain what I was talking about last night, and I want to hear all the details about your new venture."

While they were eating the Chinese take-out, Marie excitedly told Dex about her meeting and the plans she was beginning to put together. Dex let her finish her story before he said anything about his concern.

"I wish my news was as good as yours, but unfortunately it isn't," Dex said. "There is a situation developing in River City that makes me very concerned about you spending time there. Let's move over to the sofa, and I will try to explain what has happened."

Dex's tone increased the alarm Marie had been experiencing since their phone conversation the previous night. They moved to the sofa, and Dex closed his eyes and held her hand. Her first thought was that he was getting ready to break up with her, but then he took a deep breath and began his story.

"Several weeks ago someone slashed the tires on my car and spray painted a message on it indicating that he planned to also slash me."

"Why didn't you tell me about this when it happened?"

"I didn't want to worry you, but hold on, there's more. Someone also recently used an ice pick to stick a dead opossum to a tree in our front yard. It also had a note that indicated that he planned to stick me with an ice pick. My main concern so far was that he might transfer his aggression to Gigi, but if you are there, you may be in danger."

"Didn't you call the police?"

"Yes, but they don't have anything to work with. I have no idea why someone has a grudge against me, but I can take care of myself. My concern is that if he finds out we are involved, he could try to get to me by harming you. The risk will increase significantly when you start spending time in River City."

The news that someone was threatening Dex made cold chills run up Marie's back. She sat motionless and quiet for a few minutes while she digested the situation. Dex put his arm around her and asked what she thought, but it was several minutes before she spoke.

"We will have to be careful. However, if we let this person scare us into changing our lives, then he's already won, even if he never does anything else. I'm not going to let this creep keep me from opening an office in River City. The things he has done so far are pretty cowardly, so he's probably just trying to scare you. I bet the reason he slips around after dark and writes threatening notes is because he doesn't have the courage to confront you."

"You're probably right, but I had to tell you about it and let you make up your own mind. Let's not talk about it anymore tonight."

They sat quietly for a few minutes and then Dex lifted her chin, lightly brushed his lips against hers, and pulled her closer. They stretched out on the sofa face to face and temporarily forgot about the threats in River City.

Marie's hair smelled like lemon shampoo, and the fragrance of her skin reminded him of the flowers in Gigi's garden. The fragrance of her hair and skin was a pleasant but unnecessary stimulant. Just holding her was always the only stimulation he needed.

He brushed the raven hair back from her face and her soft moan when he kissed her neck hinted at years of pent-up passion. Her breath became ragged, and she murmured his name. He felt her body suddenly become rigid, and she pushed him away and sat up on the sofa with her head in her hands. He thought for a moment she might be crying, but she finally turned toward him with a slight smile and said, "Wow, where did that come from?" Dex didn't dare reply. He was still trying to regain his own equilibrium.

Marie wrapped her arms around herself, as if she was trying to contain whatever it was she was feeling. When she regained her composure, she reached for his hand.

"Dex, we've had this conversation, so you know how I feel. I was probably more caught up in the moment than you were, and I'm sorry I let it get out of hand and then pushed you away. I know it's not fair to you. I don't know . . ." She seemed to be embarrassed as she momentarily hesitated before starting again. "I don't know and don't want to know what experiences you've had, but if that's any indication of what it might be like between us, I'm not sure my heart can withstand it. Can we stay here on the sofa just holding each other for a while and not doing anything else?"

When he nodded, she stood, turned off the lamp, and again stretched out on the sofa facing him. He draped his arm around her shoulder but avoided moving his hands. They never said another word after she turned off the lamp. Her face was partially illuminated by the nightlight in the hall, and long after she fell asleep, Dex lay awake looking at the peaceful expression on the face that he adored.

They awoke the next morning in the same position. Marie made coffee and fixed breakfast while Dex shaved and showered. The conversation over breakfast was again about the precautions she should take when she came to River City. Neither of them mentioned the abruptly interrupted passion of the night before.

Chapter 16

On Sunday afternoon, Dex took the longer, scenic route back to River City. He needed the extra time to think about his weekend with Marie. He sensed that his life was suddenly speeding down a highway where U-turns were not allowed. Intimacy and love had always been the subject of locker-room humor, and that wasn't what this was about. He hadn't yet figured out the rules, and he had no idea how he was supposed to manage a relationship that was changing his life.

In his experience, intimacy was always related to something like the infamous "Louise Parties" at Georgia. When he was a freshman, an upper classman warned him not to get caught in the team's favorite hoax. But all the freshman players were not lucky enough to receive the same warning.

The first and last one he ever participated in involved Bob Seagrove, a three-hundred-pound offensive lineman from Pennsylvania. He was a fun-loving, eighteen-year-old kid whose maturity had not caught up with his girth. He also wasn't a very good football player. The coaches had taken a chance on him because of his size and speed. With maturity, he might have developed into a better player, but they never had a chance to find out.

Seagrove was sitting in the dorm lobby with Dex and two of their upper-class teammates, Burl Matthews and Lenny Cochran, when Burl said, "I wonder if Louise is home tonight?" This was the tip-off line that let the others know the hoax was on.

Lenny said, "I'll go call her and see if her husband is out of town." Rather than make a phone call, he circled through the dorm and told everyone that Bob was going to meet Louise in about thirty minutes. The dorm emptied with everyone going out the back door and scrambling into cars.

While Lenny was alerting the dorm, Burl was busy getting Bob excited about meeting Louise.

"Bob, you won't believe this girl. She's a gorgeous twenty-two-year-old country gal with a body like a dream. She's married to a long-haul truck driver that she can't stand anymore, and she is hot as a firecracker."

Lenny soon returned with the news from his phantom phone call. "She said her husband was on a long-haul trip, and she doesn't expect him back until tomorrow. She needs about thirty minutes to get ready, but she wants to see us tonight. She'll light a candle in the window if her husband's not at home. I told her about Bob, and she said, 'Bring him on, I love big boys.'"

Dex said he had to study, but after leaving the lobby, he joined the rest of the guys that Lenny rounded up to witness the event.

The house where Louise supposedly lived was actually an abandoned farmhouse ten miles out of town. A dirt road from the highway led several hundred yards across an untilled field and then passed through a stand of pine trees before ending at the house. The closest neighbor was a mile away.

Burl, a senior, had participated in numerous hoaxes at the same abandoned farm house and knew the lay of the land. The rural highway was unlit, but he easily found the dirt driveway and turned off the headlights. The light of the moon was all he needed to drive slowly up toward the house. When the car was about one hundred yards from the house, he said, "We better walk the rest of the way. Look for the candle in the window, Bob."

Burl, Lenny, and Bob all quietly slipped out of the car and started creeping up the driveway. As they went over a slight rise, they could see a vague outline of the house, and the candle burning in the window signaled that Louise's husband was not home.

Burl whispered, "There it is, and it looks like the coast is clear. Come on, Bob."

"I'm ready, let's go."

Bob didn't need any encouragement; Burl had already sucked him into the hoax. The house was a typical Depression-era farmhouse with a tin roof and covered front porch. In daylight it would have been obvious that the house was abandoned, but at night all they could see was the outline of the house and the candle flickering in the window. Bob was anxious and walking too fast.

Burl said, "Slow down, Bob; she's not going anywhere."

When they got to within about fifteen yards of the front porch, Bob was surprised by a loud voice from within the house.

"Damn it, Louise, I knewd you been messin' roun. I jest seen 'em out thar."

Suddenly, the husband, who was actually junior linebacker Jim Bradshaw, burst through the door. The accent and dialect were fairly easy to mimic for this kid from the swamps around Waycross, Georgia.

"I's has y'all now. Ain't never messin roun Louise agin."

Within a few yards, Bob was at full speed, sprinting faster than he had ever moved on a football field. He hadn't seen the shotgun, so his first notice of a firearm was when Jim pointed it skyward and pulled the trigger. Thirty boys from the dorm, including Dex, were hiding in the bushes along the side of the driveway. They were armed with handfuls of gravel that they released at the sprinting three-hundred-pound tackle just as the shotgun was fired. Somehow Bob found another gear and wasn't seen again until he straggled into the dorm during breakfast the next morning. His clothes were torn, and his face and arms were scratched from the briars he plowed through during his ten-mile trek through the Georgia woods.

The team was always unmerciful with their Louise victims. They got a bigger kick out of the victim's embarrassment than they did pulling off the actual prank. They were unrelenting with their off-color comments, and soon it seemed everyone on campus was laughing about Bob's big romantic adventure. That weekend he slipped out of the dorm before daylight and caught a Greyhound bus back to Pennsylvania.

Dex participated in the hoax but felt regretful almost immediately afterward. He did not join in any of the heckling. He felt terrible about his role in a prank that may have terminated a teammate's athletic scholarship and college career. Dex called Bob in Pennsylvania and tried to persuade him to return, but Bob said he was making plans to go to a small in-state school. The coaches never knew why Bob suddenly left school, and since his football skills were problematic at best, they did not pursue him.

Dex now knew, because of the way he felt about Marie, that he had been stupid to confuse love and lust.

Chapter 17

A week after her first meeting with the trust department, Marie delivered her proposal to Harvey Blake. They met in his office, and while he read through her plan, she looked over the three-page contract the bank legal department had prepared for her execution.

Blake finally looked up and said, "Marie, thank you for providing so much detail. This is exactly what we wanted. Is the contract satisfactory?"

"I don't have a problem with the contract, and I'm ready to sign it." She placed it on top of her briefcase and signed on the designated line.

After she handed the contract back to him, he said, "Both boards have approved the purchase contract for the River City bank, and a favorable vote by the stockholders is imminent."

"What does that mean time-wise for us in setting up the office there?"

"It would be very helpful if you could be ready to start assessing the situation there this week. We are going to consolidate the activities of the two trust departments, but before we do that, we need for you to do some preliminary work for us."

"I can go up there and get started tomorrow, but it will take me a while to hire and train staff for the office."

Blake nodded and said, "I think the initial work is only going to require one person, and it's probably something you will want to handle yourself. I'm suspicious about the number of people they have sent to nursing homes and also about the expense they are incurring for those people. I would like for you to start by focusing on that."

"Do you have a list of the patients and the nursing homes where they have been sent?"

"No, you'll have to get that from the bank. But I want you to meet with and assess the health status of each of them as soon as possible. We don't know if they even need to be in nursing homes."

"My head nurse here can handle the Atlanta office for a few days, so I can be in River City tomorrow morning."

"Very good, I'll notify the bank that you will see them tomorrow morning."

Marie thought a lot about the personal implications of being in the same city with Dex. She knew he would jump at the opportunity to share an apartment, but she wasn't ready to start playing house with him. She decided to keep her apartment in Atlanta and look for a furnished efficiency apartment in River City. She didn't intend to use it for much more than a place to sleep and change clothes.

Blake notified the trust officer at the bank how RN4U was being utilized and told him to expect Marie the following morning. When she met the trust officer, John Norton, he was far from cordial. Marie wasn't sure if her cool reception was just a reflection of his personality, if he was upset about the acquisition, or if he resented what she was going to be doing there.

"Mr. Norton, I don't know exactly what Harvey Blake told you about what my company is contracted to do here, but I need to see a list of the trust department's clients who are currently confined to nursing homes. I will also need a list of the bank's approved nursing homes."

With a demeanor that clearly demonstrated his contempt, he said, "You'll have to come back tomorrow. We're busy today and don't have the time to gather that information."

Marie didn't know what his problem was, but she wasn't easily intimidated. "Harvey Blake is expecting a preliminary report from me this week, so just give me a few of the names and the names of the nursing homes where they are living. I've already told them I would get started today."

Norton sat across the desk and glared at her for a few moments and then stood up and stomped out of the room without saying a word. She didn't understand what was happening, but she didn't have to be very perceptive to know that something beyond the man's personality was causing his hostility. She also didn't know whether he was coming back or if his abrupt departure was supposed to signal that the meeting was over. Marie chose to wait, and he walked back in ten minutes later. He threw a manila folder on the desk in front of her and said, "Maybe that'll keep you busy."

Marie thought this antagonistic meeting had gone on long enough, so without opening the folder, she mimicked his rude departure by picking it up and walking out of the office without saying a word. She sat in her car and rehashed the conversation for some clue as to his hostility, but she couldn't come up with anything in the conversation that would have prompted his deplorable attitude.

The file folder contained the names of five individuals who were all at Meadowview Nursing Home. When she arrived at Meadowview, her first thought was, *Where in the world do they come up with these names?* The nursing home was located in a seedy section of town, and there definitely wasn't a meadow in view. It appeared to have been converted from an old apartment house, a very old one.

The sign at the entrance listed Brian McPherson as the manager. Marie stopped at the receptionist's desk in the dimly lit lobby and asked to see McPherson. After calling ahead, the receptionist directed her to McPherson's office. He was sitting behind his desk, not smiling, and he didn't get up to greet her. McPherson merely motioned Marie to a chair across from his desk. Since it was obvious that he was expecting her, she could tell Norton had called him.

Marie handed McPherson a business card and said, "Mr. McPherson, I'm Marie Murphy from RN4U, Inc. in Atlanta. My company has been engaged by the parent company of Heritage Bank and Trust to assess the care of the bank's clients who have been referred to nursing homes." When he didn't respond, she continued. "I have been instructed to begin by meeting with the patients here who were referred by the bank, and I will also need to review a copy of your contract with the bank."

"We don't have a contract with the bank."

"Well, on what basis are you paid for your services?"

"Look, lady, I don't know what you mean. We just send monthly bills to the bank, and they send us a check."

McPherson was proving to be as cantankerous as Norton, so she said, "I apologize for any disruption, but if you will just clear it with the nurses for me to have access to the patients' charts, I won't take up any more of your time."

McPherson glared at her throughout the brief meeting, and again she had the impression that something strange was going on. These two men obviously didn't like what she was doing, and she didn't know why. He finally picked up the phone and told the duty nurse to let her have what she wanted and accompany her to the patients' rooms.

Marie picked up the charts of the five patients and was led to the room of the first one, Sara Barton. The door was partially open and she saw the elderly woman sitting in a wheelchair facing the window.

"Mrs. Barton, could I talk to you for a minute?" When Marie got no response, she thought the woman was sleeping, so she walked around to where she could see her face. Her eyes were open, but her head was leaning over on her shoulder and there was drool coming from her mouth. Marie instantly recognized the symptoms. She was so heavily sedated there was no way the woman could communicate with her.

Marie moved to the second and then the third patients' rooms and found each of them in essentially the same condition. All of their charts indicated some variation of mild dementia. She knew there was no reason for patients with only mild dementia to be so heavily sedated.

When she found the next two patients in the same condition, Marie returned the charts and hastily left the building. She was walking toward her car when she saw a woman sitting on the bus stop bench in front of the home. Marie sat beside her and asked, "Do you have a relative at Meadowview?"

"No, but I work there. I'm a nurse."

Marie said, "Oh, very good. I'm also a nurse, but I work in Atlanta. I'm considering putting my mother in a nursing facility here, and I wonder if you would recommend Meadowview."

"I've only been working at Meadowview for a couple of months, but I've worked at other facilities, and they certainly do things differently around here."

"What do you mean by different? Can you give me an example?"

"I really shouldn't say this, but since you're a nurse I'll tell you that I wouldn't put my mother here. Please don't repeat me saying that. I don't think I will be working here much longer, but they could give me a bad reference when I try to get another job."

"I would never tell them what you say."

"Well, the food is terrible here. It's so bad that all the nurses bring sandwiches from home. They are continually out of whatever we need, from toilet paper to medical supplies, and the administration is the worst I've ever seen."

Marie said, "Someone told me that Heritage Bank was paying for a lot of the patients here."

The nurse took the bait that Marie had dangled. "Yeah, there are a lot of bank patients here, but most of us never see them. They're all kept in one wing and stay in their rooms, and they are tended to by only certain members of the staff. They must all be pretty bad because I've been told all the bank patients are sedated as soon as they arrive at Meadowview."

Marie said, "I appreciate your help. I hope it works out for you."

She called Blake in Atlanta that afternoon and told him about the way she was received at Heritage and at the nursing home. Then she told him about the dilapidated condition of the nursing home and about the condition of each of the patients she had seen. She also told him about her conversation with the nurse at the bus stop.

Marie said, "Mr. Blake, it's obvious to me that these patients are being warehoused at Meadowview and being unnecessarily sedated. I was also told that there's no contract between Heritage and Meadowview. They haven't yet consented to give me all the records, but I doubt that the bank ever refers a patient anywhere else."

"What do you think is going on, Marie?"

"I don't feel comfortable making accusations that I can't prove, but since you're paying me for my opinion, I think someone may have their hand in the piggy bank. This is deplorable, and they are resisting everything I'm doing. I honestly think there is some type of collusion between the trust officer and the nursing home manager. Please understand, this is just supposition on my part. I don't have any evidence of wrongdoing other than that they are definitely unnecessarily sedating patients. They don't want me to see any of the records, so I'm going to need some reinforcement from you before I can prove anything."

Blake said, "Thanks, Marie. I agree something strange is going on. Back off for now, and I'll get our audit people up there to check it out financially. We'll get back to you."

Proudland immediately initiated an internal investigation and discovered that Marie's theory was correct. Norton and McPherson were siphoning funds from the trust accounts by a scam they had been running for months. McPherson submitted bills to the bank from fictitious vendors. Norton would authorize payment, and a check would be issued and mailed to the fictitious company at a post office box. Norton retrieved and cashed the checks and split the ill-gotten gains with McPherson. Both men were immediately terminated by their companies when the scam was exposed.

Marie gained access to the records and determined that the bank only referred patients to Meadowview, and none of the ones referred had close relatives in the area that could check on them. With no one to complain, the mistreatment and the scam would have probably continued for years if Marie had not discovered it.

Proudland instructed her to immediately arrange for complete medical evaluations. The exams revealed that none of the patients needed to be heavily sedated, and once they were free of the medication, it was determined that some of them did not even need to be in a nursing home. Several of those who were confined were determined to be able to function in their own homes with minimal assistance. Others were more properly relocated to assisted living facilities. Proudland instructed Marie to identify acceptable nursing homes and arrange for the transfer of the patients who did in fact need full-time care.

After Proudland notified them of the scam, the district attorney's office subpoenaed records of the two men's personal accounts. These records provided the necessary paper trail, and Norton and McPherson were arrested, arraigned, and subsequently released on bail pending a trial.

Marie was told it would be necessary for her to eventually testify at Norton and McPherson's trial. She really didn't look forward to testifying in a criminal trial, but there was an upside benefit. Her company got a lot of positive feedback from Blake for discovering the scam, and her work cemented the relationship between Proudland and RN4U.

Chapter 18

The newspaper and television coverage of the scandal led to Marie receiving calls from potential clients that she would otherwise never have been able to reach. Blake thought that their image would be enhanced because of their exposure of the scandal and arranged for Marie to be interviewed by the River City newspaper and local television stations.

Marie's appearance, poise, and intelligence made her a natural in front of the camera, and her comments positioned Proudland as an institution of high integrity in their new market area. It also introduced RN4U as a nursing home alternative that might allow elderly patients to stay in their homes longer. The public response was immediate. Marie was inundated with telephone calls for more information.

RN4U's contract with Proudland prohibited her from providing the same service to any other bank within fifty miles of an existing Proudland office. When she signed the contract, the exclusive limitation didn't seem significant, but now she actually had to turn down business from a competing bank. But the new business from individual assignments was not impacted by the contract, and it was booming.

Marie's television appearances also eased her search for new nurses. Scores of local nurses contacted her, seeking information and job interviews. It was beginning to look as if the River City office might have far more business than she had originally anticipated. This forced a decision that she did not think she would have to make so soon: should she hire a full-time business manager for River City or move there and manage it herself? Her head nurse in Atlanta was already trained and doing an excellent job managing that office, so the logical decision was for Marie to relocate.

She gave up her Atlanta apartment and became a full-time resident of River City. Marie could still handle most of the administrative duties and some supervisory oversight for both offices. And there were also personal advantages to the move. She would be in the same city as Dex, and apartment rental rates were much lower. She actually saved so much money on the different rental rates that she was able to rent a small storefront office in River City without substantially increasing her overhead.

Dex shared the excitement over Marie's business success, but he was even more concerned about her safety because of her frequent television appearances. Whoever was threatening him could now easily discover his connection with Marie.

Andrea Mitchell was also happy about Marie moving to River City, and they became very close friends. Dex had also become very close to her husband Jim. It created a problem because Jim was Dex's boss, but they made it work, and the friendship blossomed. Jim treated Dex as an equal when they were together socially, and Dex treated him with the respect due a superior when they were at the office. They defied the odds by simply not succumbing to the ego and jealousy that usually doomed this type of relationship.

Andrea and Marie often went to dinner together when the men were on the road, and despite their age difference, they discovered a lot of common interests. They also soon learned they could trust and confide in each other. One night when they were having dinner, Andrea said, "Marie, I know you've wondered but have been considerate enough not to have asked why Jim and I have never had children."

"Andrea, that's a personal question that I would never ask anyone."

"After several years of trying, we finally had the tests and the doctors discovered that I could never conceive. I was terrified because both of us wanted children, and I was afraid it would destroy our marriage."

Marie said, "Maybe I don't know Jim that well, but I'd bet he handled it with great concern for you."

"You're right. He was an absolute angel. He knew how devastated I was, and I couldn't have asked him to be any more compassionate. Tell me about growing up next door to Dex. You've said that you were just friends back then."

"Actually, we were best friends. Neither of us ever thought about a romantic involvement. I was a gangly tomboy, and Dex was already a promising young athlete. We competed in sports and everything else up until I moved to Atlanta. It was seven years before we saw each other again. I had already started RN4U, and Dex was a senior in college."

"How did you get back together? I'll bet he hunted you down."

Marie laughed and said, "You would lose that bet. He probably didn't even think about me during all those years. He had become a big college jock and had all these adoring fans, and probably a bunch of football groupies. I was at best a distant memory."

"I find it hard to believe that he hadn't kept up with you over the years."

"Well, I didn't keep up with him either. The only way I knew he was at UGA was because his name and picture were regularly in the Atlanta newspaper."

Andrea laughed and said, "Now we get to the meat of the story."

"I was alone in my apartment watching the last game of the season when Dex broke his leg. I saw them load him in the ambulance and then the announcer said he was being taken to the hospital in Atlanta where I had previously worked. I beat the ambulance there."

"Did you have some kind of premonition about getting romantically involved with him?"

"Are you kidding? That never crossed my mind. I just felt obligated to check on him because I knew he had no family in the area."

"Well, something must have happened at the hospital. Tell me how you got together."

"Something happened all right, but I'm still not sure what or how it happened. I never had a romantic thought about Dex, and I'm pretty sure he never thought of me in that way. But we talked a lot over the next few days, and it suddenly dawned on me that it wasn't friendship that was messing with my head. Before either of us knew what was happening, we were spending every possible moment together, and we've never looked back."

"Wow! That's some love story. Have you guys ever discussed marriage?"

"Gosh, no; we've both been too busy starting our careers to think that far down the road."

"Marie, would you marry him if he asked you?"

The question caught Marie off guard, and she hesitated. When she did speak, she never really answered the question. "My goal has been to spend five of six years building a comfortable business before getting seriously involved with anyone."

Although she didn't answer the question, Andrea saw the way the couple adored each other and knew the answer even if Marie hadn't yet figured it out.

Chapter 19

Dex had always heard that absence makes the heart grow fonder, but it was working in reverse with his relationship. They were growing even closer now that they were in the same town. They discovered once again why they had been such good friends as teenagers. They enjoyed doing the same things, liked the same people, and thoroughly enjoyed each other's company.

Now that Dex was making a descent salary, they dined out often, but their favorite evenings were still spent watching old movies and munching on popcorn. Every night it became harder for Dex to leave and for Marie to let him leave. He frequently left her apartment feeling agitated, but he promised himself that he would not push Marie beyond where she was comfortable. It was a vow he was finding harder and harder to keep as their passion reached levels that threatened his sanity. Dex felt like Marie was struggling as much as he was with the emotional boundaries she had established. Marie said more than once that it wasn't fair to him for her to let it go too far and then abruptly stop him. She seemed to just get caught up in the moment before she realized they were reaching the point of no return. She couldn't possibly question his love for her; he had demonstrated it in so many ways. He didn't discuss it with her, but it was always the eight-hundred-pound gorilla sharing the room when they were together.

However, finally the time came. Dex had been out of town all week and returned on a Friday afternoon. Marie rented her favorite movie, *Sleepless in Seattle,* for about the tenth time. Dex preferred action movies, but he never objected to a Meg Ryan movie. He opened a bottle of wine, and before long the tender story and merlot collectively created a mellow mood that led to whispered words of affection.

Their passion escalated rapidly. Her breathing was irregular, and she was making barely audible moans. Dex sensed they were on a plateau where Marie had never been when she finally whispered, "Please, Dex, let's go to the bedroom."

He cradled her in his arms, carried her down the short hall, and laid her gently on the bed. Over the next few hours they lost all concept of time as the world outside that one room ceased to exist.

Sometime later, Dex asked, "Marie, are you okay?"

She snuggled her head under his chin and said, "Sweetheart, I love you, and I've never been so okay in my life."

That night Dex didn't toss and turn on the sofa, as he had so many nights in the past. On this blissful night, they had no way of knowing that their shared love and commitment would be the only thing that would help them survive the turmoil of the life-changing events they would soon face.

Chapter 20

Marie was still asleep when Dex slipped out of bed Saturday morning, but after he showered, he found her in the kitchen. She was humming as she made coffee. Since he was barefooted, she didn't hear him come up behind her.

Marie jumped as Dex circled his arms around her waist and said, "Have you ever been hugged in the kitchen by a naked man?"

She answered without turning around. "Until about eight hours ago, I had never been hugged by a naked man in the kitchen or anywhere else. Go put your clothes on."

"I think I'm dressed appropriately for breakfast with my girl."

She laughed when she turned and saw that he was wrapped in a large bath towel tucked in at his waist. "I'm not serving you breakfast until you put some clothes on. Get out of here."

"Marie, do you remember Mystic Lake?"

"You're changing the subject, but yes, I remember you and Hoagie talking about it all the time; however, if you recall, my mother would never let me go up there with you."

"Well, your mother isn't here, and I think it's time you see Mystic Lake. We're going on a picnic today."

Marie smiled and said, "Dex, I know the guys used to swim in the buff up there, and I'm not going to do that."

"That sounds like fun, but it isn't the reason I want to take you up there. The mountain is beautiful this time of year, and I haven't been to the lake in years."

Mystic Lake was on top of the mountain. Over eons, the force of a spring-fed creek cascading over a waterfall had hollowed the area at its base into a crystal clear pool about the size of a basketball court. The creek that tumbled over the waterfall at the upper end of the lake flowed quietly out the other end for a few hundred yards before spilling over a massive one-hundred-foot waterfall and continuing its rush to the valley.

The lake was in a remote area of the mountain, where only the locals were aware of its existence. In the spring, mountain laurel, rhododendron, and other wildflowers adorned the area. When walking from the nearby road to the lake, the sound of rushing water could be heard a long way before the waterfall and lake finally came into view.

The lake was in a depressed area, bordered on the east and west by rock cliffs. The only access to the lake level was by carefully climbing down the cliff on the east side. The solid rock cliff on the west side was impassable.

When the couple reached the cliffs above the lake, Dex pointed to a place beside the lake and said, "That small gravel area between all the boulders is the only beach. We can spread our picnic out there and go swimming."

Marie said, "I would be happy to just stay up here and look at all the beautiful flowers, but since we both wore bathing suits under our clothes, I guess we ought to go in the water."

They climbed down to the beach area, and Dex spread a blanket on the gravel beach and set the picnic basket in the middle of it. The roar of cascading water and the light mist rising from the base of the waterfall created a surreal atmosphere.

"Come on, Marie, you've got to see this." Dex led her right up to the base of the fall, where the cold mist soaked them before they reached what he wanted to show her. The rocks were slick, but Dex supported her as he continued to pull her along. When they got closer to the falling water, the noise made conversation almost impossible, so Dex just pointed to the opening.

Marie was shaking her head, but Dex pulled her along behind him, and they slipped in behind the waterfall. There was a rock ledge where one could stand and look out through the plummeting water. A rainbow was superimposed on the inside of the waterfall, and although it was shady where they were standing, they could look through the fall and mist to the bright sunshine.

After they were back at the gravel beach, Dex said, "Let's go in the water before we eat." He dove in, and Marie was right behind him.

When she surfaced she yelled, "Great Scott, Dex, why didn't you tell me this was ice water?" She was swimming quickly toward the bank, but he grabbed her foot, pulled her back, wrapped his arms around her, and wouldn't let her get out of the water.

"Marie, you had to know this wasn't bath water. It's a mountain lake, and it's not that cold once you get used to it."

"Yeah, but it would have been nice if you had warned me to ease into it."

"If I'd told you it was cold, you would've never put a toe in the water, and you know it. Marie, you're acting like a girl."

Later she wouldn't believe she had actually done it, but she ripped off the top of her bikini and said, "Hey, buster, maybe you haven't noticed, but I am a girl."

She was laughing when she broke away from him and beat him to the edge of the water. The top was back in place before he caught up.

After they ate lunch, they stretched out on the blanket. Marie said, "I've was all over this mountain when we were growing up, but this is the prettiest place I've ever seen. I can understand why you and Hoagie liked it so much. Thanks for bringing me to your special place."

Then she smiled and said, "I can't help but wonder how many girls you brought up here when you were in high school, but I don't want to know."

Since she was smiling, Dex didn't respond. He was thinking about the hours he had spent here with DJ, and there had been others, but some things were best left unsaid. He turned over on his side, pulled her closer, and kissed her.

Suddenly she pulled away and said, "Hey, there's someone up there watching us." Two teenage boys were standing up on the cliff waving their arms, laughing, and yelling something that he couldn't understand over the sound of the waterfall. They quickly gathered their picnic gear, but by the time they climbed up to the top of the waterfall, the boys had disappeared.

Dex said, "Don't worry about them. They were just young boys having fun. That's the type of thing that Hoagie and I would have done."

"You're never embarrassed. I'm just glad I saw them before we really did something stupid down there in plain sight." Marie was still upset as they walked back to the car.

Chapter 21

The weekend ended much too soon. If Dex and Marie had known on Monday morning how the coming week would forever change their lives, they would have pulled the covers over their heads and never gotten out of bed.

Dex left that morning on a weeklong sales trip. After making several trips with Jim Mitchell, he was finally going out on the road alone, armed with extensive literature and samples of the new product. His first appointment was in Memphis, a six-hour drive from River City. It gave him a lot of time to reflect on the weekend he spent with Marie.

Dex had originally thought that his career-ending injury was the worst thing that could have happened, but now he considered it a blessing. It was what brought Marie back into his life, and he had never been happier. He was jubilant that morning as he drove west on Interstate 40. He was so deep in thought about the past weekend that he was basically oblivious of the cars and trucks whizzing by him at seventy miles an hour. He was also blissfully unaware that his euphoria was about to be tragically interrupted.

Dex's first appointment was with a young physician in private practice whom he had never met. The receptionist took his business card and said, "Have a seat, Mr. Martin, and I'll tell the doctor that you're here."

The waiting room was full, and Dex picked up a magazine and prepared for a long wait. He was sitting for less than five minutes when the receptionist said, "Mr. Martin, the doctor will see you now."

Dex followed her through the door as several pairs of angry eyes followed him. The patients didn't like the idea that a late-arriving patient was seeing the doctor before they were. As soon as he walked in the doctor's office, he immediately sensed why he did not have to wait.

There was an Ole Miss helmet sitting on the credenza directly behind his desk. The doctor was a football fan and recognized his name. Dex had already learned how to leverage his athletic celebrity to boast his sales. If these people insisted on living in the past, he would play along. They talked football for a few minutes before he started his sales pitch. Name recognition could get him in the door, but he still had to sell the product on its merits. The physicians always seemed surprised that a former jock was bright, articulate, and knowledgeable enough to intelligently discuss the efficacy of the product. Dex had done his homework well.

He was responsible for Tennessee, Georgia, North Carolina, and South Carolina, the four states in the test-market area. The company was closely monitoring the results, and since they had so far exceeded expectation, Dex was being given a lot of credit.

As part of the marketing blitz, they had a company prepare several hundred life-size cardboard mock-ups of Dex in his Georgia uniform holding a bottle of EaseFast. Starting this week they were being placed in pharmacies and supermarkets throughout the test-market states. Marie did a double take when she walked into a local pharmacy and came face to face with a life-sized clone of the man who had just shared her bed.

Dex was on the road all week but told Marie he would be home Friday afternoon. They made plans to have dinner Friday night. He was in North Carolina on Thursday night and had to make a swing through South Carolina and Georgia. When Dex realized he wasn't going to make it back for his Friday night date with Marie, he called Hoagie and asked him if would take her to dinner on Friday. Hoagie and Marie loved each other. The things that made Hoagie unattractive to all the other girls were the very things that Marie found adorable about the rotund musician. He was the one guy, other than Dex, with whom she always felt absolutely comfortable. She could show up for lunch without makeup, kid him about his weight, or just be in a terrible PMS mood and Hoagie always accepted her just as she was. Usually when she showed up in a bad mood, Hoagie could have her laughing within a few minutes. Their friendship went back to when he and Dex both thought of her as just one of the boys.

Before he called Hoagie, Dex called Marie and told her he was tied up and couldn't make it back by Friday. She was disappointed but said she understood his situation. When he called Hoagie he asked him not to tell Marie that it was his idea for him to call her.

Hoagie called Marie that night. "Hey, beautiful, how about helping me improve my reputation? If Dex is still out of town, are you free for dinner tomorrow night?"

"Hoagie, you're just what I need to get me through this week. I talked to Dex earlier, and he's not going to be back until Saturday afternoon." Hoagie didn't tell her he had just gotten off the phone with Dex.

He asked, "How about the Canyon Catfish House?"

"That sounds good to me."

Marie could have easily named a dozen other restaurants she would have preferred, but she always enjoyed being with Hoagie and she didn't want to hurt his feelings. It was a small restaurant nestled in a canyon between two mountains overlooking the river, and it was one of Hoagie's favorites. He preferred everything fried, and if it wasn't fried, it wasn't served at the Canyon. The house specialty was catfish and hush puppies. It was about ten miles from River City on a sparsely traveled, twisting road that snaked through the canyon following the curvature of the river.

Hoagie and Marie ate on the deck. After they finished eating, they continued talking and sipping on beer until they realized that they were the only customers remaining in the restaurant.

The parking lot was very dimly lit on the way out. It had been crowded when they arrived, and they had to park next to the woods at the farthest point from the restaurant entrance. The few cars remaining in the lot were all parked close to the entrance and apparently belonged to the restaurant employees. The only other vehicle next to the woods where Hoagie had parked was an older model SUV.

Hoagie walked around and put the key in the passenger door to open it for Marie; neither of them saw the man come up behind them. The butt of a heavy pistol struck Hoagie at the base of his skull, and he collapsed in his tracks. In a continuing backhand motion, the pistol struck Marie a glancing blow on the side of her head. She sprawled unconscious across Hoagie's motionless body.

The attack was so sudden that neither of them made a sound. The man lifted Marie over his shoulder and carried her to the SUV. The backseats were removed, and he placed her in the back. He gagged her with a filthy piece of cloth and put a pillowcase over her head. Even though she was still unconscious, he bound her hands and feet together. The wound on the side of her head was bleeding profusely, and blood had already soaked through the pillowcase.

The attacker went back to check on Hoagie. His position had not changed. He was lying on his side with his head in a pool of blood. There was a wide, gaping laceration at the base of his skull. He knelt beside him to check his pulse. There was no heartbeat, and he started to panic. The attacker hadn't intended to kill Hoagie. He had done some crazy things in his life, but he had never committed murder. His first thought was to leave the body in the parking lot and run, but he quickly discarded that idea. He dragged the body to the SUV and struggled to lift and push the dead weight into the vehicle beside Marie.

Exiting the parking lot, the attacker turned away from River City. His mind was working overtime. He had to dispose of the body, but he needed time to be far away from there before it was discovered. He had only driven a few miles from the restaurant on the mostly deserted highway when he noticed the road beyond the guardrail fell off sharply. He stopped and struggled to get the body out of the SUV and over the guardrail. It was so dark he could barely see the river at least a hundred yards below. He pushed Hoagie's lifeless body over the edge and listened as it splashed into the dark water. He got back in the SUV and sped away. The attacker headed for his original destination with Marie still bound and unconscious.

Marie slowly began to regain her senses, but she didn't recognize her surroundings. She was in a small room with what looked like log walls. She had a blistering headache that worsened as she slowly sat up. Then she saw that she was tethered to a log column that extended from the floor to the ceiling. A logging chain was wrapped tightly around her ankle and fastened with a lock.

The last thing Marie remembered was walking across the restaurant parking lot with Hoagie. Her head was pounding, but she tried to ignore it and reconstruct what had happened. She had a vague recollection of being carried over someone's shoulder like a sack of flour and having a gag in her mouth and something like a bag over her head.

Maybe she was dreaming. She wasn't gagged now, and there was nothing covering her head or face. She put her hand on her throbbing head, and it felt wet. Her hand was covered in blood when she removed it. She knew then that this wasn't a dream. Someone hit her in the head, knocked her out, and chained her in the cabin.

Marie thought about Hoagie and wondered where he was. Had he also been hit in the head? The questions continued to run through her mind, but she had no answers.

She began to survey her surroundings. She was lying on an army-type cot. The only light was from an oil lantern that cast an eerie glow over the semi-dark room. She struggled to her feet and found that the chain was not long enough for her to reach the cabin door. It had apparently been carefully measured to allow her to only reach a makeshift toilet in the corner of the room. The toilet was constructed like an outdoor john with a large pipe that slanted down and passed through the wall to the outside. Next to the toilet there was a small metal tub sitting on a wooden crate. It was apparently supposed to function as a washbasin, because there was a small mirror and towel over it. There was a bucket filled with water sitting on the floor beside the toilet. She assumed it was for drinking, washing, and flushing the toilet. The idea of drinking from the bucket was repulsive to her.

The last thing she noticed was a small pet door that was too small for an adult to get through. It was cut out of the logs almost at the floor level. There was fresh sawdust around the opening. She pushed against it and could feel it give slightly, but it would not open. When she pushed it there was a noise like metal against metal, and she assumed it was a lock on the outside.

"Help, help! Is there anyone out there? I need help." Marie cried out repeatedly but there was no answer, and she heard no movement outside the cabin.

She was still somewhat disoriented, but she again dragged the chain over to the wash basin to look in the mirror. She immediately wished she hadn't looked. Her hair was caked with blood, and when she parted it she could see a large gash just above her right ear. It was still oozing blood, and even in the dim light she could see that it needed several sutures. She took the towel from the back of the basin, dipped it in the water bucket, and very carefully tried to clean the wound. She had nothing with which to disinfect the wound, but she was able to get a lot of the congealed blood out of her hair.

The effort exhausted her, and she finally limped back to the cot, dragging the chain behind her. She had no choice but to try to relax while she waited for someone to come. Thankfully her clothing was still intact. She had not been molested while unconscious. She had no idea why she had been abducted, but she was afraid some sort of sexual deviate had captured her and that it was only a matter of time before the molestation began. She looked around the cabin for anything she could use as a weapon but didn't see anything.

Chapter 22

Dex returned Saturday afternoon and immediately called Marie. He got her answering machine and left a message for her to call him. His phone rang an hour later, and he was sure it was her. It was Gigi, and he could tell from her voice that something was terribly wrong.

"Dex, Hoagie's mother called. He didn't come home last night, and she is very worried. He was supposed to have met Marie for dinner, and she has been calling her all day but she hasn't answered her phone." A cold chill griped Dex as he hung up and headed for the door.

He left his car double parked, ran up the steps to Marie's apartment, used his key, and opened the door. She wasn't there, but thankfully there were no signs to indicate a struggle had taken place. Maybe she was just out shopping; Saturday afternoon was her only time to do that. He saw the message light blinking on her answering machine. He hesitated to invade her privacy, but worry trumped that concern. There were several recorded messages beginning with one from her mother on Friday night. He listened to the three calls from Hoagie's mother and his own call earlier that afternoon. She had not answered any of them, and she always returned calls promptly. He was really frightened now.

Dex called the police and both local hospitals but didn't find out anything. Then he noticed a note pad beside her phone. There was a note in Marie's handwriting: "Dinner/Hoagie-7 pm @ Canyon." He knew the Canyon Catfish Restaurant was one of Hoagie's favorites. He ran to his car.

At the restaurant, Dex saw Hoagie's car parked at the far end of the parking lot. It was locked, but the keys were dangling from the passenger side door. That didn't make sense. Questions were tumbling through his mind: Where were they? Why would Hoagie leave his keys in the door? Why would the keys be on the passenger's side? The manager of the Canyon was an old classmate, and he found him inside.

"Ron, have you seen Hoagie?"

"Not today. He was here last night with some good-looking woman, but we were busy and I just waved at him from across the dining room. I believe they were still on the deck when I left about thirty minutes before closing time."

"He didn't come home last night, and his car is still in your parking lot with the keys hanging in the door. I was out of town and called to ask him to take my girlfriend to dinner. She was the one who was with him last night. She's also missing. Something bad has happened, and we need to call the police now."

A county cop responded to the call about fifteen minutes later. Dex hurriedly told him what had happened, but the officer said, "We don't usually investigate a missing person case until after forty-eight hours, but I'll check out the car and look around."

They walked to the car together, and the officer walked around it without touching anything.

"Excuse me, Mr. Martin; I need to make a call." He went to his car and returned in a few minutes.

"I've called for the crime scene unit. They should be here in a few minutes."

"So you are going to go ahead with the investigation without waiting forty-eight hours?"

"Yes, I think we will get started on this one. It would be best if you wait in the restaurant until we finish here. I may need some additional information from you."

The officer had not told Dex that he had spotted what appeared to be a pool of dried blood on the pavement and an intermittent trail of droplets leading away from the parked car.

When the crime scene unit arrived, the original officer pointed out what he had seen and said, "That looks like dried blood. You'll want to get a scraping."

The CSU officer said, "Yeah, I agree. We'll also dust the car and the keys. Fingerprints may not help, but I'd rather get them than now than wish later that we had dusted." They also photographed the car and the surrounding area and then walked all over the lot searching for other evidence. Dex was watching from a window in the restaurant.

The officer walked back inside and questioned the manager. None of the waitresses there were on duty the previous night, so he said he would be back later to interview the night shift.

The officer led Dex to a table in the back of the restaurant. "Now tell me again exactly what your relationship is with the two people who are missing?"

"The man, Tom 'Hoagie' Hogan, is my best friend, and the woman he was with, Marie Murphy, is my girlfriend."

"And why was your best friend out with your girlfriend?"

"I know how that must sound, but we all grew up together in River City, and there's no love triangle here. I was out of town on business and was supposed to be back in time to take Marie out to dinner on Friday night. When I realized I couldn't get back until Saturday, I called Hoagie and asked him to take her to dinner. We've all been close friends since we were in elementary school."

The cop still seemed curious, but he didn't pursue it. They exchanged business cards and agreed to contact each other if there were any further developments.

Dex checked Marie's apartment again, but everything was just as he had left it. He left a note asking her to call him at Gigi's, but he had already decided that it was probably hopeless.

Dex was terrified, but there was nothing else he could do. He went to see Gigi because he knew she would be frantic, and he needed to talk to someone just to get his own mind around what had happened.

"Gigi, I found Hoagie's car at the restaurant where they went last night, but no one has seen them since they left. I called the police and they're investigating, but they don't have a lot to go on."

"Do you think they've been kidnapped? Why would anyone do that? They're not rich, so they couldn't be after a reward."

"I don't know. It could just be a random act, but what's worrying me is that it could be linked to whoever slashed my tires and nailed the possum to the tree."

"But those just seemed like pranks compared to kidnapping."

"Yeah, but the notes didn't sound like pranks. They were pretty threatening, and whoever wrote them could be trying to get back at me by hurting Marie and Hoagie."

"Do you know of anyone who was mad at either of them?"

"Gigi, you know Hoagie. He didn't have an enemy in the world. Those two guys at the bank and nursing home that Marie exposed probably hate her, but I don't know if professional people would get involved in something like this. And before we started dating, she dated a doctor in Atlanta who threatened her when she dumped him, but he's working in Birmingham now."

"Dex, everybody has their feelings hurt and gets mad when someone breaks up with them. A doctor isn't going to do anything this dumb."

"Gigi, I've never felt so helpless in my life. I know I ought to be doing something, but I don't have any idea what to do. I've got a million questions but no—" Dex stopped for a minute and then said, "Oh no, Gigi, I forgot to tell the investigating officer about any of these incidents. I was excited at the time, but the officer may not accept that excuse."

He was right. When Dex called and told him, it was obvious that the officer was upset and didn't completely buy his story about forgetting to mention any of the incidents. Dex really couldn't blame him. Excitement or panic was a stupid excuse for omitting what was obviously pertinent information.

Dex dreaded calling Hoagie's mother, but he knew he had to do it. He would prefer to see her in person, but he was afraid to leave the phone in case Marie or the police called. He hated the feeling of being paralyzed with fear. He had always been proactive and never just waited for things to happen. It was driving him crazy because he couldn't figure out how to speed up the process.

When she answered the phone, Dex could tell Hoagie's mother was crying.

"Mrs. Hogan, I don't have much information, but I found Hoagie's car at the Canyon Grill. The manager told me that he and Marie were there last night, but no one saw them after they left the restaurant. I called the county police, and they're investigating."

"Why would his car still be there, Dex?"

"I don't know. There may be some logical explanation, but we've got to remain positive. I'll keep you posted on any news I hear."

"Please pray for them, Dex."

"I started praying as soon as I found out they were missing."

He gave her the name and phone number of the officer and tried to reassure her, but Dex knew his words sounded hollow. How could he reassure her when he was so terrified himself?

Chapter 23

During the long, lonely hours in the cabin, Marie became concerned about her mental state. She started talking to herself, and her mind was playing tricks on her. Her paranoia was rampant; she jumped at all the normal forest sounds from outside the cabin. Every time she dozed off, she would have a frightening nightmare that would jolt her awake. She couldn't sleep because of the stifling heat, humidity, and continuing nightmares. There was no air circulation in the small windowless cabin. Her headache had eased up some, but the iron chain had rubbed her ankle raw, and it was painful when she moved it.

Marie delayed as long as physically possible but was finally forced to start using the makeshift toilet. The experience was disgusting, and only slightly less demeaning than the alternative. Her clothes were filthy and caked with dried blood.

Marie was always personally well groomed, even when she was alone, but the combination of filthy clothes, perspiration, and dried blood created a putrid body odor that thoroughly repulsed her. Trying to bathe using water in the bucket was cumbersome and ineffective. If her personal body odor and the pungent musty odors in the cabin were not enough to disgust her, there were spiders crawling everywhere.

After another clumsy attempt to bathe herself, Marie dragged her chain back across the floor and stretched out on the cot. The excessive blood loss from her head injury made her weak, and the effort of dragging the heavy chain back and forth from the cot to the toilet or washbasin completely exhausted her.

She continually looked for ways to free herself, but without tools she had no options. The chain was too thick to be broken by being stressed or twisted. Her ankle had started oozing blood. It was so sore that she started bending at her waist when she moved so she could pull the chain with her hand.

Marie was dozing on the cot when she heard someone walking outside the cabin.

"Hey, out there. Can you help me? I need help to get out of here."

She called out repeatedly but got no response even though she could still hear movement. Then she heard metal being rattled near the small pet door. When it was pushed open, a shaft of daylight poured through the small opening, but whoever was out there still wouldn't respond to her pleas for help. Marie got down on her knees to peer out the opening but couldn't see anyone. Whoever was there was apparently standing close to the wall to prevent being seen.

A can of lantern fuel and matches was pushed through the opening. That was followed by a gallon jug of water and a sack with the ubiquitous McDonald's golden arches on it.

"What do you expect to accomplish with this silly game? Where am I? What have you done with Hoagie?"

Marie still received no response and finally lost her patience. Although she was not a profane person, she certainly sounded like one when she screamed at her abductor.

"You gutless bastard, if I could get my hands on you I'd show you what it's like to be hit in the head and locked up in this hellhole." She continued her tirade. "If you'll open the door, you damn coward, I'll claw your eyes out."

Marie was mad enough to kill, and she would have if she had had the means with which to accomplish it. She was suffering pain and humiliation, and the lack of a response was infuriating. The small door closed, she heard the lock being rattled, and she heard footsteps fading away. She continued yelling long after there was any sound of movement outside the cabin.

Marie was once again alone with only the dim light from the flickering oil lantern. The bold anger that had allowed her to scream at her abductor soon gave way to fear and desperation. Although she was starving, she ignored the McDonald's sack and lay back on the cot. The realization that her abductor intended to keep her in the cabin indefinitely finally summoned the tears, and she cried herself to sleep.

Marie didn't know how long she slept. She had no way to keep time. The only way she could tell the difference between night and day was by a little light seeping through a couple of cracks in the chinking between the logs.

She racked her brain trying to remember exactly what had happened at the restaurant. She remembered everything about her dinner with Hoagie and being surprised when they realized that all the other customers were gone. She also remembered starting to walk across the restaurant parking lot. But from then until she woke up in the cabin, her memory was blank, except for some slight recollection of being carried over someone's shoulder.

Marie was worried about Hoagie. He wasn't a fighter, but he would have never let anyone take her without doing everything he could to prevent it. If Hoagie had also been abducted, why wasn't he in the cabin with her? She was trying to avoid thinking about her greatest fear. He was a big teddy bear who never hurt anyone, and she couldn't bear the thought of him being seriously injured.

Dex was also never far from her mind. He would be home from his trip by now and would have called her. What would he do when he couldn't find her? She didn't doubt that once he realized something was wrong he would do everything possible to locate her, but what could he do?

He had a key to her apartment, but there wasn't anything there to let him know what had happened. She hadn't talked to him after Hoagie called to invite her to dinner, so he wouldn't know that she had been with Hoagie.

Marie's family was in Atlanta, so no one but Dex would miss her until she didn't show up at the office on Monday morning. Dex was her only hope, but what could he do? He would surely go to the police, but without any information they wouldn't be able to do anything. They probably wouldn't even start an investigation for several days.

Marie ran all of these details over and over in her mind, but she couldn't come up with anything that was reassuring. She was at the mercy of her abductor, and her only hope was to figure out some way to escape. And escape didn't seem possible since she was chained inside a windowless cabin, didn't know where she was, and had no tools or weapons with which to aid her escape.

Every time Marie drifted off to sleep, the dreadful heat and humidity forced her awake. She couldn't understand why she was perspiring so much, because so far she had not forced herself to drink water from the bucket. She was afraid of becoming dehydrated, but the thought of drinking from the bucket was gross and disgusting. She had no idea where her abductor had gotten the water. She decided to continue to wait until she had no choice before she held her nose and drank from the bucket.

Time was crawling, and the silence inside the cabin was deafening. She thought about the old philosophical question of whether or not a tree falling in the woods would make a noise even if no one was there to hear it. She would love to hear a tree fall; she would love to hear any type of identifiable noise.

Marie was finally so ravenously hungry that she opened the McDonald's sack and found three cold burgers. She reluctantly unwrapped one of them and bit into it. It was awful, but since she needed the sustenance, she forced herself to eat the entire sandwich. Trying to choke down the dry hamburger finally forced Marie to put her face in the water bucket and drink. She gagged and almost lost what she had just eaten.

It was dark outside and eerily quiet when Marie heard the first mournful sound. It sent chills up her back. She was frightened until she recognized the sound she had heard so many times in old Western movies. She assumed she was still in Tennessee, but she had never heard of coyotes in Tennessee. The howling coyotes made her realize once again that she really didn't know where she was being held captive. She had no idea how long she had been unconscious, and therefore, she didn't know whether she had been moved to some distant state or was still near River City.

Chapter 24

The fisherman had launched his bass boat before sunrise. He was alone and enjoying the early morning calm. Somewhere in the distance a rooster was noisily announcing the beginning of a new day, but as the boat eased along, the only nearby sounds were the soft hum of the trolling motor and the buzzing of insects just wakening to the new day.

As the first light filtered through the trees, a deer bounded unseen up the steep bank from his watering spot, and every so often a squirrel shook the morning dew from a tree as it scrambled for breakfast a hundred feet overhead.

When the fisherman's line grew taut, he leaned back and jerked to set the hook. The instant exhilaration died when nothing pulled back. He mumbled a curse because he figured his lure was caught on another underwater stump. When he got closer he saw that it was tangled up in a large mass of debris floating on the surface. He leaned over the boat's gunwale to free the line, and his heart momentarily stopped. This debris had once been alive.

He tried to collect his senses and figure out what to do, but he knew he shouldn't touch the body. He fumbled for his cell phone and nervously dialed 9-1-1.

"I just discovered a dead body floating in the river. I need to report this to the police."

"Sir, tell me where you're located?"

"I'm in a boat on the river about four miles downstream from Running Water Marina."

"Hold on, sir. I'm going to connect you directly to the county police office."

The fisherman repeated the information to the dispatcher at the station.

"Sir, do not move the body. Where can you meet one of our deputies?"

"The best place is at Running Water Marina. I can be there in about ten minutes."

He cranked the bass boat's powerful outboard motor and got to the marina about fifteen minutes before the sheriff's deputy arrived.

"Are you the one who discovered the body?"

"Yes, it's about four miles down the river."

"Our marine unit will be here in a few minutes, but can we get to the body from the bank?"

"Not without getting wet. It's floating about twenty yards from the bank."

When the marine unit arrived and launched their boat, the fisherman led them down the river to the body. They took photos and then pulled the body into their boat. The fisherman followed them back to the marina.

Several emergency vehicles had arrived, and there seemed to be blue lights flashing everywhere. The lights had caused a crowd to congregate in the marina's parking lot. The county coroner was there, and an ambulance was standing by. The coroner examined the body and made the official death pronouncement. He also preliminarily identified the body by the contents of the wallet.

When Hoagie's mother saw the two policemen on her front porch, she knew by their sad expressions that Hoagie would not be coming home. She collapsed when the policeman confirmed what she had already surmised. The officer caught her as she fell and carried her into the house, and the second policeman went next door to ask a neighbor to stay with her.

Gigi was concerned about Dex and pleaded with him to come over for lunch. She knew how worried he was even though he was putting up a brave front for her. They were sitting at the kitchen table eating a sandwich, and the television was playing in the background. Suddenly the notice of a special bulletin caught their attention. The reporter announced that a body had been discovered floating in the river. Before waiting for additional information, Dex jumped up so fast he overturned his chair and was out the front door before Gigi could get up from the table. An ominous sense of doom swept over him.

He didn't want to think that the body could be Marie's or Hoagie's, but he had to find out. Without making a conscious decision to go there, he pulled up in front of the city police station. He double parked, ran up the station steps, and stopped at the window in front of the desk sergeant.

"My best friend and girlfriend are missing, and a special bulletin on television said that a body was found in the river."

"We had a report about the body being discovered, but it was in the county so it's not our jurisdiction."

"Can you get an identity from the county?"

"Not unless the next of kin have already been notified."

"Please call and see what you can find out. I'm desperate."

The sergeant hesitated but finally pointed across the lobby and said, "Have a seat over there. I'll see what I can find out."

From his seat across the lobby Dex could see the sergeant on the phone, but he could not hear the conversation. When he hung up, the sergeant motioned for Dex to come back to the window.

"Mr. Martin, the preliminary indication is that the body was that of Tom Hogan. Is he the friend you were concerned about?"

Dex couldn't speak for a moment so he just nodded. When he somewhat regained his composure, he asked, "Was there only one body found?"

"Yes, but you really need to go to the county sheriff's office to get any further information. Detective Lester Morgan is handling the case. I know Morgan. He's probably the best detective in the sheriff's department. Just ask for him when you get there."

Dex staggered to his car in a daze, but he didn't get over a block away before he had to pull over to the side of the road because he couldn't see. He couldn't remember the last time he had cried, but he had just lost his best friend and was terrified that Marie might have met the same fate. After a few minutes, he wiped his eyes and started his car again. He drove directly to the sheriff's office and was directed to Detective Morgan.

"Mr. Martin, the preliminary investigation indicates Mr. Hogan died from blunt trauma to the base of his skull. He was probably dead before his body was put in the river."

"He was with a woman when he disappeared; was there only one body found in the river?"

"There was only one body found, and our marine unit searched the river for two miles in each direction after retrieving Mr. Hogan. A fisherman discovered him about two miles downstream from the Canyon Grill. The city police informed us that he and the lady had dinner there the night they disappeared."

"What's your relationship to these two people?"

"We all grew up together and have been friends since elementary school. Marie Murphy is my girlfriend, and I had asked Hoagie to take her to dinner because I was out of town."

"That's what the city policeman told me; it sounds like an unusual situation. I will need to talk to you later, but I have an appointment now. Here's my card. Give me a call if you think of anything that will help the investigation. I'll be in touch."

Following the time-honored tradition of "if it bleeds, it leads," what had previously been downplayed as a missing person incident was now the lead story on the television news that evening. The following morning the front page headline boldly announced, "Local man's body recovered from river—Female companion still missing."

Dex had seen headlines like this countless times, but this was Hoagie and Marie, and he suffered through every word of the accompanying article. He thought it was disgusting that the reporter felt it was necessary to punch up the intrigue by pointing out Hoagie and Marie's connection to him because of his athletic accomplishments. One line in the article stated, "Hogan was entertaining Martin's girlfriend while the athlete was out of town on business." The detail was correct, but the insinuation was purposely used to titillate the readers, and it infuriated him.

Dex wanted to know more about Detective Morgan since he was going to be handling the investigation. That night he called a former teammate who was on the city police force and asked if he knew him.

"Dex, I've met him a couple of times when our investigations merged, but I know him mostly by reputation."

"I've heard he's supposed to be very good."

"Everyone thinks he's the best investigator around here. He started as a rookie and worked his way up to the lead homicide detective on the force. They say he's an aggressive interviewer with unrelenting tenacity, and if the person he's interrogating is guilty, he'll get a confession from him. I've also heard that he knows he's perceived as a mean son-of-a-bitch and he enjoys the reputation. The conviction rates on his cases make him a favorite with the district attorney's office."

"Well, I'm probably going to be in for one of his fierce interrogations. He said he would be back in touch with me."

"Before you go let me tell you a funny story I heard about him. He's about thirty-five years old and has been divorced a couple of times. He has a German shepherd that rides with him all the time. He's doesn't have anything to do with the canine unit; he just likes the dog. The story that is told about him is that his last wife said he had to choose between her and the dog, and he chose the dog. He said he wished all of his decisions were that easy because the dog had a better disposition and was more company at the foot of the bed than his wife was in it."

"He sounds like a real peach. I'll look forward to my interrogation."

Morgan called the next morning and asked Dex to meet him at the sheriff's office at eleven o'clock.

Dex was ushered into an interrogation room where Morgan was sitting at a small table in the center of the room flipping through some notes.

"Are you going to sit down, or just stand there like an idiot?"

"This is your meeting and your agenda. I was waiting for you to tell me what you want me to do."

"I asked you to come back today because I want to get to the bottom of this cock-and-bull story about you asking your friend Hogan to take your girlfriend to dinner."

"It's not a story; it's exactly what happened."

"Do you really expect me to believe that you invite other men to entertain your girlfriend while you're out of town?"

"You're trying to make something dirty out of a simple act of friendship. I told you that we all grew up together and Hoagie was my best friend."

"I don't care if he's your best friend or your damn cousin, it's still strange. You're just going to get into more trouble by lying, so why don't you just admit that you were jealous about the relationship between them?"

Dex was now officially pissed, and if Morgan wasn't a cop, he would have slugged him. But he obviously wasn't the bumbling cop who had investigated the tire slashing and opossum incidents. Morgan was slick, and he was purposely trying to get Dex riled. So far, he had been pretty successful.

"Detective, you can believe whatever you want to. I can't prove a negative, and you can't prove that fairy tale you've made up about a love triangle. Why don't we stop this stupid interrogation game of yours and concentrate on trying to find Marie and whoever murdered Hoagie?"

"Martin, in case you haven't noticed, I'm the one with the badge, and you're a suspect in a murder investigation. You'll sit there and answer my questions until I'm satisfied with your answers, or we'll take a little walk back to the cell block."

"You can ask me a hundred different ways, but my answers are all going to be the same. I didn't have anything to do with Hoagie's murder and whatever has happened to Marie, and I have no earthly idea who's responsible."

Morgan wasn't accustomed to having a suspect challenge him like Dex was. His size and menacing personality usually overpowered suspects and earned him a degree of reluctant respect. He was well over six feet tall, weighed over two hundred pounds, and had a close-cropped black beard that gave him an ominous appearance. His facial expressions suggested perpetual rage. Most suspects thought he would explode if they crossed him. It wasn't working out that way with Dex, so Morgan changed his tactics.

"Okay, Martin, why don't you tell me again where you were when Hogan and Ms. Murphy disappeared?"

"I was on a business trip. My last appointment on Friday was in Greenville, South Carolina, at four o'clock, and it was over at about five. My next appointment wasn't until eight o'clock the next morning in Atlanta. I stopped for the night at a small motel outside Greenville and checked in at about six."

"What did you do from then until the next morning?"

"I ate dinner at a small country restaurant near the motel and then caught up on some paperwork. I had paid in advance for the motel because the clerk said the office wouldn't open until six on Saturday morning, and I planned to leave at about five-thirty."

"How long does it take to drive from Greenville to River City?"

"It would probably take about four hours if I drove straight through, but I drove into downtown Atlanta for a meeting."

"Okay, tell me about Saturday morning."

"I left the motel at about five-thirty and ate breakfast somewhere on the interstate at a Waffle House. I don't remember the name of the small town, but it was the next one after the motel. I met with the manager of

Cross Town Pharmacy in Atlanta at about 8:15 a.m. and left for River City at about 9:30 a.m."

Morgan had been taking notes during Dex's recounting of his activities. He looked up and stared at him for a moment.

"Let me make sure I got this story straight. From six o'clock on Friday afternoon until your eight o'clock meeting in Atlanta on Saturday morning, you saw or talked to no one who can verify where you were. Is that correct?"

"I guess that's correct, but why would you think it's unusual? I doubt if many people can account for their time if they are asleep in a motel."

"Whether it's unusual or not isn't for you to decide. What is important is that I have investigated several homicides where the husband or boyfriend comes home unexpectedly, finds the love of his life making whoopee with his best friend, and takes matters into his own hands."

"That is not what happened here, and when you quit wasting time accusing me and start an actual investigation, you just might find out what really happened."

"I'm conducting the investigation, and I don't need suggestions on how to do it from a suspect. By tomorrow morning I want you to bring me a complete itinerary of your week's activities, with the names of people who can verify where you were during the week."

Dex was relieved when he walked out of the station. He had been subjected to the full force of one of Morgan's fabled interrogations, and he was pleased that he had held his temper fairly well. Despite Morgan's unpleasant disposition and what he had said, Dex was pretty sure that the detective believed him. But he couldn't resist the temptation to let Morgan know that his intimidation tactics hadn't scared him. Dex called him the next day.

"Detective, this is Dex Martin. I wanted to check and see if your investigation has turned up any new leads yet?"

"No, and we haven't found your girlfriend. You'll know if and when we come up with something; you don't need to call unless you have some information."

Chapter 25

Marie's parents had come to River City as soon as they were notified of her disappearance and had been there ever since. Dex kept them updated on information he was able to get from the police. He had nothing else to do, and since he had to keep his composure around them, it helped him maintain his own sanity.

Morgan's personality was so screwed up it was difficult to read anything into what he said or how he acted, but Dex thought he had been more amiable since the interrogation. He was at least sharing some information from his investigation. He told him that blood found in the parking lot was matched to Hoagie during the autopsy and that there was no water in his lungs. That confirmed he was already dead when his body was dumped in the river. He said fibers found on the body were sent to the crime lab in Nashville for analysis, but they would probably not help unless a suspect was captured and they had something to which the fibers could be matched. He also told him Hoagie's wallet still contained money and credit cards, which would seem to rule out robbery as a motive. Unfortunately none of these details really moved the investigation forward. They didn't even suggest additional avenues of investigation.

Morgan kept poring over the information he had, but all known facts could be summed up in a several short sentences: Hoagie and Marie had eaten dinner together at the Canyon Restaurant. Hoagie's car was discovered the next day in the restaurant parking lot. Blood found in the parking lot matched Hoagie's. His body had been recovered from the river a few miles from the restaurant. Death was not due to drowning but rather to a blunt-object blow to his head. Robbery was unlikely as a motive since his wallet was found intact. Marie's whereabouts were still unknown. That was it, the sum total of their investigation. There were no other clues.

The moment Dex dreaded finally arrived. With more self-control than he thought he possessed, he helped Hoagie's mother plan the funeral. So far he had struggled through the gut-wrenching, emotional pain, but he knew the worst was yet to come. He had almost lost it when he had to help select a casket. If he hadn't had to help Mrs. Hogan deal with her grief, he would not have been able to bear his own.

Dex and several of his high-school classmates were asked to serve as pallbearers. He loved Mrs. Hogan, but she finally asked him to do something that he refused to do.

"Dex, I want you to deliver a eulogy at the funeral. Hoagie would want you to do it."

"Mrs. Hogan, I love you and you know how I felt about Hoagie, but I can't do it. There's no way I could get through it without completely breaking down, and Hoagie would understand that."

"Okay, I understand, but I need your help with a decision the funeral home is asking me to make. They want to know whether or not I want to have an open-casket viewing and funeral, and I don't know what to do."

"I hope you aren't offended when I tell you what I think, but I would never open the casket if it was left up to me. I think funerals are the most inhumane ceremonies in our culture. No one benefits from them except the funeral homes that prey on grieving relatives and charge outlandish prices for the minimal service they provide. They claim to provide comfort to the family, but I've never known anyone who was comforted."

"I appreciate your honesty and don't disagree, but we've got to have a funeral. I don't want to open the casket either. I would like to try to remember Hoagie in happier times, but I felt like the funeral home was pressuring me to do it."

"If you want me to tell the funeral home that the casket will not be opened, I'll be happy to do it."

"Thanks, Dex, but I'll take care of it."

The television and newspaper coverage was unrelenting. It was most likely responsible for a lot of the curious onlookers who showed up at the funeral. Dex saw high-school classmates there who wouldn't have accepted Hoagie into their little cliques, but now they wanted to act as if he had been their friend. Dex greeted his old friends but was not in a mood to socialize. He suggested to those who tried to engage him in a more lengthy conversation that they should get together when times were better.

The media coverage made Hoagie's death the "celebrity funeral" of the season. The church was packed. Dex didn't look around to see who was there. He stared at the closed casket, and a thousand memories ran through his mind. At the end of the service he couldn't have repeated a single thing the minister had said.

It was raining at the cemetery, and Dex was thankful that his tears were indistinguishable from the raindrops peppering his face. He knew that gravesite services were supposed to bring closure and a sense of relief, but he felt no such relief or closure. Hoagie would always be a part of his life, and there was no way he could close out all the years they had spent together. But as he walked away from the grave, Dex was thinking of Marie. Finding her was now the single focal point in his life.

He had mixed emotions when he saw Morgan writing down tag numbers of cars in the funeral procession. It was sad that even this solemn occasion was under police scrutiny, but he was at least glad that Morgan was pursuing the investigation.

Dex went to the sheriff's office the next day to see if there was any news about Marie. Intellectually, he knew there was a good possibility that she had also been killed, but in his heart he could not accept that possibility until there was unequivocal physical evidence.

Morgan had chosen not to tell Dex, but an additional blood scraping from the restaurant parking lot had been typed. It matched traces from a Band-Aid that was found in a waste basket in Marie's apartment bathroom. He thought it was probably from something like a minor leg shaving incident. The blood match confirmed that she had also been injured in the abduction, but there was no way to determine the extent of her injury. Morgan didn't know if she was dead or alive, but with each passing day, he knew the possibility of her having survived the attack was lessened.

The daunting questions were in the forefront of Dex's mind as he tossed and turned through sleepless nights. Every time he drifted off to sleep, he was abruptly awakened by a recurring nightmare of Marie floating in the river. Was she already dead? Was her body actually floating somewhere in the river? Where else could she be? If someone was holding her captive, was she being abused? And the constant questions underlying all the others were who was responsible and what was their motive?

Dex had been checking by his office, but there was no way he could concentrate on anything related to his job. Jim Mitchell, his boss and friend, was very understanding. He told him to take as much time as he needed but to check for messages at least once a day.

Morgan got a list of all Hoagie's friends from his mother and talked to everyone on the list, but they had not provided any clues. Everyone seemed to have the same opinion: Hoagie didn't have an enemy in the world.

Marie's parents had returned to Atlanta, and Morgan drove there to interview them. They were visibly distraught but wanted to assist him in finding their daughter.

"Do either of you know of any difficulties or disagreements your daughter was having with anyone? Had she recently been involved in a dispute or argument that you know about?"

"We talked to her several times a week, but she didn't mention anything in particular. She had an argument with an old boyfriend some time back, but he moved out of town and she hasn't mentioned him in a long time."

"Do you remember his name?"

"His name was Dr. Bill Bishop, and he worked at Munson Hospital. Marie told us that he started acting weird and she told him that she didn't want to see him again. Apparently he didn't like the idea of being rejected and caused some more trouble, but she wasn't specific about what he had done."

Dex had already told Morgan about the situation with Dr. Bishop, so he didn't pursue it with Marie's parents. Her mother suggested he might want to check with her friends at the hospital and with her employees at the Atlanta office of RN4U. He already had that on his list of things to do while in Atlanta.

Her father said, "The only other argument or dispute in which Marie was involved, as far as I know, was over a recent business situation in River City."

Dex had also told Morgan about that situation, but he wanted to hear it from a different perspective.

"Do you know what the dispute was about?"

"What Marie told me was that during a medical review audit she discovered a financial scam between a bank and a nursing home, and that due to her audit, the managers of both facilities were arrested. While you're in town, you should talk to Harvey Blake at Proudland Bank. He knows about this situation and could give you a lot more information."

Morgan started asking questions about Marie's relationship with Hoagie and Dex. Her father thought he was suggesting the possibility of a love triangle, and he interrupted him.

"Look Morgan, it's pretty clear where you're going with this line of questioning, so let me save you some time. Those three have been friends since they were all in elementary school. We've known their families for twenty years. Marie and Dex have been dating for several months, and her mother and I think that the relationship may be pretty serious. Hoagie was like a brother to both of them, but she has never dated Hoagie."

The detective continued to take notes while Marie's father was talking. When he finished, Morgan offered no response to anything that had been said. He merely thanked them for their time and said he would keep them posted on any developments.

Morgan's next stop was at the hospital personnel office, but they told him that hospital rules allowed them to only confirm employment and give the dates of employment.

He went to Proudland and talked to Harvey Blake. Blake was cooperative but didn't have any information that Morgan didn't already know. Blake confirmed that both men involved in the scam were furious with Marie, and he had extremely high praise for the work she was doing for the bank. He also told Morgan that if he thought a reward offer might produce some leads the bank would be happy to contribute to it.

So far Morgan's investigation was bumping up against one dead end after another. Dr. Bill Bishop might prove to be another dead end, but Morgan had no intention of letting it go. He had investigated too many crimes involving terminated romances to not at least consider Marie's rejection of Bishop as a motive. Dex had told him that Bishop was working in a public health clinic in Birmingham, and he had already decided to make the trip to Birmingham before returning to River City.

Chapter 26

As far as Lester Morgan was concerned, Birmingham was not a destination city. It was simply a place one passed through, or more accurately, around en route from the mountains of Tennessee to the snow-white beaches along Florida's panhandle. Although he had driven past it on many occasions—it was only two hours from River City—Morgan could never remember actually visiting Birmingham.

The city had spent a lot of money reinventing itself from the time when it was known as the "Pittsburgh of the South." The steel mills were now shuttered, and the sky over the city no longer resembled the smog-choked Los Angeles basin. One could now actually take a deep breath in Birmingham without worrying about lung damage.

Morgan wasn't there to appreciate or evaluate the city's urban renewal program; he was there in search of information. However, he didn't get what he wanted. Bishop had resigned from the clinic several months earlier and left no forwarding address. He was told Bishop said he was leaving because he had not felt challenged by the work at the clinic and needed a change. The director described Bishop as a loner who had apparently developed no close friends while at the clinic.

The only physician at the clinic who was willing to talk described him as "sort of weird." He also said that his bedside manner sucked and he had a hard time relating to his coworkers. But he did say that Bishop was a competent doctor.

The only address they had for him was the one listed on their payroll records. Morgan checked but found that Bishop had moved from the apartment on or about the same day he resigned from the clinic. Again, he left no forwarding address and none of the people in the surrounding apartments knew anything about him. Morgan had bumped up against another dead end.

During the two-hour drive from Birmingham to River City, Morgan rehashed the investigation in his mind. He had interviewed dozens of people in Tennessee, Georgia, and Alabama, and he still didn't know much more than he did the day Hoagie's body was pulled from the river.

The only people he could even remotely consider as persons of interest were Dex, Dr. Bishop, Norton, the bank trust officer, and McPherson, the nursing home manager. He hadn't interviewed Bishop, Norton, or McPherson, and he really didn't consider Dex a prime suspect. Dex seemed believable during the interrogation, but he needed a lot more information than he had so far before he could eliminate anyone. Morgan still didn't even know if the primary target in the attack was Marie. It could have been Hoagie or Marie. He also wasn't sure if he was investigating a single or double homicide. Locating Marie, or her body, was a priority.

As he drove, Morgan summed up all that he really knew about the case. The only physical evidence was the blood scrapings from the parking lot and the fibers recovered from Hoagie's body, which were basically useless until they had something to match them against. The restaurant witnesses could testify to nothing except that they had seen Hoagie and Marie together before the abduction. He had identified four possible suspects, but he didn't have enough evidence against any of them to even consider an arrest. That was his entire case in a nutshell, and it was basically useless from a prosecution standpoint.

Chapter 27

Bishop had disappeared. Morgan had run out of ideas, and the investigation was at a standstill. One of Morgan's defining characteristics as a law enforcement officer was his ability to definitively profile suspected felons. Other officers, even those from surrounding states, frequently sought his advice in this area. He was somewhat amused that others believed he had some sort of special talent. He knew, even if others didn't, that it wasn't unusual ability that made him successful. It was simply that he was willing to spend more time developing the details that allowed him to accurately profile the bad guys. With no wife and no hobbies, he didn't have a life outside of his work anyway. His complete devotion to the job had already destroyed two marriages, and his only real friend was a dog. But he rather liked the idea that everyone thought he had extraordinary talent, so he didn't tell anyone his secret.

Bishop was the subject of Morgan's latest profiling project. He had gathered a lot of background information on him online and by telephone. He was born and grew up in Lynchburg, Virginia, as the only child of hourly textile workers who were both deceased. He had started to excel academically at an early age, but his social skills didn't develop at the same rate. He was a loner and never participated in athletics or any other extracurricular activity. The photo in his high-school annual was of a normal-looking teenager, but the caption under it told the story of his young life: "Billy is a scholar with little time to enjoy life."

Bishop was valedictorian of his high-school graduating class, received a full scholarship to the University of Virginia, attended classes twelve months a year, and graduated in three years with a bachelor's degree in biology. He was accepted at the Medical College of Virginia when he was only twenty years old and entered medical school a month after graduating from UVA.

Morgan talked by phone with staff members at UVA and the medical school. Those who remembered Bishop confirmed that he was an excellent student but also remembered him as a loner. An anatomy professor recalled that he had a volatile temper and did not work well with other students on joint assignments. A chemistry professor related an incident where his lab partner said Bishop had blamed him for the failure of an experiment and threatened to pour a beaker of sulfuric acid on him.

The recurring theme from high school through medical school was of a brilliant student that had no interest outside of academia and few, if any, friends. Even considering the alleged lab incident, there was nothing in his background to indicate he was capable of premeditated murder. He couldn't be prosecuted for having a volatile temper or being antisocial, and so far that was about all Morgan knew about him. He wasn't likely to gain a lot more insight into his psyche unless he could get him into an interrogation room.

The big break happened several days later. Morgan had left his card with the director of the Birmingham clinic and asked that he be contacted if they came across any additional information. The director called Morgan and told him they had just received an inquiry from a hospital in Dalton, Georgia, requesting previous employment information on Bishop.

Dalton, a north Georgia mill town, was only a few miles south of River City. Morgan called the hospital and confirmed that Bishop was an emergency room doctor there and was currently on duty. His shift was scheduled to end in about two hours.

Morgan made the short drive to Dalton, was at the hospital in time for the shift change, and had a nurse identify Bishop as he was leaving the hospital. Morgan followed him into the parking lot before he approached him and flashed his badge.

"Dr. Bishop, my name is Lester Morgan. I'm a detective investigating a case involving Marie Murphy, whom I understand is a friend of yours."

Morgan always watched the initial facial reaction of a subject when first approached. He was surprised that Bishop had no visible reaction when he first heard Marie's name.

Bishop looked at the detective's shield, nodded, and said, "Yeah, I know Marie. We dated for a while when I was working in Atlanta. What's she done? Is she in some kind of trouble?"

"Why don't we go in the hospital cafeteria and talk?"

After they were seated, Morgan said, "Marie has disappeared, and she was last seen with a man who has been found murdered."

There was still no reaction from Bishop. This made Morgan think he was either one hell of an actor or he really didn't know anything.

"Well, I hope she's okay. I can't imagine why anyone would want to hurt her."

Was he feigning this response? Had he rehearsed the reaction in anticipation of being questioned?

"Since all the television news in Dalton comes from River City, I'm surprised you haven't heard the news about this."

"I rarely watch the local news since I'm new in this area. In fact, I don't watch much television, and when I do it's usually CNN or the History Channel."

Morgan got the first reaction from him when he said, "I understand you and Marie had some kind of lover's quarrel in Atlanta."

Bishop put his hand over his mouth and coughed nervously but seemed to instantly regain his composure.

"Detective, most romances end with some kind of dispute; ours wasn't any different. We had a disagreement and decided to stop seeing each other. I haven't thought about Marie in a long time. We've both moved on. I assume she still has Dex."

Morgan said, "Yeah, I understand you and Dex also had a confrontation."

"Well, you know, boys will be boys. He was acting like a bullying miscreant, and I objected to it."

"I understand your objection ended up in a fist fight. Is that scar under your chin from the fight?"

"No, Detective, I cut myself shaving," Bishop replied sarcastically.

"Dr. Bishop, I had a hard time finding you. You seem to move around more than most physicians I've known."

"I haven't decided where I want to set up my practice, so I've been using the hospital jobs to try out different areas of the country."

Morgan decided that this cat-and-mouse game wasn't getting anywhere, so he followed his instinct to go for the jugular and see if it would jump-start the interrogation.

"I've been told that you threatened to kill Ms. Murphy."

Bishop stared at Morgan, hesitated for a long time, then smiled and said, "In the passion of the moment, we all say ridiculous things. I'll bet that on occasion even you have said something like, 'I could kill that guy.' It's a damn figure of speech. I was angry at the time, but I certainly have never tried to kill anyone. For God's sake, I save lives not take them."

"Several people have told me you have a problem with your temper." It was not stated as a question, but one was clearly implied.

Bishop simply shook his head and said, "I don't know why anyone would say that. I certainly don't think I have a problem."

"Several people have also said you don't get along very well with people."

Bishop just shook his head but didn't reply. This technique of goading a suspect to get him rattled had worked many times for Morgan, but since Bishop wasn't rising to the bait, he intensified the questions. When he did, Bishop stopped readily responding and resorted to merely shaking his head.

"Why did you and Ms. Murphy break up? What was the disagreement about? Did you ever have a physical altercation with her?" All of these questions received only a headshake or one-word answers, but Morgan could tell he was beginning to break through Bishop's calm demeanor.

He finally asked the question that set him off. "When you were dating Ms. Murphy was it an exclusive arrangement or were you seeing other people?"

Morgan had been told this was the reason for the breakup, but he didn't expect the outburst with which Bishop responded. Bishop's face suddenly flushed, and his raised voice attracted the attention of other people in the cafeteria.

"I thought it was exclusive until I caught her sleeping around on me. I thought she was different and then I found out she was just like every other damn woman I've ever met." He pounded his fist on the table for emphasis.

Morgan looked up from his note pad and said, "And you don't have a problem with your temper?"

Bishop stood up and said in a raised voice, "I'll tell you what I do have a problem with. I have a problem with your damn accusations. I have a problem with you thinking I'm stupid enough to still be moaning over some young girl I haven't seen in a long time. And I have a problem with a backwoods cop who thinks he's Sherlock Holmes. This interview is over. You can arrest me, or do whatever the hell you want to do, but any additional answers to your stupid questions will come from my lawyer."

Bishop walked out of the cafeteria with everyone there watching. When Morgan stood, he smiled, bowed to all the people staring at him, and whistled a tune as he slowly ambled out of the cafeteria. There was a thespian with a flair for drama under the hardened exterior of Detective Lester Morgan.

On his drive back to River City, Morgan thought about the conversation. He had established that Bishop definitely had a volatile temper, was not reluctant to lie, and was still furious with Marie for dumping him. It might not be enough for an arrest, but he had investigated a lot of murders committed with far less passion than what Bishop had just demonstrated.

Chapter 28

Her abductor showed up at the cabin every day with a bag containing three McDonalds' hamburgers. They were always cold so Marie figured it took some time to drive from wherever they were purchased. This made her think the cabin must be in a fairly remote area since the golden arches were everywhere in urban areas. The coyotes howling each night reinforced that hypothesis. The water he brought each day was still cool, so she assumed it was coming from a nearby mountain spring or stream. She had a lot of time to theorize about all these things, but she didn't know if any of her theories were correct. In fact, the only thing she knew for sure was that she was chained to the wall in a log cabin and she was going nuts.

Marie quickly learned to ration the three sandwiches she received each day. A cold Big Mac for breakfast wasn't very appealing, but at least it kept her from starving, and she didn't worry about the calories. She still didn't like drinking water out of the bucket, but she didn't have a choice.

After several days, the man slipped a sack containing two cotton dresses through the access door. They were ugly and shapeless, but they were clean and not soaked in blood and could easily slip over her head. Interestingly, there were also several pairs of snap-on panties in the sack. She was surprised that he had thought about the fact that she wouldn't be able to step into regular ones with the chain on her ankle.

The dresses were made from an appalling floral pattern, which confirmed Marie's suspicions that a man had selected them. No woman would have ever selected anything that ugly. When personal feminine supplies arrived without being requested, she realized that he wasn't planning to release her anytime soon.

After the screaming fit she had the first day, Marie realized she was not going to get anywhere by yelling at the abductor. For days she had tried pleading with him each time the small door was opened, but her pleas fell on deaf ears. The access door was opened once a day, her food and supplies were delivered, no comment was made, and the door was closed and locked once again.

Marie actually found herself looking forward to his arrival each day since it was the only thing that broke the monotony of her captivity. But she wasn't going to become too comfortable with this character. She had read about the Stockholm syndrome and wasn't about to pull a Patty Hearst stunt and start identifying with this nutcase.

She had dragged the chain behind her so long that her ankle had gone from just being raw and sore to the point where it was now an open wound. It was swollen, inflamed, and oozing blood. She was sure it was infected, but she had no antibiotics with which to treat it. For days her pleas to have the chain moved to her other ankle went unanswered.

Marie had explored every crack, crevice, and nail hole she could reach but had not discovered anything that might aid her escape. Her efforts did nothing but occupy her mind and further damage her ankle.

The only encouraging thing was that the wound above her ear seemed to be healing from what she could see in the small mirror. She was pretty sure she had a concussion because she had suffered loss of consciousness, severe headache, loss of memory surrounding the incident, fatigue, and other symptoms. Unfortunately there wasn't enough light on the mirror to check for the unequal pupils that would confirm her diagnosis.

Marie usually went to the gym three times a week, but her confinement kept her from doing any exercise and she felt miserable. She finally discovered she could do sit-ups without hurting her ankle. She stopped counting, but she figured she was doing a thousand a day; it helped to pass the time and hopefully get some health benefit.

Each day was a repetition of the previous one. There was no relief from the agonizing boredom of her nonexistence. She recited every poem and piece of prose she had ever learned in school. Then she started at her toes and moved up her body trying to remember the name of each bone she had memorized in her nursing school anatomy classes. When she got to the skull, she started back down her body naming muscle groups, veins, and arteries. Then she started all over again. She realized that she had to keep her mind active so that she could quickly react if she ever got the chance to escape.

Marie continued to worry about Hoagie. She was afraid he might have been seriously injured or worse when she was abducted. She assumed Dex was her only hope for rescue. He wouldn't let the police rest until they had exhausted every possible effort to locate her. She didn't doubt that he was thinking as much about her as she was about him and that he would never give up. There was nothing she could do but sit and hope she was found before she was killed by her captor, lost her mind, or died of boredom.

Chapter 29

To keep the investigation on the front burner, Dex pestered Morgan relentlessly. His repeated calls were beginning to get under Morgan's skin. He had told Dex several times that he wasn't helping by taking up so much of his time, but the calls continued unabated.

Dex knew his name was still on the suspect list, but he didn't think Morgan actually though he was involved. He had developed a level of respect and an arm's-length rapport with the detective. He had discovered that despite his crotchety exterior, Morgan was a very good cop who cared for people and took his work seriously. He pursued leads like a cat stalking a mouse; there just weren't many leads to follow on this case.

Morgan would have been furious if he had known that Dex was thinking about starting an investigation of his own, and if he caught him doing it, he would probably arrest him for interfering with an official investigation. He would eventually find out and there would no doubt be hell to pay when he did, but Dex would worry about that later.

Dex started by talking to every waitress at the restaurant and even some of the customers whom the waitresses remembered were in the restaurant that night. Prior to the abduction, none of the waitresses had known Hoagie, and the only reason they remembered seeing him was because they had wondered how the chubby, red-headed guy had gotten a date with such an attractive woman. No one had seen what had happened in the parking lot.

Dex's friend, the restaurant manager, pulled copies of credit card receipts from that night and read off the names. None of them were familiar to Dex, and for legal reasons, the manager would not give him copies of the receipts. He was told that Morgan had also reviewed the receipts, and he assumed that the detective had followed up with all the customers.

After visiting the restaurant, Dex drove to Atlanta and spent several hours with Marie's parents. He asked them to walk him through everything they could remember about high-school or nursing-school friends who might have had a disagreement with her. They also talked about the friends and contacts she had made in her business, but Dr. Bishop was the only one they were aware of who had ever had a serious disagreement with her.

Marie's mother took Dex up to Marie's old room. He suggested they look through her high-school annuals to see if it might prompt her mother to remember a long-forgotten instance. They also looked through a large scrapbook Marie had kept during her high-school years. Dex was impressed but not surprised with her prowess on the basketball court. There were also copies of a lot of articles she had written for the school paper, but there was nothing in the room that helped with the investigation.

After reviewing Marie's life, from high school up to the present time, they were still able to come up with only one person who might want to harm her. Mrs. Murphy had never met Bishop, but Marie had told her while they were still dating that it wasn't a serious relationship. She did not tell her mother about Bishop's threat until much later and then only when she was asked about what had happened to the young doctor.

Marie's father called the Atlanta office of RN4U, told them Dex was on his way there, and asked them to cooperate with him. Dex had never met any of the nurses, but they all knew about his relationship with Marie. The head nurse reviewed the firm's clients with him, and he also talked individually with each nurse, either in person or by phone. There was nothing in the records or the interviews that shed any light on why Marie was abducted.

The only other person he wanted to interview in Atlanta was Harvey Blake, the trust officer at Proudland. Marie's father told him Blake had been her connection to the bank in River City. He called Blake and was invited to come to the office. Blake told him the story of how they had decided to utilize RN4U and how he had encouraged Marie to open an office in River City. He also repeated the story about Marie discovering the fraud there and confirmed that both Norton and McPherson were furious with her after her discovery of their fraudulent scheme. He was highly complementary of her and the job she had done. What Blake said matched what Marie had already told him. Dex, after his admittedly amateur investigation, had the same suspects as Morgan with one notable exception: he wasn't on the list.

From Morgan's perspective there were four possible suspects: a bank officer, a nursing home manager, a physician, and a boyfriend. He couldn't have imagined a more eclectic group of possible felons. Of course, there was always the possibility that the perpetrator was none of the above.

Back in River City, Dex contacted one of his fellow suspects by showing up unannounced at Norton's home. He got a terse response to his first question. Norton said, "I'm represented by counsel; any information will have to come from my lawyer." Dex later got the same response from McPherson.

Dex knew the lawyers weren't going to tell him anything, so he didn't even bother trying to contact them. After his earlier altercation with Bishop, Dex didn't think it would be a good idea to contact him. He had now reached the same dead ends Morgan had encountered, and he had no idea what to do next.

Dex wasn't going to give up, but he needed to sit back and try to make some sense out of what he had learned. One thing he had learned was that it was a lot easier to criticize the police than emulate them. Logic should dictate that he stay out of the way and let Morgan do his job, but the detective's interest and his were not parallel. Morgan wasn't in love with Marie.

Chapter 30

The arraignment of Norton and McPherson had been a media event in River City. The people were initially shocked and embarrassed that anyone in their town would defraud the area's sick and elderly; then they got angry. Sordid schemes like this just didn't happen in their town. When network television picked up the story, the citizens were ready for a public lynching.

The two men were demonized in the press and on television, and Marie, who had uncovered the elaborate scheme, was portrayed as a hero of the elderly and oppressed. To properly set up the story, the media had to explain why a nurse was doing the audit that uncovered the fraud. This included discussing the relationship between the bank and RN4U. The exposure was extremely beneficial for both organizations. Before her abduction, Marie was busier than she had ever been.

The criminal trial was not scheduled to begin for several months, and in the interim between the indictments and when Marie was abducted, the national media quickly lost interest and the area newspapers soon relegated the story to the back pages. But when Marie was abducted and her companion was murdered, the story immediately became an intriguing mystery. It was picked up and followed by the wire services and was a topic of conversation around office water fountains across the country.

The story might have been buried or used as back-page filler if it had happened in a large metropolitan area, but since it was taking place deep in the storied mountains of southeast Tennessee, it created a media carnival. Add an all-American quarterback in the mix, and the felons became bit players in a soap opera featuring Marie and Dex.

Morgan wasn't really interested in the fraud case; his forte was homicide. After the fraud arraignment, he tried to arrange interviews with

Norton and McPherson, but their lawyers immediately shut him down. Both men claimed, through their lawyers, to know nothing about the murder or abduction. The assistant district attorney handling the fraud investigation discussed his case with Morgan, but it didn't shed any new light on the homicide case.

Morgan began to develop profiles on Norton and McPherson. If either or both of them were involved in the abduction and murder, Morgan thought there should be something in their background to indicate a tendency for violence. Norton was from Asheville, North Carolina, and McPherson was from Norfolk, Virginia. He wondered how they had come together to plan the fraud scheme and if there might be some connection in their background. His question was answered when he discovered they had been fraternity brothers at North Carolina State in Raleigh.

Morgan knew that with the tight budget under which his department was working he could never get approval for trips to Asheville and Norfolk. Instead he used the Internet and telephone, as he had with Dr. Bishop, to profile the men. He discovered that although they did not graduate in the same year, they were in school together for three years and in the same fraternity. McPherson graduated first with a degree in sociology. Norton graduated the following year with a finance degree. In River City both men had been working in careers that were related to their degrees.

Norton's first job was at a bank in Charlotte, where he worked for a year before accepting the job in River City. McPherson's first job was in the personnel department of a nursing home management company based in Norfolk. There was no indication that the two men had any contact with each other in the years since leaving college until McPherson turned up in River City two years ago as the manager of Meadowview Nursing Home.

The past connection between the two men had to somehow be material, and that made Morgan want to explore their backgrounds in more detail. The Raleigh police had no arrest information on either of them while they were at North Carolina State.

The Asheville police only had Norton on record for a couple of minor traffic violations as a teenager. He spoke to the principal and guidance counselor at Norton's high school and learned that he had been a good student but prone to mischief. The guidance counselor remembered that Norton had led a gang of pranksters that had used a thirty-foot extension ladder to drop used tires down over the school flagpole. He laughed when he described how the tires were already stacked nine feet high when the prank was discovered by school officials. All of his friends ran, but Norton was trapped at the top of the ladder. The school had agreed not to press charges after his parents paid to have someone use a chain saw to remove the tires.

There was nothing in the police or school records to indicate any homicidal tendencies. Of course, there was also nothing to indicate that he would later be involved in bank fraud.

Morgan's next call was to the Norfolk police station, and this one proved more interesting. McPherson had once been charged with assault, but the charge was later dismissed because the victim wouldn't press charges. An assault charge was the type of thing that Morgan needed to start his investigative juices flowing.

According to the records, Wanda Langley, the woman who had initially made and later dropped the charge, had been eighteen at the time and alleged that McPherson had struck her repeatedly with his fist during an argument. Morgan used a people search site on the Internet and found the telephone number for a W. Langley listed in Norfolk. When he dialed the number, a woman answered.

"Are you Wanda Langley?"

"Who wants to know?"

"Ms. Langley, my name is Lester Morgan. I'm a detective, and I need to ask you some questions."

"What's he done this time? You know we're divorced now, and I don't know anything about him."

"I'm not sure I understand who you're talking about."

"I'm talking about Maynard, my good-for-nothing ex-husband. You people should know all about him; you've arrested him enough times."

"Ms. Langley, I'm not calling about your ex-husband. Do you know a man named Brian McPherson?"

"Hey, I told the police years ago that I didn't want to press charges against him. I haven't seen him in years, so why are you bringing this up again?"

"I'm not with the Norfolk police. I'm calling from Tennessee, and I'm investigating a case involving McPherson. Your name has come up in reference to an assault charge you made against him."

"I don't know how I could help you, and I don't want to get involved in anything to do with him."

"Look I can easily get a subpoena, drag you into court, and compel you to testify, but you can save yourself a lot of trouble if you will just cooperate by answering a few questions. All I need to know is exactly what happened between you and McPherson and if there are any similarities between what happened to you and the incident I'm investigating."

"I don't want to go to court. If I talk to you now, will you promise not to make me?"

"I can't answer that until I hear what you have to say, but I promise you that if you don't talk to me now, you will end up in court."

Morgan was bluffing, but he doubted that she would think it was a bluff. She only hesitated for a minute before she started to tell the story.

"I was very poor and extremely shy in school. I never felt like I fit in with the other girls because they had so much more than me. Brian was the first boy who ever took an interest in me. He was a senior and I was a sophomore, and he had a car and money. We dated for several months and became very close."

Morgan assumed that "very close" was code for sleeping together, but he didn't interrupt her.

"When he graduated that spring, we continued to date until he went away to school in Raleigh and then I didn't see him again for a whole year. I dropped out of school and married Maynard. He was five years older, and the marriage was crap from the beginning. You sure you want to hear all this?"

"What I need to know is what happened when you charged McPherson with assault, but you can tell me the story any way you wish."

"Well, after we were married, I found out that Maynard was still seeing other girls. I had been thinking about divorcing him, and Brian came home from college and called me. I told him up front that I was married, but he said he just wanted to have lunch and catch up because we hadn't seen each other in so long."

Morgan was getting a little bored with the soap opera and was hoping that she would get to the assault before he had to start prompting her. For a woman who had been reluctant to talk, she sure was wound up now.

"Although I agreed to meet him for lunch, I was afraid and excited at the same time. Brian was my first love, and compared to Maynard, he seemed so sophisticated after being away at college that it confused me. He asked if he could take me home and then before I knew what was happening he had me in bed."

"You mean he raped you?"

"No, Maynard wasn't paying any attention to me and I needed someone to love me, so I didn't tell him to stop. He left about an hour before Maynard came home, but he called again the next day. It went on for two weeks. He told me he loved me and even hinted that we might get married after he graduated."

While she was telling her story, Morgan stopped taking notes and was actually feeling sorry for this naïve, love-starved girl that McPherson had so easily seduced.

Langley continued her story. "After Brian said he loved me, I was getting ready to tell Maynard I wanted a divorce, but then Brian went a week without calling me. I needed that week to come to my senses. He was just playing around with me before he went back to school. When he finally called, I told him that our summer fling was over and asked him not to call me again."

"Ms. Langley, you haven't said anything about an assault."

"Damn it, I ain't finished. I'm getting there. An hour later he knocked on my door and forced his way into the apartment. He was boiling mad and screaming at me. I tried to run, but he grabbed my arm and started hitting me with his fist. I finally got a good knee into his crotch, and while he was on the floor moaning and gagging, I ran outside and hid behind a dumpster in the parking lot. A few minutes later he staggered out and drove away. I ain't seen him since."

"So that's when you reported it to the police, but why did you later refuse to press charges?"

"I didn't want the neighbors or Maynard to find out how stupid I had been to get involved in this mess. Maynard was drunk as usual when he came home that night, and I explained the bruises on my face by telling him I had fallen down the steps. We stayed together for several more months before I finally divorced him, and I ain't wanted a man since."

Morgan thanked her for her help and was ready to end the phone call when she asked him about McPherson's problems in Tennessee. He told her it was an ongoing investigation that he couldn't discuss. He was now even more concerned about what might have happened to Marie Murphy. McPherson's former girlfriend had convinced him that he had a volatile temper and would not hesitate to attack a woman.

Chapter 31

It occurred to Marie that although she hated the man who was holding her in this cabin, the worst thing that could happen was for him to die or get killed. She had always been a believer, but since graduation from high school she had not regularly attended church. She had also fallen into the habit of only praying when a relative or friend was gravely ill, but now she found herself praying for the safety of the one person she hated above all others.

She was alone in the cabin and totally dependent on him for survival. She couldn't survive long without the food and water he provided. No one else knew where she was or even if she was dead or alive. If anything happened to him, she would surely die of starvation before she was found.

The loneness of the cabin was brutally painful for Marie. She thought most women were collegial, social beings like her and actually needed social interaction. In her opinion, men were different. They could more easily adapt to being alone for long periods of time. But even Dex, who appeared to be fairly comfortable in his own skin, would probably prefer a public flogging to a long-term sentence in this place.

She had seen prisoners in the movies check off their remaining days in captivity on a calendar, but she not only didn't have a calendar, she didn't even know if there was going to be a release date. The length of her sentence was yet to be determined.

Marie thought about all the tired phrases she knew for dealing with unpleasant situations: Tomorrow will be a better day. This can't go on forever. Just let me make it through the night. All black clouds have silver linings. Unfortunately, repeating worn-out axioms didn't seem to be helping.

When Marie really began to question her sanity was when she started looking forward each day to watching a large spider weave its web in a corner of the cabin. She had never been squeamish about bugs and insects. They were just pests that had not yet been exterminated. But the spider had become a source of entertainment. She sat for hours and watched the inexhaustible spider design his intricate web. She marveled at how he set his trap for flying insects and how rapidly he could move across the web to claim his prize.

Then one day Mortimer suddenly appeared. She named the tiny field mouse on the day of his first visit, and he made regular calls each of the following days. She didn't know where he had come from, but she was grateful for the companionship. He scampered back and forth across the cabin floor and appeared at odd hours of the day and night to claim the bread crumbs she saved him from her hamburgers. When she started talking to him, she was pretty sure she had finally slipped around the bend. Who in their right mind talked to a mouse and was happy to have it share a bedroom?

Marie was struggling to maintain perspective; it was becoming increasingly difficult. These bizarre activities were the extent of her morning and evening activities in the cabin. She invented games in a vain attempt to keep her mind active. In addition to her anatomy-naming game, she tried to name all the kids in her third-grade and fourth-grade classes.

When she thought about the poetry and prose she had committed to memory, one thought kept reoccurring to her. It was something she had read years before in a philosophy book. She didn't remember the exact quote or who had said it, but she did remember the thought. It was that one of the things that differentiated humans from other living creatures was the ability to reason and choose among alternatives. Man, unlike lower forms of life, could refuse to accept outcomes that were imposed on him and could instead choose alternatives.

Marie didn't know why she remembered that particular hypothesis when she didn't remember much else from the philosophy class. She could easily shoot holes in the theory, but she kept trying to relate it to her present situation. She made up her mind that she would not allow her abductor to impose an outcome on her. She decided she would choose her own, and her choice was freedom. Of course, she didn't have a clue about how she was going to accomplish it, but it was comforting to have a positive thought.

At that point, Marie quit playing the endless mind games and devoted her time entirely to considering how she might ultimately gain her freedom. It dominated her every waking hour.

Chapter 32

Marie listened as her abductor made his daily delivery of hamburgers and water. When he closed and locked the access door, she could hear his footsteps as he walked away.

She yelled sarcastically, "Thank you. Come to see me when you're in the area." Her regular sarcasm never seemed to affect him.

About twenty minutes later she heard footsteps again approaching the cabin. In the same sarcastic tone she yelled, "Hey, you came back. I guess you just couldn't stand to be away from me."

She didn't expect a reply and didn't receive one. But she heard the lock on the main cabin door rattling. She was terrified, but she tried to make a joke by saying, "Did you decide to finally come in and spend some time with me?"

"Who's in there? What are you doing in my cabin?"

"Aren't you the one put me in here?"

"Lady, I don't know what you're talking about. Is this some kind of game you're playing? If you don't tell me what's going on, I'm calling the cops."

Marie realized that this wasn't the man who was holding her captive, and she said in a half sob, "Oh, thank God! Someone chained me to the wall in here, and I thought you were the one who did it. Please help me get out."

"Okay, stand back. I'm going to shoot the lock on the door. This better not be a trick because when I open the door, I'll still have five more rounds in my pistol."

The deathly quiet inside the cabin was shattered by the gunshot. She heard the lock being removed just before the door began to slowly open. Bright sunlight flooded the cabin, momentarily blinding Marie. She looked away and blinked her eyes several times. When she could see more clearly, she looked toward the door and saw a man in camouflaged fatigues standing in the doorway pointing a pistol at her. The man saw the chain extending from Marie's ankle to the wall and slowly lowered his pistol.

"Thank you, sir. I've been locked up in here for days and was beginning to think I would never get out."

"Who did this to you?"

"I don't know. Someone hit me on the head and knocked me unconscious. When I woke up, I was chained to the wall. He's been bringing food and water and pushing it through that small door over there, but I've never seen him or heard his voice."

She was pointing to the access door, and the man noticed it for the first time. "This is my hunting cabin, but that door has never been there. He must have just recently cut through the logs."

"Mister, can you get this chain off my leg?"

"I don't have any tools, so I'll have to shoot the lock like I did with the one on the door."

He warned Marie to turn her head, close her eyes, and hold her hands over her ears. When he fired the shot, the resulting impact of the chain against her ankle caused her to scream in pain.

"Are you okay?"

"Yeah, but it hurt like the dickens when the chain jerked against my ankle."

Marie was standing, and the man was kneeling down examining her ankle. "I need to get you to a hospital. That's a pretty angry looking wound where the chain has been rubbing against your ankle. Do you think you can walk?"

"I think so, if you can help me."

He stood and took her by the elbow, but after a few awkward steps, it was obvious that Marie wouldn't be able to walk to where his truck was parked several hundred yards away.

"Do you mind if I just pick you up and carry you? It's quite a ways to my pickup."

She agreed, and he put one arm under her knees and the other behind her back and swept her up into his arms. He was a big man, and he seemed to carry her rather effortlessly. When they reached his truck, he helped her into the passenger seat.

When he was seated behind the steering wheel, he said, "I'm going to take you directly to Bradford Memorial in River City. That ankle needs immediate medical attention."

"Yeah, I think it's infected. I'm a nurse, but I didn't have anything with which to treat it."

He had already put the truck in gear, but he stopped abruptly after only moving forward a few feet.

He turned toward her and asked, "What's your name?"

"Marie Murphy."

"Oh my God! You're the one that everyone has been looking for. Your picture has been on television every day, but I didn't recognize you. I'm Bob Nichols from River City."

"I hoped that people were looking for me, but I had no way of knowing. Where are we anyway?"

"We're on Dogwood Mountain about twenty miles from River City. I'm going to call the hospital and notify them that we are on the way."

He pulled a cell phone out of his fatigue pocket and called information to get the hospital number. He then called the hospital and told them that he had found the missing nurse and was en route to the hospital with her.

When he ended the call, Marie asked, "May I use your cell phone?" She dialed Dex's cell number, and he answered on the first ring.

"Dex, I'm okay. I've just . . ." She started sobbing uncontrollably and handed the phone to Nichols because she was so choked up she couldn't speak.

He took the phone and said, "Hello, this is Bob Nichols. I just found Ms. Murphy. She was chained to the wall in my hunting cabin on Dogwood Mountain. She appears to be all right except for a nasty looking wound on her ankle and a cut on her head. I'm taking her to the emergency room at Bradford Memorial, and we should be there in less than thirty minutes."

"Thank God she's safe. Are you sure she's okay?"

"I think she's going to be just fine."

"Okay, I'm on my way to the hospital. I'll meet you at the emergency room entrance."

Marie was still crying softly, but she managed to thank him for completing the call.

"Was that Dex Martin I was just talking to? You called him Dex, and he's the only one I know by that name."

"Do you know Dex?"

"No, I've never met him, but I watched him play football all through high school and also followed his career at Georgia."

Marie nodded but was too choked up to continue the conversation. They drove the rest of the way in silence. At the hospital, Nichols pulled his pickup right up to the emergency room door. Before they came to a stop, Marie saw Dex standing there beside a nurse with a wheelchair. He quickly opened the door and grabbed Marie before the nurse could get to her. The news that she had been found had spread throughout the hospital and a lot of people were standing in the background watching the reunion.

Dex gently lifted Marie out of the truck but was reluctant to turn her loose long enough for the nurse to get her into the wheelchair. They were whispering back and forth, and Marie was now smiling through her tears. The nurse finally prevailed on Dex to put her in the wheelchair. She quickly pushed her through the emergency waiting room directly to the treatment area, but they stopped Dex at the door.

He went back outside to thank Nichols and met him walking from the parking lot back to the hospital entrance. He had parked his truck and was coming back to check on Marie.

"Mr. Nichols, I'm Dex Martin. I didn't mean to ignore you when you brought her to the door. I was just so relieved to see that she was okay that I forgot what I was doing. I don't know how I can ever thank you for taking care of her."

"You don't owe me any thanks. I was happy to have been able to help her. I wanted to see you again though to tell you that I don't think she knows what happened to her friend. She never asked me about him, and if she had asked I wouldn't have told her anything. You probably ought to talk to her before she finds out from someone else."

"Thanks, I thought she already knew about Hoagie. We've all been close friends for years, and she is going to take the news very hard. Are you sure there isn't anything I can do for you?"

"Well, if you don't mind, I would like to have an autograph for my son. He's a big fan of yours, and he plays at your old high school."

"I'd be honored to give him an autograph, and when this is all over, I would love to meet him. I'm still very close to Coach Delaney, and I'll make sure he knows that the father of one of his players is a new hero of mine."

Dex called Marie's parents to let them know she had been found and was going to be okay and then called Gigi to give her the good news. While Dex was waiting for Marie to be moved to a room, what seemed like every reporter in town arrived and cornered him in the emergency room lobby.

The reporters wanted Dex to make a statement, and he finally said, "I saw Marie only briefly, but her injuries did not appear to be too serious. She is being treated in the emergency room, and there isn't anything else I can tell you until I've had an opportunity to talk to her."

He started to walk away but saw Morgan motioning for him to follow him to a corner where they could talk privately.

"Who found her? Where was she?"

"A man named Bob Nichols has a hunting cabin on Dogwood Mountain, and he found her chained to the wall inside the locked cabin. He brought her here to the hospital. I talked to him briefly before he left, and he told me she didn't know who had abducted her. Apparently she was knocked unconscious and woke up in the cabin."

"How badly is she hurt?"

"The chain that was wrapped around her ankle left an ugly looking wound, and she has a cut on the side of her head. By the way, Nichols told me that she apparently doesn't know about Hoagie. I would prefer that you let me tell her, because it's going to really hit her hard."

"Yeah, I think you should be the one to tell her, but I need to talk to her as soon as she's moved to a room. Do you know how to get in touch with this Nichols fellow?"

He handed Morgan a piece of paper and said, "Here's the address and phone number he gave me, but I need this back so I can contact him later."

"Do you think he is on the up and up? You don't think he had anything to do with her abduction do you?"

"No, absolutely not. He couldn't have been any more helpful. He ought to get some kind of recognition for rescuing her."

Morgan walked with Dex to the nurse's station to see if there was an update on Marie. The nurse told them that she had just been moved upstairs and gave them the room number. On the way to the room, Dex said, "You better let me talk to her first because she's going to ask about Hoagie."

Morgan stayed in the hall beside the door when Dex went in the room. He couldn't hear their conversation, but Marie suddenly screamed, "No, not Hoagie. He can't be dead."

After that, all Morgan heard for the next ten minutes was Marie sobbing loudly as Dex tried to console her. Dex finally came out of the room and said, "Morgan, she's not in any condition to talk to you now. Is there any chance this can wait until tomorrow morning?"

"I just need to ask her a few questions, and it won't take but a few minutes."

"Okay, go ahead and try it, but I'm not sure she can be of much help right now."

Dex walked back in the room with Morgan and said, "Marie, this is Detective Lester Morgan with the county police. He has been working on the case since the beginning and he needs to ask you a few questions. He promised this would only take a few minutes."

Marie nodded at Morgan, but didn't say anything.

"Ms. Murphy, I'm sorry to bother you at such a time, but I need to find out anything you might be able to tell me about the man who did this."

She was still crying softly but managed to say, "I don't have any idea who he was or why he did it. I never saw him or heard him say a word."

"I understand he hit you in the head. Were you unconscious when he took you to the cabin?"

"Yes, I don't remember anything until I woke up in the cabin. I was chained to the wall."

"You were there for a long time. How did you survive with no food or water?"

"There was a small opening about the size of a pet door that he had apparently cut in the wall near the floor. It was locked from the outside. Every day he shoved three hamburgers and some water through the door. He avoided being seen by standing next to the wall when it was open. I tried to get him to talk, but he never said a word."

"Had you ever seen this Bob Nichols who rescued you?"

"Not until he opened the cabin door today, but next to Dex he was the most beautiful man I had ever seen."

Morgan and Dex both smiled at her attempt to make a joke, and Morgan told her that he would come back when she was feeling better.

Dex had asked Nichols for directions to the cabin, and he now relayed that information to Morgan, who said he was familiar with the area. Morgan immediately called his office and asked them to place a hidden sentry on the road up the mountain in case the abductor came back. Unfortunately the news media was already all over the story. Special news bulletins were broadcast throughout the afternoon and evening, and it seemed the kidnapper saw them. He never returned to the cabin.

The next day Morgan went with the crime scene unit when they were dispatched to check the cabin. They found the place on the dirt road where all the recent truck tracks stopped and noticed a partially obscured trail leading off into the deep underbrush. After following the trail for several hundred yards, they came to the clearing where the cabin was located. The lock, with a bullet hole in it, was hanging in the door hasp. They found the chain and the other busted lock inside the cabin. Marie had told him that the man never came inside the cabin while she was imprisoned there, so he didn't think there would be much evidence available, but he still asked the crime scene investigators to check it out.

Morgan went back outside the cabin and slowly circled it, looking for any evidence that might help identify the abductor. Other than footprints leading to the front door, he only saw tracks that led to the small access door on the left side of the cabin. He noted the new hinges and the sawdust on the ground under the door. There was no way anyone could be seen from inside the cabin if they stood close to the cabin wall.

The crime scene people fingerprinted the area around the door and then they all packed up and left the mountain.

Chapter 33

Marie had been given a light sedative, and she appeared to have finally drifted off to sleep. But when Dex got up from the chair beside her bed, she again started to cry softly.

"Dex, I worried about Hoagie every day I was in that cabin. We were together when I was taken, and I couldn't figure out why he wasn't being held captive with me. I just can't believe he's gone. What kind of monster could have done this?"

Dex sat on the side of bed, and she sat up and buried her face in his shoulder. As he held her he repeated her name over and over as if trying to be sure she was really safe and in his arms.

He finally said, "Sweetheart, we'll talk about all of it later, but right now I just want to hold you. Thank God you're safe. I've been so afraid that I would never get you back."

They held each other for a long time before he released her and she lay back in the bed. She was still feeling the effect of the sedative, but she obviously wanted to talk about her ordeal.

"Dex, it's my fault. I'm responsible for what happened to Hoagie."

"What are you talking about? You didn't kill him. You were both attacked, and there was no way you could have prevented what happened to Hoagie."

"But he wouldn't have even been at the restaurant if he hadn't been trying to cheer me up. I feel responsible."

"Marie, that's nonsense; you are no more responsible than I am. I really think you should wait, but if you insist on doing this now, just start at the beginning and tell me everything you remember."

When she started talking, it seemed to provide her with at least a momentary reprieve from her agony. She stopped crying.

"Dex, I don't remember anything about the actual attack. I remember walking out of the restaurant with Hoagie, but nothing after that except for a vague recollection of having something like a pillowcase over my head and someone carrying me over their shoulder. I didn't fully regain consciousness until I was by myself and chained to the wall inside the cabin."

"So, there's no way you can identify who attacked you?"

"No, I never saw him, and I never heard his voice. I tried every way possible to get him to talk, but he never said a word. I honestly don't have a clue about his identity. I wouldn't even be sure it was a man rather than a woman except I don't believe a woman could have carried me over her shoulder like that."

"And he never hurt you after the initial attack?"

"No, but I was terrified every day that he would kill or sexually attack me."

Dex nodded at the bandage around her ankle and asked, "How badly did the chain damage your ankle?"

"I was so angry the first few days that I drug the chain all over the cabin and it rubbed all the skin off my ankle. After that it bled every time the chain touched it. It's raw, bruised, and swollen, and now the doctor says it's infected. He applied a topical ointment and gave me an antibacterial injection for the infection." She pulled her hair back and said, "This cut above my ear is actually the most significant injury. I was apparently hit on the head with something that knocked me unconscious. I had all the symptoms of a brain concussion. Since it wasn't sutured when it should have been, I'm going to have a large scar above my ear but my hair will cover it. It's too late now to do anything about the wound or the concussion, but it will all be okay."

Dex could see the effect of the sedative as Marie's eyes became droopy, and he said, "You need to get some rest. I'll sit here with you while you sleep."

He sat in the chair and held her hand as she drifted off to sleep. She had been sleeping for about an hour when her mother and father arrived. It was an emotional family reunion, and Dex stayed for only a few minutes before leaving to give the family some time alone. Her mother had already said she was going to spend the night with her, so he kissed Marie on the cheek and told her he would see her the following morning.

Dex had been on an emotional roller coaster for days and had not taken time to collect his thoughts. When he reached the parking lot, he didn't immediately start the car. He sat for a while and thought about everything that had happened in the past few weeks. Thankfully, Marie had been spared, but he had lost his best friend and he still didn't know who had attacked them or what the motive might have been.

Seeing Marie in the hospital and realizing that she was at least safe for now made him wonder all over again what in the world he would have done if she had been killed along with Hoagie. He could no longer imagine his life without her. He couldn't understand why she had been spared and Hoagie had been killed.

He once again started wondering why he had never felt romantically inclined toward Marie when they were younger. He had certainly been interested in girls before Marie moved away, but he had only thought of her as his buddy. Even today in the hospital when she was an emotional wreck, wore no makeup, and her hair was a tangled mess, she was still the most desirable woman he had ever seen. How could he have not recognized that when he was a teenager?

Even though Dex had called Gigi shortly after he first saw Marie in the hospital, when he got to her house late that afternoon, he had to reassure her again that Marie was going to be okay. Then Gigi wanted to hear the whole story. They turned on the television to watch the evening news, and the lead story was about Marie's rescue. He was surprised when the short interview with him in the emergency room lobby was featured in the story.

Marie's mother was still in her hospital room when the doctor came by just after seven the next morning. "How are you feeling this morning?" he asked.

"I slept well for the first time since I was abducted. Thanks for the sedative."

"We're running a culture to identify the bacteria in your ankle. The lab should have the results this afternoon, and we can start you on the appropriate antibiotic. I checked the X-rays we made yesterday, and you did not have a fractured skull, but the head injury still concerns me. I'd like to monitor you for another twenty-four hours before you're released."

Marie's mother asked, "Doctor, will it be okay if I get the hospital beautician to wash her hair today?"

The doctor grinned and said, "Yeah, it is sort of in a mess, isn't it?"

By the time Dex arrived, Marie was sitting in a chair beside the bed with her hair shimmering and her usually flawless light makeup in place. The telephone had been ringing all morning. The media was clamoring for an interview with Marie, and her mother had been running interference for her. After Dex arrived, he called Detective Morgan to see if he had any suggestions on dealing with the media. He didn't want Marie to do or say anything that might jeopardize the investigation.

Morgan said he knew the media would be all over the story, and he realized that Marie would have to say something. His only request was that she confine her remarks to her captivity and rescue and not speculate about Hoagie's death. That wasn't a problem since she couldn't remember the actual attack.

Marie was started on an antibiotic that afternoon, and after the doctor checked her the next morning, she was released from the hospital. Dex pushed her wheelchair through the hospital exit and saw that the area around the door was stacked three deep with reporters and cameramen. Someone on the hospital staff had leaked her imminent release to the media. Questions were being yelled from all directions as microphones were shoved in her face.

Dex stepped in front of her and said, "Folks, if you will back off for a minute, Ms. Murphy will make a statement."

Before leaving the room they had prepared a statement because they knew she would have to say something if she was confronted. However, they had not expected the size of the media blitz she now faced.

Marie started by saying, "I want to read a brief statement, and then I will take a few questions. There are some areas that the investigating officers have asked me not to discuss, and I hope you understand that I don't want to do anything to interfere with their investigation." She then started to read the prepared statement. "I had dinner with my dear friend, Tom 'Hoagie' Hogan, and I remember leaving the restaurant and starting to walk across the parking lot. The next thing I remember was waking up in a cabin on the mountain. I was kept chained to the wall of the cabin for the entire time of my captivity. I was not physically or sexually abused while I was in captivity, but I was knocked unconscious by a blow to my head while being taken captive. The owner of the cabin, who had nothing to do with the abduction, found me and brought me to the hospital. I have no idea about the identity of my abductor. I never saw him or heard him speak. That is basically all I can tell you, but I will take a couple of questions."

An attractive brunette, whom Dex recognized from the evening news, asked, "Ms. Murphy, do you have any idea what the motive might have been. Did he threaten to harm you while you were held captive?"

"I have no idea what his motive was, and he never said a word to threaten me or anything else during my confinement. He passed food and water to me through a small opening in the cabin wall, but I never saw him."

The next question came from a reporter whom Dex did not recognize. "Ms. Murphy, can you describe your injuries?"

"I have a severe abrasion around my ankle from the chain, and it's infected. I also have a rather severe cut above my ear where I was struck with some type of heavy object during the abduction."

A reporter in the back yelled, "Can you tell us why Mr. Hogan was killed, and you were not?"

"I was knocked unconscious in the attack and didn't know Hoagie had died until I was rescued. I don't know why I wasn't also killed. Now if you will excuse me, I really need to get home so I can start to recover from this ordeal."

One of the reporters asked, "Ms. Murphy, what can you tell us about your relationship with Mr. Hogan."

Dex started to push her wheelchair away, but Marie said, "Dex, wait a minute."

She looked directly at the reporter who had asked the question and said, "I've known Hoagie since we were in elementary school. He was a wonderful friend to Dex and I, and the three of us were very close. If your question was intended to imply some type of romantic involvement, I can assure you that Hoagie and I were never romantically involved and never dated. He was simply a very dear friend whose memory I will cherish forever."

Dex turned the wheelchair away and pushed her to where her father was waiting with the car door open. As she was being helped from the wheelchair, one of the reporters yelled the question they had both been expecting. "What's your relationship with Dex Martin?"

Before she got in the car, she smiled for the first time and said, "Very, very close."

Dex helped her into the car and kissed her good-bye while the reporters watched. She whispered, "Hopefully that will end any ugly speculation."

The plan was for Marie to go home with her parents for a couple of weeks to fully recover and stay away from the intense media attention in River City. Dex told her he would call her later that day and closed the car door.

When Marie and her family drove away, the media descended on Dex. "Dex, how would you describe your relationship with Ms. Murphy?"

"I have known Marie all my life. We grew up next door to each other. I care for her very much, and as she said, we are very close. Now I have to go."

The reporters continued to yell questions at him as he trotted to his car, but he left without answering them.

Chapter 34

Marie loved her parents dearly, but after getting used to living by herself for several years, there had just been too much togetherness the last couple of weeks. She was bored to death. Her wounds were almost healed, and she was thoroughly rested. Her ankle was still sore, but she was tired of sitting and ready to get back to work.

She missed Dex. They had talked on the phone every night, but it wasn't the same as seeing him every day. Her car was still in River City, so she called and asked him to come pick her up. The two-hour drive from Atlanta to River City was the first time they had really been alone since before her abduction.

During the drive, Dex cautioned her repeatedly about how careful she should be since whoever had abducted her had still not been apprehended or even identified. She had listened to this same lecture from her parents for two weeks, and she was ready for another subject.

"Okay, Dex, that's enough. I understand the danger and I promise to be careful, but we can't let this idiot dictate our lives. What if he's never caught?"

"They'll catch him. We've just got to give them time." He said it with more conviction than the he felt.

"Dex, I'm more concerned about you. You're probably the one he's really after. He had ample opportunity to kill me while I was helpless in that cabin, but he didn't. Remember, it was you that got the threatening notes, had your tires slashed, and had a dead animal nailed up in your yard."

"That still doesn't lessen your need to be careful."

"I thought a lot about this while I was in Atlanta. I don't think he actually intended to kill Hoagie. He probably just hit him harder than what he intended. I think he was after me because he wanted to use me as bait to get to you. He just hadn't figured out exactly how to do it before I was rescued. This guy's a mental case, so it's useless to try to predict what he might do next. I'm not going to let him control what I do or don't do every day."

They were almost to River City when Marie said, "Before we go to the apartment, I want to visit Hoagie's mother and go to the cemetery."

"Marie, you don't have to do that today. You need to rest now."

"I'm tired of resting. I haven't done anything but rest for two weeks. Stop by the florist before we go to her house."

Dex had talked to Hoagie's mom regularly since the funeral, but Marie hadn't seen her since she was in high school. She was on the porch when they got out of the car.

"Marie, I would have never recognized you if I hadn't seen you so many times recently on television."

Marie searched for the right words but finally just embraced her. When she stepped back, they both had tears in their eyes. Mrs. Hogan invited them to sit with her on the porch, and they talked for a while before Marie stood up.

"Mrs. Hogan, we stopped by the florist and got some flowers. We're going to the cemetery, and it would mean a lot to me if you would come with us."

Mrs. Hogan initially hesitated, but Marie and Dex both encouraged her and she finally agreed.

Dex parked the car and they walked up the hill to the grave. Grass had been planted in the newly turned soil and straw had been spread to protect the seeds. There was a single wreath of artificial flowers next to the newly erected tombstone. Dex hadn't been back to the cemetery since the day of the funeral, and when he saw the name on the tombstone, his eyes began to water. The two women were so consumed with their own emotions that they didn't notice the tears slipping down his cheeks.

Marie said, "We were all three so close when we were growing up. I loved Hoagie like a brother. That's probably why I feel so guilty. This wouldn't have happened if he hadn't been entertaining me at that restaurant."

Mrs. Hogan was overcome with grief, but she said through her tears, "Marie, this was not your fault. No one can blame you for the action of a crazy person."

When Dex returned to the car after walking Hoagie's mother to her front door, he said, "Marie, I love you for doing that. You will never know how much that meant to her and to me."

They drove in silence to Marie's apartment, each lost in their own thoughts. Dex had gone by to check on the apartment several times while Marie was in Atlanta, but he wasn't a housekeeper. Marie immediately noticed the accumulation of dust and started the housekeeping chores as soon as her bags were unpacked. They ordered a pizza for dinner, and Marie started dozing off while eating.

"Dex, I'd love to spend more time with you tonight, but I'm exhausted from the trip. I'm still not used to staying up all day. Would you mind terribly if we wait until tomorrow to celebrate my homecoming?" She walked him to the door, and he kissed her good night.

"Marie, before I leave I want to tell you one more time to be sure to lock—"

"Good night, Dex. Go home."

Dex was in his office the next morning by 7:00 a.m. While Marie was in Atlanta, he had been working long hours trying to make up for the time he lost from work during her captivity. He had made several day trips to nearby towns and spent a lot of time with the marketing department on two new commercials that were almost ready to be released.

EaseFast sales continued to exceed expectations, and the revenue was going to have a larger-than-expected impact on Argon's quarterly earnings. Jim Mitchell, Dex's boss and biggest supporter, made sure that Dex's name was at the forefront of any discussion about the product that took place within the company. He made sure Dex was viewed as a rising star, because Dex's success was his success.

When Dex called Marie at noon, he got her answering machine. She was supposed to stay in and rest all day, but when he called RN4U, she answered the phone. He was both angry and relieved at the same time, and she picked up on his mood.

"Look, Dex, you can't panic every time you can't find me for ten minutes. We've both got to get over this and go on with our lives. I've got a business to run, and I'm going to be in and out of the office every day. Don't worry about me."

"Okay, you are obviously not going to rest, so let's get dressed up, go to dinner, and celebrate tonight."

"Do you think we should? Morgan warned us about being in public places before they catch the guy that kidnapped me."

"You're the one who said we couldn't let this nut control our lives."

"If we're going, we should go early and try to miss the crowds. Pick me up at five-thirty."

Dressing up was always a simple process for Marie. She had the type of body that made off-the-rack dresses look like designer originals. When Dex arrived at her apartment, she was wearing a pale-blue silk dress. It was beautiful on her, but it also revealed that she had suffered some weight loss on her recent hamburger diet. The slacks she was wearing the day before covered her injured ankle, but tonight the wound was clearly evident, even though her hose softened the appearance. Dex had made reservations at Harbor Lights, a restaurant overlooking the river in the downtown area. It arguably served River City's finest French cuisine and had elegant European décor and a romantic atmosphere. They had to park several blocks away and walk to the restaurant because the day-trip tourists were still clogging the streets and had taken all the nearby parking spaces.

It was a beautiful fall afternoon, and Marie and Dex walked hand in hand, happy to be together again after her terrible ordeal. At the restaurant, they sat on the deck overhanging the river and lingered over the excellent food and wine. They enjoyed the setting sun and even danced for a while on the small floor in the back of the restaurant.

The rather pricey, upscale restaurant was patronized by an older clientele. The big band music carefully selected to appeal to this group actually created a romantic ambiance. They were probably the youngest couple in the restaurant, but this was a special night. Dex and Marie weren't interested in anyone but each other.

When they left the restaurant, Dex noticed the slight chill in the air that promised winter was not far away. They held hands and strolled along the dark street toward their car. Even on this backstreet, three blocks from the restaurant, parked cars had been jammed bumper to bumper on both sides of the street when they arrived. But now that most of the tourists had left for the night, there were only a few cars parked along the street.

They were so consumed by each other that they failed to notice the car parked directly behind theirs had its motor idling. Just as they walked abreast of the car, a man with a bandana tied over his face leaned out the window and pointed a pistol at Dex. The shot shattered the stillness of the evening and was so close it was deafening. The car sped away before

Marie realized what had happened; then Dex collapsed face-first onto the sidewalk.

Marie screamed as she dropped to her knees beside him. She knew he had to have been hit, but she saw no blood until she rolled him over on his back. The blood pumping from his chest soaked his shirt and jacket.

Marie's nursing instinct took over. She spread his jacket apart and ripped open his shirt. The bullet had entered the right side of his chest a few centimeters below the nipple. She immediately placed her thumb over the entrance hole and pressed as hard as she could to stem the blood flow.

People attracted by the gunshot were running from several directions to where Marie was working feverishly on Dex. She yelled for someone to call 9-1-1. Several cars stopped, and a crowd began to build as Marie continued to work on him. The emotion had not yet seized her, and she was reacting as she had when she had worked in the emergency room.

Dex had lost consciousness. She checked his heart rate. The rate was steady but weak. His breathing was labored, and she could tell from the entry site and the sucking sound that his lung had been punctured. She covered his mouth with hers and continued to blow her breath into him in an attempt to supplement his airflow while continuing to pressure the entry wound.

Fortunately the downtown fire station and rescue unit was only four blocks away. The EMTs got there quickly and took over for Marie. She climbed into the back of the ambulance where the EMT personnel were working on Dex, and they left the scene before the police arrived.

A trauma doctor met the ambulance at the emergency room entrance, and Dex was rushed directly into the hospital. Marie was stopped at the door to the treatment area and told she would have to stay in the ER waiting area.

The cool, professional efficiency with which she had attended to Dex now gave way to raw emotion. Unfortunately she knew how seriously he was injured and that he might not make it. She also realized she must be in shock because so far she hadn't shed a tear. She was covered with his blood and had to explain to two different nurses who passed through the waiting room that it wasn't her blood.

When the police arrived, a nurse pointed out Marie, who was sitting by herself in a corner of the waiting room. He wrote the personal information that Marie furnished in his notes and then asked, "Ms. Murphy, can you tell us what happened and who shot your friend?"

"We were walking toward our parked car, and without any warning, a man leaned out of the window of the car parked behind us and shot Dex. He had a red bandana over his face, and he didn't say a word. He sped away, and I immediately started working on Dex."

"Can you give me a description of the man and his car?"

"No, I don't even know the color of the car, but it was a dark color and it was parked directly behind us. The only thing I remember is the red bandana. This wasn't a random shooting; this man was waiting for us."

"I agree. I know who you are and what happened before. Who's handling the case in the county?"

"Detective Lester Morgan. Someone should get in touch with him right away."

"I'll take care of that. I will need to talk with you again, but right now I need to get back to the scene and see what I can find."

Marie had called Gigi when she got to the emergency room, and after finishing with the policeman, she turned and saw her walking toward her. The two women held each other and waited for some word from the trauma team. Finally the doctor who had met the ambulance came out to talk to them.

"Mr. Martin has lost a lot of blood, and we've already given him two replacement units. He has a collapsed lung and has been taken upstairs for surgery. It will probably be a while before they can give you more information. You should wait in the surgical waiting room."

Marie said, "Thank you, Doctor. We appreciate the update. Where's the waiting room?"

"It's on the fourth floor. Ms. Murphy, I recognized you from all the recent television reports. The EMTs told me what you did at the scene, and in my opinion, you saved his life by reacting so quickly. If you hadn't been there, he probably wouldn't have even made it to the hospital."

After the doctor walked away, Marie said, "Gigi, the good news is that they wouldn't even attempt surgery unless they thought he was strong enough to withstand it. They can take care of the collapsed lung, but they won't know what other injuries he has until they start the surgery."

It was almost three hours before the surgeon finally walked into the waiting room. Marie held her breath as she saw him approaching.

"Hello, Ms. Murphy, they told me who you are and about your nursing background, so I'll try to explain to you where we are in dealing with his trauma. He made it through surgery and I believe he will pull through, but he has some substantial problems. The bullet entered the upper right chest wall, passed through, and collapsed his right lung and nicked the subclavin artery before lodging against the scapula. I removed the bullet and put in a chest tube so we could use negative pressure to inflate his lung. We've repaired the damage as well as we could, but he's not out of the woods yet. He'll be in recovery for an hour or so and then taken to the surgical ICU unit. The next twenty-four hours will be critical. If we can get through that period and avoid a serious infection, I believe he will recover."

"Doctor, when we will be able to see him in the ICU?"

"You are not going to be able to see him tonight, and I suggest you get some sleep and be back here early in the morning."

Gigi didn't fully understand what the doctor had said about Dex's condition, so Marie explained it to her as well as she could. When they began to relax for the first time in hours, the conversation slowed and Marie realized just how tired she was.

Neither Marie nor Gigi wanted to leave the hospital. Although visiting hours had been over for hours, she bluffed her way up to the ICU desk. The duty nurse would have been frightened by her blood-soaked clothes if she had not recognized her. Dex and Marie's continuing tragedies had been reported so much that the news of the new event had quickly spread throughout the hospital.

Marie started to introduce herself, but the nurse said, "I know who you are, Ms. Murphy. We have already been notified to expect him to be transferred here from surgery."

"The surgeon just told us that he is in recovery now, but we won't be able to see him until morning. His grandmother is here with me, and she won't leave until she's sure we will be notified if there's any change. Will you take my number and give me a call if anything happens?"

"You probably know I'm not supposed to do that, but since you're a nurse, and with all you been through lately, I'll give you a call if anything changes." She wrote down Marie's number and told her to try to get some sleep.

Marie finally convinced Gigi there was nothing either of them could do, and they walked out to the car in the early morning darkness. Gigi drove Marie to her apartment, and they agreed to meet later that morning at the hospital.

Marie wasn't sure she could sleep, but she got out of her blood-soaked clothes and took a shower. It was after 3:00 a.m. She set her alarm for six-thirty and stretched out on the bed. Her mind was in overdrive even though her body was exhausted. She replayed the tumultuous evening in her head before gradually drifting off to a short, restless sleep.

Chapter 35

Marie was already dressed before her alarm sounded at six-thirty the next morning. She was at the hospital thirty minutes later, and Gigi pulled into the parking lot right behind her.

There was a different nurse at the ICU desk, but she recognized Marie.

"Good morning, Ms. Murphy. He was moved here from surgery at about four o'clock this morning. He is still heavily sedated, but he seems to be resting comfortably. Visiting hours start at eight, and family members can go in for ten minutes every two hours."

When she saw Marie's disappointed expression, she grinned and said, "You're his sister, aren't you?" She winked and said, "If you would really like to see him, I'll take you in now but you can only stay a couple of minutes."

Dex looked about like what she had expected. He was on oxygen, had an IV in one arm and a blood pressure cuff on the other, and was pale as a ghost. The sheet only came up to his waist, and his torso was wrapped like a mummy.

The ICU nurse was standing beside her when Marie said the first thing that came to her mind. "After surviving refrigerator-sized behemoths regularly pounding him into the turf for years, a small bullet has rendered him completely helpless."

The nurse said, "I went to high school with Dex. It's hard for me to see him like this, so I can appreciate what you're going through."

During her years in nursing, Marie had become callous to a lot of suffering, but this was Dex and she suffered with him. He briefly opened his eyes when she held his hand, and she thought he smiled slightly before drifting off again.

Gigi was allowed in the room for ten minutes at eight o'clock, but she said he never woke up while she was with him. Marie reassured her that it was the medication and not the injury that was keeping him asleep.

They both went in at ten o'clock, and there was no change in Dex's condition. Marie sneaked a look at the chart hanging on the foot of his bed, but there was nothing there that she didn't already know about his condition.

The doctor came in about noon, and after examining him, said, "So far so good. His breathing is very much improved, and there's no sign yet of any infection. He should be coming out from under the heaviest anesthesia pretty soon, but we will keep him somewhat sedated for another twenty-four hours."

The next time Marie was allowed in his room, Dex's eyes were open, and he reached for her hand as she stood beside his bed. He had a tube down his throat so he couldn't talk but he mouthed, "Thank God, you're okay. I love you."

"And I love you, Dex."

He then mouthed, "What happened?"

Marie could tell that he was alert enough to communicate even if he couldn't talk. He apparently didn't remember anything about being shot. They had always been honest with each other, so she told him what had happened.

"We were walking from the restaurant to the car, and someone leaned out of a parked car and shot you at close range."

He pointed to his chest and mouthed, "What's wrong?"

"The bullet punctured your lung and hit an artery. They operated on you last night to repair the damage and remove the bullet. The doctor says he thinks you're going to be okay."

He mouthed, "Stay with me."

"Dex, you're in ICU and they will only let Gigi and me come in for ten minutes every two hours. You need to rest. You won't have to stay in here too long."

That afternoon Detective Morgan showed up at the hospital to talk to Marie. It wasn't his case since it happened in the city, but he still had a murder and abduction to close, and it appeared the same perpetrator was involved.

"Detective, all I can tell you is the same thing I told the city police last night. We were walking to our car when this guy with a bandana over his face leaned out of a parked car and shot him."

"Since his face was covered, I assume you can't identify him, but can you identify the car?"

"No, I don't even know what color it was. It all happened so fast, and Dex was on the sidewalk bleeding. All I concentrated on then was trying to keep him alive."

"What's the doctor told you?"

"He had surgery last night and is still out of it, but the doctor told us this morning that he thought he was going to be okay unless he develops an infection."

"I'll leave you alone for now, but as soon as he's released, all three of us need to sit down and talk. We need to go over everything again because there's got to be something we're missing. This guy can't be smart enough to do all these things without leaving a clue."

Each time Marie went in to see Dex, he struggled to talk. He was agitated by his inability to do so, and she tried to soothe him. "Dex, just let me talk. Maybe by tomorrow they will be able to remove the tube and then you can tell me whatever it is you're trying to say."

When Marie left for the night at eight o'clock, Dex was only running a low-grade fever. She told Gigi this was the best news they could hope for because it indicated that he had not developed a serious infection. She had not told her how common serious infections were with puncture wounds, particularly gunshots.

Marie had to run by her office the next morning before she got to the hospital. When she arrived, the doctor had already been in and removed the tube from Dex's throat. He could talk, but his throat was sore and talking irritated it. Marie assured him that this was normal and it would improve rapidly.

The first thing he said was, "Marie, thank God it was me and not you that got hit."

She leaned over the bed, kissed him, and said, "I was so scared for you that I thought I'd die."

"The doctor told me that you saved my life. How can I ever repay you for that?"

"By getting well and loving me."

"The doctor said that if I continue doing well, they will move me out of ICU tomorrow. Gigi said she is going to stay at the hospital all day today, so you can go to your office and just come back after you close tonight."

Marie had been avoiding the media, but when she got back to her office they were camped outside. She knew she would eventually have to make a statement, so she decided to do it now. There was a television crew and two newspaper reporters she recognized.

"What can you tell us about Dex's condition?"

"He had surgery last night and is in ICU. The doctor thinks he will make a full recovery."

"Do you know who shot him?"

"No, if I could identify him, he would already be in jail."

She briefly told the reporters what had happened and then said, "The reason I couldn't identify him was because his face was covered with a bandana. The street where it happened was not well lit, and I was frankly more concerned with Dex's injuries than identifying his attacker. I have no idea what the motive might be, but it must in some way be related to everything else that's happened to us lately."

"The doctor has said that your fast action saved Dex's life. What did you do?"

"Look, don't portray me as a hero in your stories. I'm just a nurse who happens to be in love with a man who desperately needed my help. I would have done the same thing for a stranger, but I admit that I wouldn't have been nearly as terrified."

That quote introduced the story on the television news that evening, and it also appeared in print on the sports pages of newspapers all over the South.

Chapter 36

Dex was finally convinced that he had been the primary target all along. He tried not to dwell on it, but it crushed him to think that Hoagie would still be alive and Marie would have never been abducted if it was not for him. Marie was right; she and Hoagie had just been targets of opportunity for whoever wanted to punish or kill him.

Marie made several trips a day to the hospital. She timed her visits to be there during the few minutes the family was allowed in ICU. The doctor had said it would take two to three weeks for the lung to heal but that Dex would continue to be partially incapacitated for longer than that. Gigi spent most days at the hospital. Marie relieved her at night and stayed until the last ICU visitation period ended.

Dex made steady improvement, did not develop an infection, and was sitting up and taking a few steps by the third day. Two days after that he was so restless they were having difficulty keeping him for overexerting. The doctor said the speed of his recovery was remarkable and attributed it to his physical condition prior to the attack. He wanted to go home, and after five days the doctor released him with precautions about what activities he could attempt.

Several days later Dex and Marie were walking in the neighborhood when his cell phone rang. He answered it and then said, "Yeah, she's here with me now. Where do you want to meet us?" He listened for a few seconds and then said, "We can be there in twenty minutes. We'll see you there."

Dex put the phone back in his pocket and said, "That was Morgan. Something has come up, and he wants to see us in his office right now."

"Did he say what it was about?"

"No, he just said it was important and that he wanted to talk to both of us as soon as possible."

When Marie and Dex walked into Morgan's cubical at the sheriff's office, his first question was, "Do either of you know a man named Buford Wilson?"

Dex and Marie looked at each other with puzzled expressions and both shook their heads.

Dex said, "I don't remember anyone by that name. Are we supposed to know him?"

"Apparently he's also known as Snake."

They both reacted immediately, and Dex said, "I didn't know his name was Buford, but the only one I've ever known as Snake is a creep who went to high school with us. He was sent to a juvenile detention center for carrying a gun to school."

Morgan said, "Yeah, that's him, and we've discovered some evidence that links him to your shooting. The officers who did the on-scene investigation found an empty shell casing and an empty cigarette pack. The shell casing had a partial fingerprint, which probably wouldn't have been much help except it was matched to a full set of prints on the cigarette pack. They traced those prints through the database and identified them as Wilson's."

Dex and Marie looked at each other, and Marie asked, "You haven't seen him since he was arrested, have you?"

"No, I never saw him again, except possibly one time just before I graduated from high school. Hoagie and I discovered a moonshine still on the mountain, and I thought Snake might have been one of the people we saw working at the still. They fired a shot to scare us away, and we left in a hurry. I couldn't swear it was him because Hoagie didn't recognize him."

Morgan was looking at a sheet of paper and said, "This guy has quite a rap sheet for someone no older than you. After he was released from detention on his eighteenth birthday, he was charged with assault for attacking a girl at a fast-food restaurant, but she later refused to press charges. After that he was charged with stealing a toolbox from a truck, although the owner later said it was just a misunderstanding. When multiple victims refuse to press charges, we are always suspicious that they may have been threatened and intimidated."

Marie said, "He's the type of person who would do something like that."

Morgan continued referring to his notes. "Then he was nailed for grand theft auto and spent two years in prison. He was paroled about six months ago and has never checked in with his parole officer. We don't know where he is now, but the evidence points to him being the one who shot you. Do you know any reason why this character would have it in for you?"

"Well, several people said he brought the gun to school to shoot me because of a fight we had, but that was seven or eight years ago. Surely that idiot wouldn't still be carrying a silly grudge from a high-school fight."

Morgan said, "Wait a minute, back up and start at the beginning. I want to hear the whole story."

Dex looked at Marie and asked, "May I tell him everything that happened?" She nodded that it was okay.

"When we were in high school, Snake followed Marie home one afternoon. Her parents weren't there, and he tried to molest her. She was able to get away, ran next door to my house, and told me what had happened. I went after him, but he was already gone and I couldn't find him that afternoon."

Dex kept glancing at Marie who was visibly uncomfortable, but she said, "It's okay, Dex, that was a long time ago."

"Marie was embarrassed by what had happened. She said she could never go back to school because someone would find out about the incident and think that she had encouraged it. I talked her into going to school the next day by telling her that I would make sure Snake never bothered her again and no one would ever know about what happened. When classes were over that afternoon, I caught up with him in front of the school where a crowd of students were waiting on the school bus. I pounded him pretty good until several people pulled me off. It really wasn't much of a fight, but he had several cuts on his face and one eye swelled closed. One of the students got him in a car and took him to the hospital.

"I was told later that he was treated and released. He didn't come back to school for several days and then on his first day back he was arrested for having the pistol. As far as I know, the police were not notified about the fight. All the people who were waiting for the school bus saw the fight, so he was probably so embarrassed by the beating he took that he didn't tell anyone what had happened to him."

Marie said, "I didn't see the fight, but a couple of weeks after that I moved to Atlanta with my family. I've never seen Snake since the day he tried to assault me."

Dex added, "Hoagie had nothing to do with the fight, but he was the only one other than us who knew what it was about. I told Hoagie after Marie had moved, but I told him he could never tell anyone, and I don't think he did."

They talked for a while longer, and when they stood up to leave, Morgan said, "I wish I had known about this earlier, but I understand that it had been so long you didn't think it was important. I think Wilson must be our man."

Dex asked, "What about the investigation into Marie's abduction and Hoagie's murder?"

"I've interviewed all the people we identified as potential suspects, and we don't have anything to connect them with the crimes. Of course, we also don't yet have the evidence to link Wilson to anything other than shooting you, but it seems reasonable to assume that he was the culprit in all of it. His motive may have been his high-school obsession with Marie or hatred of you for embarrassing him in front of the other students. It may not make sense to us, but I learned a long time ago that those who think logically can't always understand the irrational impulses of a criminal's mind. I'm not yet going to eliminate McPherson, Norton, or Bishop, but right now we have nothing to link them to any of these situations. What we need to do is locate Wilson."

Chapter 37

Years of athletic conditioning and an indomitable spirit had hastened Dex's recovery thus far, and the doctor told him if he continued to improve he would soon be released to return to work.

Marie and Dex had tried for days to go for neighborhood walks, but the media was driving them crazy. Every time either of them ventured outside, some representative of the media latched onto them. They were both tired of responding to questions for which they had no answers.

"Dex, the only way we are going to get away from reporters is to slip out of town for a while. We need to go somewhere where there aren't any reporters who recognize us, and maybe you can relax for a few days before you go back to work."

"Where do you suggest we go?"

"I don't care as long as it's at least ten miles from the nearest TV or newspaper reporter."

"I had a friend at Georgia who talked all the time about his family's place on Lake Burton in the north Georgia Mountains. He said it was his favorite place in the world."

"Okay, I'll go online and see if I can find out anything about Lake Burton."

Marie got on the Internet and found a rental agent in the general area. The agent told her most of the houses around the lake were private summer residences, but she knew one family that would accept short-term or even weekend rentals. She booked the house before ending the conversation.

The three-hour drive took the couple through several small, picturesque mountain towns. The scenery on the trip through the beautiful mountains of north Georgia made the trip worthwhile, but it did nothing to prepare them for their first breathtaking glimpse of Lake Burton. The lake, nestled in the heart of the Blue Ridge Mountains, was a bucolic paradise that virtually whispered tranquility.

After the problems they had encountered recently, they were in serious need of a place where they could simply kick back, relax, and let the world pass them by. Lake Burton looked like just the place to do it.

The residents around the lake were apparently not too interested in encouraging tourists to invade their sanctuary. Street signs were almost nonexistent. They had to stop twice for directions, such as, "Turn right at the white house and left at the big rock, and it'll be down there a ways." After wandering around trying to follow the directions they were given, they finally located the rental house. It faced the water and was surrounded on the other three sides by white pines that essentially isolated it from neighbors. They loved the privacy, boat dock, and unobstructed view of the lake.

Marie made Dex watch as she unloaded the car and carried their two small bags into the house. Although the doctor had said his medical condition was significantly improved, his nurse and lover refused to allow him to lift anything heavier than a beer bottle. He murmured a comment under his breath about bossy nurses but acquiesced to her temporary authority.

They had not brought any food with them, and it was almost time for dinner. They were both hungry after their long drive.

Dex said, "There's probably not an abundance of restaurants in the mountains. We better get started; we may have to search for a while."

Fortunately, they stumbled on a small restaurant only a few miles from where they were staying. They wouldn't have recognized it as a restaurant except for the sign. Buffy's Place looked like a campground with one large cabin surrounded by several smaller ones. The rustic setting was interesting, but they didn't hold out much hope for the quality of the food.

"Marie, do you want to take a chance on this place?"

"We might as well try it. There probably isn't another restaurant for miles."

As soon as they went inside, they were enthusiastically welcomed by Buffy herself, who was working behind the bar near the front entrance.

"Good afternoon, folks. Are you just passing through?"

Dex said, "We're staying at a place on the lake for a few days."

"Well, I'm Buffy, and we're happy to have you stop by tonight. Are you here for dinner or can I get you something from the bar?" Dex looked to Marie for approval, and when she nodded, he said, "We're going to stay for dinner. Maybe we'll have something from the bar after we're seated."

They were ushered to a larger dining room. It had seats for perhaps two dozen people, but since it was still early, only a few of the tables were occupied.

Dex asked the waitress, "Can we have a couple of Coors Lights while we look over the menu?"

Marie only looked at the menu for a few seconds before saying, "I didn't expect anything like this here in the mountains. Look at the descriptions of the entrees and the number of choices. If they are as good as they sound, this place would rival some of Atlanta's better restaurants."

In a few minutes, people began drifting into the restaurant, and before Marie and Dex were served, the room was almost at capacity. From the snippets of conversation they overheard, it was obvious that most of the people knew each other. And they weren't local mountain people. The casual but trendy way they were dressed, together with the urbane chatter about market conditions and social events, clearly identified them as some of Atlanta's movers and shakers.

Marie whispered, "These people probably own all those expensive homes we saw on the lake. They look like permanent residences, but I bet they're just used on the weekends."

This wasn't the type of place where one would expect entertainment with dinner, but while they were eating, a man was setting up a portable CD player and microphone. He was a solo vocalist, and his only accompaniment was CDs of popular recordings from past decades. He had just started his routine when some of the restaurant patrons starting singing along.

One diner, with a questionable voice and a vague knowledge of the lyrics, soon stood and joined him on the microphone. In any other setting, he would have been roundly booed, but the joyful crowd at Buffy's laughed and loudly applauded his efforts before the DJ finally convinced him to sit down. The quality of the food, festive attitude, and friendliness of the staff created a perfect ambiance for two young lovers seeking some normalcy for their recent chaotic lives.

When they walked outside after dinner, Marie said, "Remind me to never judge a restaurant by what it looks like from the outside. Buffy's was wonderful."

The remainder of the weekend was everything Marie and Dex had hoped it would be. Each day they bundled up and braved the chill of the mountain air to spend time in the Adirondack chairs on the dock. But most of the time they were content to stay in the cabin. They spent long hours together sitting, talking, and reading on a plush rug in front of the fireplace. And they kept the promise they had made to each other before leaving home: they didn't mention their problems until they started the trip back to River City.

Chapter 38

Their self-imposed ban on discussing their problems was over, and Dex and Marie used the return trip to talk about the events that had happened and what they could anticipate in the coming weeks.

"I haven't thought about Snake in years, but I'm inclined to agree with Morgan," Dex said. "He's just the type of creep who could be behind everything."

"I agree, Dex. But the only thing that continues to bother me is that I would have never thought he was smart enough to pull off the abduction or resist the temptation to attack me while I was helpless in that cabin."

"Thank God he didn't follow through on that, but that doesn't mean he wouldn't have eventually attacked you. You may have just been rescued before he did anything. What I don't understand is why he would still hold a grudge when we were only fifteen years old at the time of the fight. He must be insane to still be harboring anger about something that happened so long ago."

"Don't forget what Morgan said about trying to understand an illogical mind."

"Marie, do you even still remember what he looked like in high school?"

"You've got to be kidding. Yes, I remember exactly what he looked like. He was the ugliest guy in school. He was tall and had a scrawny body with this lumbering way of walking. He didn't have any hips, and he kept his pants clinched tightly around his waist, like he was afraid they might fall down to his ankles. I even remember that lump of an Adam's apple on his scrawny neck and the elongated nose that shaded his upper lip. There was nothing pretty about Snake, but what turned my stomach was the inflamed acne all over his pockmarked face."

"Wow, you really do remember him."

"After what he tried to do that day, it would be pretty hard to forget him. I can't believe it now, but before he attacked me I actually felt sorry for him. No one would have anything to do with him, but I at least spoke to him when we passed in the hall. He must have got the wrong signal from my friendliness, but the only time I was ever within three feet of him was the day he tried to force himself on me. I can still remember the putrid stench of his breath when he tried to kiss me . . . Oh, for God's sake let's change the subject. He's just vermin that needs to be eradicated."

Snake was the last of the three sons of Hobart and Daisy Wilson. Rufus and Elroy were older siblings. As the baby in the family, he learned to defend himself at an early age. He actually got his nickname at age five when he bit Rufus on the leg for taking one of his toys. His mother said, "Buford, you just bit him like a snake." The nickname stuck.

Rufus was five and Elroy was three when Snake was born, and he was tormented by his older brothers his entire childhood. He was on the receiving end of all their pranks and constantly berated about his appearance and intelligence. When he tried to follow his brothers around the neighborhood, they would throw rocks to chase him back home.

Snake's parents knew he was mentally challenged before he ever started to school, because he didn't walk or talk nearly as early as his brothers. Rather than improving, his diminished intelligence became more noticeable as he grew older. He was a miserable student and as socially inept as he was dumb. He had his first skirmish with the police at age twelve when he was caught shoplifting candy at a local supermarket. The store didn't press charges, but when the police drove Snake home, his father beat him unmercifully with a leather belt. It never occurred to Snake that he was being beaten for his thievery; he thought it was because he got caught. He had several other run-ins with the police, so when he was caught with the pistol at school, the local police already knew that he was simply a young criminal in the developmental stage of what would probably be a lifetime of crime.

It was a seminal moment in his criminal life when the juvenile judge sentenced Snake to the detention center until he turned eighteen. The first night of his incarceration he got into a fight for stealing another inmate's cigarettes. It was only the first of several such incidents. The other inmates despised and shunned him. He was an outcast even among other society outcasts. Although he was surrounded by dozens of other young juvenile delinquents, he might as well have been in solitary confinement. None of them would associate with him.

Snake was finally released on his eighteenth birthday. As he walked through the gate, his counselor made what would prove to be a prophetic statement: "We should just transfer him directly to prison; that's where he'll spend most of his life." Snake was arrested a couple of years later for grand theft auto and spent two years in the state prison.

His father died while he was incarcerated, and his two brothers got married and moved out of the house. Rufus and Elroy never visited Snake while he was in detention, and his mother, who neither drove nor owned an automobile, had only been able to visit a few times. She was the only one in the family who had ever had any sympathy for Snake. She welcomed him home, even though she could barely support herself on the social security checks that were her only source of income.

Snake's mother told him that his brothers didn't come around very often, and she was afraid they were getting into some kind of trouble. Snake was able to track them down and found that his mother's suspicions were right. They were distilling moonshine at a still tucked into the side of a nearby mountain. Since he couldn't get a regular job because of his record, and didn't want one anyway, Rufus and Elroy agreed to hire him. He had long ago decided that the only people with regular jobs were those that weren't smart enough to make money without one.

The brothers needed a packhorse to carry the raw ingredients that were used to distill the moonshine and to then carry the jugs of moonshine back to the mountain road where the bootleggers picked them up. Snake had the right qualifications: a strong back and a weak mind.

He had been working at the still for less than a week when Dex and Hoagie stumbled on the operation. When the sentry's shot scared them away, they were moving so fast that he didn't recognize them. He had intended to shoot Dex the day he was arrested at school, but some kid saw him put the pistol in his locker and told a teacher. That was the beginning of all his problems. In his mind, if it hadn't been for Dex, he would have never been incarcerated, and he vowed every day he would get even with him.

Snake could never understand why Dex got so mad about him trying to make out with Marie. She wasn't related to him, so why did he care? Anyway, she had been asking for it. She obviously wanted him because she said hello every time they passed in the hall, and none of the other girls ever spoke to him. He was just going along with what she wanted, but then she got scared and ran to tell Dex. When Snake was released from juvenile detention, it was too late to carry out his vow to get even with Dex because he had already left for college.

Chapter 39

Snake obviously never understood Albert Einstein's definition of insanity: doing the same thing over and over and expecting a different result. He started stealing cars again less than a week after serving two years for doing the same thing. This time he joined his brothers in what they euphemistically called their "automobile business." A chop shop by any other name was still an illegal auto theft operation.

After federal agents destroyed their moonshine still, the brothers stumbled onto the demand for used parts and had already started their new venture before Snake was released from prison. Elroy had been serving as the point man, the one who actually stole the cars and drove them to the mountain. It was the most dangerous job in the operation, and he was glad to relinquish it to his dim-witted baby brother.

Their shop was portable, and they operated it from the top of a desolate, uninhabited mountain. Every night they loaded their tools in a pickup truck and left the mountain before daybreak. They didn't set up the operation again until after dark.

The only access to their shop, other than a long steep hike, was an abandoned logging road from the valley to the top of the mountain. It was unpaved, steep, narrow, and crooked until it reached the summit. A half-acre area on top of the mountain was level and clear. It had been cleared a half-century before to allow logging trucks the space to turn around and start their long descent to the valley lumber mills. The road came to a dead end in the clearing at a precipice overlooking the valley. The Wilson brothers' "automobile business" operated in the clearing. Stolen cars were disassembled, the useable parts were salvaged, and the carcasses were pushed over the escarpment.

It had been over fifty years since the last log was hauled off the mountain. Lately the road was only used during the day by an occasional off-road explorer and by the Wilson brothers, who only used it after dark. The mountain's isolation was a necessity for their illicit enterprise.

The brothers worked by the light of gasoline lanterns and moonlight when it was available. The only sounds to disturb the mountain's solitude was the occasional poignant hoot of a distant owl calling its mate, the hiss of their acetylene torch, the metallic clink of tools bumping against metal parts, and an occasional mumbled curse from a thief with a skinned knuckle.

The day after he joined the operation, Snake discovered a vintage Corvette in the parking lot of a movie theater in downtown River City. While the owner of the Corvette and his date were enjoying the movie, his cherished sports car was hot-wired and delivered to the chop shop. In less than an hour, Rufus and Elroy disassembled it, salvaged the parts for which they already had an order, and pushed the remnants of the once beautiful Corvette over the escarpment. It would rust at the bottom of the cliff with the hulls of dozens of other cars that had met their fate in the same manner. Before daylight the parts from the Corvette were already en route to an auto body shop in north Georgia that had ordered them.

The mountainous terrain around River City was an auto thief's paradise, and the city's theft rate was among the highest in the south. A vehicle parked in front of a resident's home at bedtime could be stolen and disassembled before it was ever discovered missing.

The Wilsons' operation had made a bad situation worse in recent weeks. The local media had been warning citizens about a significant increase in the number of thefts. A former car thief, who had served his time and was now supposedly reformed, was interviewed on television. He explained that the cars were not just randomly stolen but were taken in response to orders received for specific parts. He said that after receiving an order, the thieves would cruise the streets until they found the exact make and model to fill the order. Rufus and Elroy wouldn't know a business model from bread pudding, but the ex-thief had accurately described their operation.

Chapter 40

The murder and abduction in River City had already been thoroughly covered by the southern media. But when one of the South's best-known athletes was shot, the story took on new proportions. The law enforcement agencies hadn't confirmed or even publically discussed it, but the media had already concluded that the cases were related. The story had been revived and was now being followed in network news reports.

Dex had dodged the ongoing media frenzy at every opportunity, but his low profile efforts ended when he returned to work. The marketing department had already started developing a new television spot to capitalize on the heightened attention he had received.

They told him the decision was his to make but tried to convince him that they would be sensitive to his dilemma by taking advantage of the opportunity in a very subtle manner. He was skeptical at first but took a wait-and-see attitude before deciding if he would allow them to use his misfortune as a marketing tool. They talked him through what they planned to do and showed him the script before he finally agreed to go forward with it.

The new ad featured Dex holding a large bottle of EaseFast while looking into the camera lens and saying, "When life occasionally knocks you down, depend on EaseFast to quickly get you back on your feet." The camera then faded to an old game film clip showing him bouncing back up after getting clobbered by a huge linebacker.

Dex was impressed by the adroit merging of the product with his career as a player. There was no mention of his recent adversity, but most people would instantly make the connection with bouncing back from being shot. Hopefully that was the connection made by most people, but it wasn't what Snake thought. He fumed all night when he first saw it, and his irrational fury increased with each additional airing of the spot.

Dex had received a letter from the manager of the restaurant where they had dinner the night he was shot. He wished him a speedy recovery, invited them to have dinner at the restaurant, and enclosed two gift certificates for free meals. Since the television spot was running every hour, it didn't make much sense to continuing trying to keep a low profile. They hadn't been out to dinner in River City since the shooting and decided to take advantage of the gift certificates. He made reservations and they returned to Harbor Lights, but this time they utilized the valet parking.

Dex and Marie had become a couple of interest and were recognized by everyone in the restaurant when they followed the maître d' to their table. Several of the diners came by their table to wish them well.

They were having coffee after their meal when the restaurant manager came over and thanked Dex and Marie for coming. He grinned and said, "I appreciate all the publicity we received from your last visit, but you really don't have to go to that much trouble tonight." He also made a joke about how much valet parking had increased, and they all laughed together. It was nice to be at least temporarily far enough away from their problems to once again laugh and enjoy an evening out.

The restaurant's ambiance, the river setting, and the superb cuisine were all as appealing as they remembered. But just being together would have made it enjoyable even if they had been in a hamburger joint. They even danced to a couple of old big band selections before leaving the restaurant.

Marie was a catalyst to Dex's libido. As a star college athlete, he had dated a lot of girls in school and pretty much had his pick of campus queens, but none of them had ever excited him like she did. Marie was far less experienced, but she didn't need experience to appreciate what she and Dex had together. They enjoyed a wonderful dinner and evening together. Of course, the only thing they ever needed to make an evening successful was to be together.

Chapter 41

The elected officials were beginning to take a lot of heat from constituents because the investigation of the high-profile cases appeared to be stalled. Political pressure always follows a predictable course; it flows downstream. This time it eventually piled up on the desk of Detective Lester Morgan. It wasn't the first time politicians had dumped on him as they scrambled to cover their own butts. He didn't appreciate being unfairly singled out, but he had learned that in politics the boss takes the credit for successes and blames underlings for failures.

He and the sheriff were jointly summoned to a meeting with the mayor and district attorney. The mayor, who Morgan doubted knew the difference between investigation and indigestion, started the discussion.

"Morgan, we're getting some pretty bad publicity because you haven't made an arrest in any of these high-profile cases. What's keeping you from getting the investigation off dead center?"

"Mr. Mayor, it's a very difficult and complex case. We're doing everything possible to apprehend the person or persons responsible for these crimes." He didn't even try to explain the difficulties because he knew the explanation would fall on deaf ears. The politicians were under pressure, they didn't like it, and they were looking for someone to take the blame. Morgan was the most convenient target.

"If the cases weren't difficult and complex, you wouldn't have a job. We'd let rookies handle them. We expect more from the people we put in positions like yours. I've got people clamoring for answers from my office, and you haven't given me anything to tell them."

Morgan didn't want to discuss the details of the investigation with the mayor because he was fairly certain that whatever he said would wind up in the newspaper the following day. But he finally realized the mayor wasn't going to let up on him until he gave him more information.

"Mr. Mayor, I've identified four possible suspects and interrogated three of them. We don't yet have enough evidence to bring charges against any of them. We do have enough evidence to charge the fourth suspect with the shooting of Mr. Martin, but we have not been able to find him."

"Well maybe that will satisfy them for a little while."

"Mr. Mayor, it would be helpful if you could just respond by telling them we have identified four potential suspects. If we release too much information, the one we are trying to locate will likely flee the area and further complicate the investigation." He assumed that his request for confidentiality would fall on deaf ears, but the limited information he gave them at least allowed him to escape the contentious meeting.

Morgan didn't tell them, because he didn't have enough evidence yet to get a conviction on anything except the shooting, but he was already convinced that Snake Wilson was the single culprit responsible for the murder, abduction, and shooting. The only thing he could prove against the other three was that they all had motives. Norton and McPherson were certainly guilty of the white collar crimes for which they had been indicted, but there was nothing linking them to the crimes he was investigating. Dr. Bishop was guilty of making a fool out of himself over a younger woman who detested him, but there was nothing linking him to these events. Everything, including his usually reliable gut instinct, led him to believe that Snake was the only perpetrator.

Morgan had talked with Snake's mother and his two brothers. His mother told him that her son no longer lived with her, and that she hadn't seen him in several weeks. His gut feeling was that she was probably telling the truth, but when Rufus and Elroy said they hadn't seen him and didn't know how to contact him, he was pretty sure they were lying.

"If I catch you guys concealing your brother, I will personally arrest both of you for obstruction of justice and do my best to get the district attorney to throw the book at you."

His instinct about the brother's truthfulness was correct. Snake had delivered a car to them the previous night. They really didn't know where he was staying because he refused to tell them, but they could easily contact him by cell phone.

After Morgan left, Rufus said, "We'uns done always been scaret bout Snake gittin us in one of his dadbum crap piles. Now he dun dun it. We'uns gotta shet down the bizzness."

"Rufus, you be who calls him. I ain't got his numer. Jes don't call him agin."

"I's gotta call and tell him we shet down."

Snake answered his cell phone on the first ring and Rufus told him they were going to shut down the chop shop because Detective Morgan was getting too close.

"Snake, you be the cause we shet down. Git outta town fore theys fries you ass."

"I's ain't goin' nowheres. It be none of your nevermind what I's do. Mind your own bizzness and stay outten whas mine. Theys comes atta me, I's take sum of 'em wit me. Theys ain't gonna get me live, so you'ens don't fret bout my ass gitin' fried."

Snake was never more than twenty-five miles from Detective Morgan's office, but he only surfaced when protected by the cover of darkness. Rufus had told him about the all-points bulletin Morgan had issued, but Snake ignored the warning.

Despite operating outside the law for their entire careers, neither Rufus nor Elroy had ever been convicted of a crime. In their illegal business ventures it was important to be able to operate without police scrutiny. Even before being contacted by Morgan, they had been nervous about doing business with their baby brother because he was so dumb and unpredictable. The risk was probably even greater now that he was being actively hunted by the authorities.

The brothers had always been afraid that Snake would eventually draw attention to them, because they knew it was inevitable that he would eventually do something stupid and get caught. They didn't think he would intentionally involve them, but since they had been outsmarting him his entire life, they knew that the police could easily outwit him.

His brothers had known for years about Snake's hatred for Dex Martin, although he never told them why he hated him so much. After Dex was shot, Rufus grilled him about the shooting, abduction, and murder.

"Snake, youse dun bin hatin' Martin fer years. Did youse shoot 'em?"

"I's ain't know nuttin bout no shootin', but I's wish he was kilt."

They never accepted anything he said at face value because he had been a liar his entire life. They knew he was capable of murder and dumb enough to do it, so they weren't convinced of his innocence. The only reason they gave Snake the benefit of the doubt was because they didn't think he was smart enough to pull it off without being caught.

Even though he had denied shooting Dex, he told them he laughed every time he saw a news report about the shooting. He also told them that Dex and Marie was "gittin it on" in high school, and that they both deserved what had happened to them.

The concept that Dex was trying to protect Marie's honor was beyond Snake's comprehension.

His brothers didn't know where Snake was hiding, but they knew that he was as familiar with the mountains around River City as anyone. He had grown up on the side of one of them and was the best hunter in his family. His mother had depended on his squirrel hunting to feed the family when he was younger. He hunted twelve months a year. Legal hunting seasons had never meant anything to Snake. He hunted for food, and his family didn't just get hungry during the season.

Chapter 42

Morgan figured the most logical place for Snake to hide was in the mountains, but unless a search area could be more narrowly defined there wasn't much chance of finding him in the heavily forested woods. The all-points bulletin (APB) hadn't produced any results, so a chance sighting by someone who had seen the TV broadcasts was probably the next best hope for catching him.

In many of his investigations Morgan had been uncanny in his ability to think like the suspect he was chasing, but thinking like Snake was proving challenging. He didn't seem to plan anything and simply reacted to whatever situation developed. Morgan wanted to do something proactive, but he had no idea what he could do to flush Snake out of hiding.

Morgan's intuition was partially correct about Snake hiding in the mountains. He was more accurately hiding under them. For months he had been living in a cave within the city limits of River City. The entrance to the cave was only about a hundred yards from several upscale residences located on a well-traveled city street.

There was a solid six-foot-tall wooden fence at the back of the manicured lawns and thick underbrush on the mountain side of the fence. The entrance to the cave was a small hole barely large enough for a grown man to squeeze through. The small opening was almost completely camouflaged by the thick underbrush and several large boulders. Snake had never seen evidence of anyone else having been in the cave and was pretty sure the nearby residents didn't even know it existed. He felt secure inside the cave. He had discovered it when he was a young boy, years before the houses were built. He had always thought of it as his special place and often hid there when he was younger to get away from the torment of his abusive brothers.

Beyond the narrow entrance, the cave broadened into a room almost as large as the houses on the other side of the fence. A crystal clear, subterranean stream flowed through the center. He never knew the origin of the stream or if it ever rose to the surface. It entered the room from an opening in the cave wall and disappeared into a similar opening in the opposite wall. The stream's entrance and exit were both too small to allow him to trace it.

Snake's living quarters were set up beside the stream. He had a gasoline stove, two lanterns, and an army cot. He also had metal pans, plates, and cutlery and had fashioned a table from sticks he had brought into the cave. It was at least as well equipped as most deer hunting camps, and it had several attractions that deer camps did not have. The year-round temperature did not vary more than a few degrees, and there was permanent protection from rain, snow, and all the other inconveniences of nature.

The only thing Snake didn't like about his temporary home was that he had to share it with a colony of bats. He hated the sight of the flying rodents hanging upside down on the cave's ceiling and really detested the way they whizzed around his head on the way in and out of the cave on their nocturnal feeding sprees.

Snake wasn't accustomed to a lot of creature comforts, and the cave had everything he needed. It was a luxury suite compared to his cell in the state prison. He had become as nocturnal as the bats, so he read, or more accurately just looked at the pictures in his comic books during the daylight hours. His library consisted of at least one hundred of the brightly colored books filled with pictures of super heroes. The words in the comic books tested the upper limits of Snake's literary skill. He was living proof that an individual could be dumb as a wart and still be cunning and devious.

Since he had started living in the cave, Snake parked his stolen car in the crowded parking lot of a twenty-four-hour superstore located only a few blocks from his hideaway. To keep it from attracting attention, he had been moving it from one spot to another within the same lot every night, but after his last conversation with Rufus, he decided to change cars.

After dark he drove to the chop shop location on the mountain, removed all personal items, wiped the car down with an old shop cloth, and pushed it over the cliff. It would be the only intact vehicle in the mass of rusting metal. The precautions he had taken probably weren't necessary.

There was little chance it could be traced to him, but he went through the process of removing evidence anyway.

After pushing the car over the cliff, Snake walked all the way down the dark logging road to the foot of the mountain and crossed the highway. There was a wide wooded area separating the highway from the river. He stayed in the woods, out of sight from the highway and walked upstream about a quarter mile to a boat dock. As he approached, he could see there was no one at the dock. Several boats were moored there, but most were chained and locked. He finally found a small fishing boat that was only secured by a rope. There was a paddle lying in the boat. He got in, pushed it away from the dock, and used the paddle to move several hundred yards up the river before cranking the small outboard motor. Using only moonlight, he guided the boat up the river for about ten miles before pulling to shore inside the city limits of River City. He wiped down the paddle and the boat to remove his fingerprints and then pushed the boat back out into the river to let the current take it away.

It was only a few blocks from the river to another large shopping center where Snake planned to steal a replacement car. He found a car he liked in the parking lot and used his Swiss Army knife to exchange the license plate with the car parked next to it. Within minutes he had hotwired the car and driven it directly to the superstore where he regularly parked. As he walked back to the cave, he was proud of himself. He had been able to ditch one car and then steal a new one all within one night's work.

Chapter 43

Rufus and Elroy had not talked to Snake since they had temporarily suspended the chop shop operation, but they closely followed the news to see if he had been arrested. They were convinced that he had shot Dex and were surprised that he had thus far avoided arrest. He hadn't gotten smarter, but he had apparently become more cunning and cautious since his previous incarcerations.

Snake's only entertainment in the cave, other than his comic books, was a small battery-operated TV. By sitting near the cave's entrance he could get local TV reception. He used earplugs to suppress the sound. He followed developments on the case by watching the news in the morning, afternoon, and evening. With the leaks coming out of the mayor's office, it was almost like being tuned into the police radio band. He laughed at some of the reported responses to the APB. He had supposedly been sighted in Lexington, Tupelo, and Waycross. He didn't even know in what states those cities were located. In fact, he had never been far enough away from River City to lose local TV reception.

Snake was ready for the chop shop to get back in business. He was quickly running out of money and had no other source of income. After waiting two weeks he violated Rufus's strict orders and called him at home. When Rufus answered, Snake simply said, "Call me," and hung up. A few minutes later Rufus returned his call, and he was furious that Snake had called him at home. He launched into a tirade of verbal abuse, but as usual, Snake wasn't fazed by his brother's diatribe.

"Damn it, Rufus, you'ens ain't called me in nigh on two weeks. I's ain't got no money, and I's needs smokes. Ain't you'ens needin' any cars?"

"Snake, you idiot, has you not been eyeballing the news? We's gonna stay shet down til it be safe. Dem cops still be atter you."

Snake tried to protest, but Rufus had already hung up.

He was broke and he needed cigarettes, food, and gas. That night after midnight he drove across the nearby state line into Georgia and spotted a service station and convenience store sitting several hundred yards from any other buildings.

He pulled up and stopped at the pump with the least visibility from inside the store. There were no other customers at the pumps, and he didn't see any inside the store. An older Asian man was the only clerk on duty.

Snake pointed to the rack behind the counter and said, "Gimme a pak of dem Malberrys."

The clerk turned his back to get the Marlboros from the rack, and when he turned back around Snake was pointing a pistol at him. "Open up dat dere cash box and fill up this here sack."

The clerk hesitated, and Snake reached across the counter and hit him on the shoulder with the barrel of the pistol. The man cried out in pain, and Snake pointed the gun directly between his eyes. The register was opened, and Snake jumped over the counter and told the clerk to lie face down on the floor. He pulled a roll of duct tape from the pocket of his cargo pants and taped the man's hands behind his back. Then he taped his ankles together before rolling him over and putting tape over his mouth.

Snake filled the paper sack with the money in the cash drawer, picked up several cartons of cigarettes from a display counter, and started walking toward the door. He turned around and said, "Ifen you moves yor ass 'fore I'm gone, I's come back and kill you dead."

Snake ran to his car and was several miles away before a customer discovered the clerk still lying behind the counter. When the responding officer arrived, the store clerk told him he had not seen the robber's car and didn't know which way he came from or where he was headed when he left the station. By that time, Snake had already crossed over the state line and was back in Tennessee. He pulled into a service station, took forty dollars from his paper sack, and filled up his car. Then he drove to an all-night store and bought a fresh supply of comic books and the food he would need for the next few days.

Snake was back in his cave before 3:00 a.m. He sat down and counted his money for the first time. After his purchases at the store and the gas station he still had about seventy dollars. Maybe he didn't need Rufus and

Elroy anymore. He had made as much that night as they paid him for a night's work, and he didn't have to listen to their abuse.

Still keyed up from the robbery and not sleepy, Snake got his TV and moved to the front of the cave. As soon as he turned it on, Dex was doing one of his new EaseFast commercials, and it ruined the good mood he had been in since the robbery. It made him furious when he was reminded that he was living in a hole in the ground and could only go outside after dark, while Dex was appearing on television and making big money. Snake truly believed that Dex was responsible for everything that had gone wrong in his life. If it wasn't for him, he would have never gone to juvenile detention, would still be in the "automobile business," and wouldn't have to rob gas stations to get money for food. Snake vowed once again that he would still get even with Dex.

He couldn't believe Dex had survived the gunshot. The muzzle of the pistol was almost touching his chest when Snake pulled the trigger, and he still didn't die. The next time he went after him it would be with something bigger than the .22-caliber pistol that had failed to kill Dex. He was going to steal something a lot more powerful before he tried it again. Snake wished now that he had also shot Marie. The television news had reported that she had saved Dex's life, and she was also responsible for his problems in high school. She ran to her boyfriend when he tried to kiss her. He had been watching television when she made the remark about being in love with Dex. It almost made him smash his TV.

After he shot Dex, Snake watched television nonstop to see if he was going to survive the gunshot. He was mad at himself for firing only one shot and for not making sure that Dex was mortally wounded. He had been ready to go after him again, but he had to wait until Dex was released from the hospital. Even Snake wasn't crazy enough to attempt a hit in the hospital while Dex was under constant police protection.

Chapter 44

The Lexus was traveling way too fast on the rural highway's rain-slicked surface. The teenager, behind the wheel of his mother's two-year-old Lexus, had his left hand on the steering wheel while his right was cuddling the girl close by his side. The road wasn't his primary focus, and he didn't see the sharp curve until he was already in it. He slammed on the brakes, and the Lexus had almost completed its second 360-degree spin when it left the road and struck a telephone pole. The two kids escaped with only minor injuries, but the Lexus was not as lucky. The entire right front of the car was demolished.

The insurance company appraiser calculated the cost of repairs at a little over forty-seven hundred dollars using all new parts. The independent body shop, where the car had been towed, agreed to repair the car based on the estimate.

However, the woman who owned the car came by the shop and told the owner she was going to have it towed to the Lexus dealer. The shop owner really wanted to make the repairs, so he played his ace in the hole.

"Lady, I'll absorb your deductible if you'll let us repair it."

"I have a five-hundred-dollar deductible. How can you do that?"

"The appraiser figured new parts, and I can use replacement parts just like what was on the car. I guarantee your car will look just as good and you'll save five hundred dollars."

"But isn't that cheating the insurance company?"

"No. The insurance company doesn't care how you repair the car, or even if you decide not to repair it. They're on the hook for the amount of the estimate, and that's all they care about."

"But if the used parts are as good as new ones, why didn't the appraiser figure on using them?"

"Now, that gets to the crux of the situation. The court makes them use new parts. They can't seem to understand that a car does not lose value when a two-year-old fender from the damaged car is replaced with a two-year-old undamaged fender from another car."

"I just don't understand all this. Are you sure it's okay?"

"Lady, if you had to buy an automobile one new part at a time, the cost would approach the national debt. The insurance companies know what's going on. They just spread the cost out and pass it on with higher premiums. Save your five hundred dollars and let us worry about the parts."

Conversations like this take place every day, and most transactions for used parts are with legitimate salvage dealers. But there is also an opportunity for chop shop operators like the Wilson brothers to significantly undercut the legitimate dealers who have to buy the wrecked cars from which their parts are salvaged.

The Wilson brothers had never bought a car in their lives. Rufus and Elroy were flat broke. When they received the order for Lexus parts, they decided to accept it and at least temporarily reopen for business. Rufus called Snake and told him the model of Lexus they needed and warned him to be careful. The last thing they needed was for the police to follow him to the mountain and discover their operation. Three brothers in the state penitentiary at the same time might be a Tennessee state record.

That night Snake roamed through most of the large parking lots in town searching for the correct make and model of Lexus. He hadn't had any luck and was about ready to quit for the evening when he spotted one. He had to hide the car he was driving so he drove two blocks away and parked it at a twenty-four-hour pharmacy. He ran back to the lot to get the Lexus, but it was no longer there.

Now completely disgruntled, Snake started to walk back to his car, but before he got out of the lot another Lexus like the one he was searching for pulled in. It passed where he was standing, and he saw it was being driven by an elderly woman who was alone in the car. He watched as it moved up and down the long parking lanes as the driver apparently searched for a space close to the store in which she planned to shop. Snake easily kept up with it by walking diagonally across the lanes and was only a few feet away when he saw the woman pull in and park between two SUVs.

Snake grabbed her when she opened the door, clamped his hand over her mouth, and forced her to sit on the pavement between the SUVs. He showed her the pistol he was holding and said, "I's ain't gonna hurt you lessen you holler out or try to run. Ifen you do, I's blow your head plum off."

The elderly lady was too old to run and too scared to scream. She sat there and trembled as he took a roll of duct tape from the pocket of his cargo pants and put a piece over her mouth. He then wrapped the tape around her ankles and wrists. She was completely immobilized when he took her keys, got in the Lexus, and headed for the mountain.

Snake figured he would be far away before anyone discovered the old woman sitting between the vans. Unfortunately for him, she was spotted only moments later when a man started to pull into the vacant parking space. He removed the tape from her mouth, and she told him what had happened. He immediately called 9-1-1 on his cell phone and let the woman give the operator a description of her car, including the tag number.

Within minutes, a police officer in his cruiser spotted the Lexus, moved up behind the speeding car, and confirmed the tag number. He flipped on his blue flashing lights and gave pursuit. Snake assumed the cop was trying to stop him for speeding since he didn't think there had been enough time for the carjacking to be reported. However, it really didn't matter because he had no intention of pulling over. With his record, he might as well just drive himself up to the prison gate and save the cop the trouble of arresting him.

He slammed the gas pedal to the floorboard, and the Lexus responded. The police cruiser was no match for the high-powered Lexus as the cars screamed through the city streets. The Lexus handled the corners with ease, and when they hit the highway leading out of the city, it was gradually moving away from the cruiser.

Snake was traveling between eighty and ninety miles per hour when he came up behind a gasoline tank truck. He swerved into the opposite lane to pass the truck, but the high speed caused him to misjudge the distance. The right front of the Lexus clipped the left side of the tanker, snapping off one of the discharge valves. The impact caused him to lose control, and he sideswiped two cars and spun around several times before rolling over the guard rail and coming to a stop on the front lawn of an apartment complex. The tanker had stopped, partially blocking the road, and gas was gushing from the severed valve. The police car that was following Snake slid in the discharged fuel and crashed into the guard rail on the opposite side of the highway. The officer was unconscious for a few minutes, and this allowed Snake to escape.

Shattered glass from the side window of the Lexus had cut Snake's arm and the airbag had stunned him when it deployed, but he had no serious injuries. The door was jammed so he slithered through the side window of the Lexus, much like his namesake would have done. He was running full speed and was out of sight before the people in the apartment complex had made it outside.

The accident happened two blocks from the foot of the mountain and about two miles from the entrance to his cave. If he could just make it to the mountain without getting caught, he thought he would be safe. Snake's galloping stride wasn't very fast, but he did make it to the foot of the mountain and was quickly swallowed up by the underbrush; he was now on home turf.

The accident site was alive with policemen; flashing blue lights lit up the area. Cops swarmed all over the neighborhood looking for the driver of the Lexus, but Snake was on the mountain and still running toward his cave.

The police interviewed the elderly victim, who gave them a detailed description of her assailant, and they retrieved fingerprints from the wrecked Lexus. The woman's description closely matched Snake's mug shot, and the fingerprints later confirmed that Snake Wilson was still in the area.

That was Snake's first attempt at carjacking, and he decided it would be his last. It was much easier to steal parked cars. The following night he found a parked Lexus, delivered it to his brothers, and collected his fee.

Chapter 45

When Dex was twelve years old, Gigi offered him some sage advice. A boy who was helping him on his paper route had missed two houses, and the customers called to complain.

"If you want a job done right, do it yourself."

She was talking about him letting someone else deliver his newspapers. She would be horrified if she knew that her admonition to him as a child was about to launch him on a mission that could get him killed.

Intellectually Dex knew that going after Snake by himself was ill-advised, but at some point emotion overrides intelligence. Dex had reached that point. Sometimes the school bully pushes a little too hard and the timid child comes at him with fists flying. Snake had pushed him too far, and Dex was ready to go on the attack.

The police investigation was based on an intellectual process, and it wasn't going anywhere. In fairness to Lester Morgan, he was forced to follow specified procedures, but Dex didn't have that handicap. If he had to break a few rules to stop the madness, he was ready to start.

The idea of conducting an individual, unauthorized manhunt didn't just suddenly occur to him. It began to form in his mind the day he finally came to the conclusion that Snake was the only one who was both crazy and depraved enough to have created all the mayhem.

Dex was ready to go after him, but he wasn't ready to discuss his plans with anyone. If he did decide to discuss an action plan with anyone, Marie Murphy and Lester Morgan would certainly not be on the list of confidants. Marie would panic, and Morgan would arrest him for obstruction. He had a lot of respect for Morgan, but the detective was hamstrung by official protocol and he played by the rules.

Actually, at this point Dex didn't have anything to discuss with Morgan anyway. He hadn't decided what he was going to do; he had just decided what he would not do. He would no longer sit around and depend on someone else to solve his problem. As Gigi had said, "If you want it done right, do it yourself."

Until Snake was either behind bars or dead, and right now he didn't care which of those options removed the threat, Dex would never have a moment with Marie without having to look over his shoulder and anticipate another attack.

He had a few days to come up with a plan because he had been selected to run Argon's booth at a trade show in Jacksonville, Florida. He had already worked the booth at a couple of trade shows, and his sports popularity was like a magnet drawing people to the booth. He actually enjoyed intermingling with people at trade shows, and the Jacksonville show was particularly important. Argon was poised to kick off the nationwide sales campaign for EaseFast, and this was a national show that would be well attended by health-care professionals from all over the country.

As soon as Dex walked into the trade show, his attention was drawn to a giant banner designed by his marketing department. It was hanging from the ceiling and high enough to be seen over the maze of other booths. It read: "Meet All-American Dex Martin, Argon Pharmaceuticals, Booth 112." By the time the two-day trade show was over, Dex thought most of the two thousand attendees had accepted the invitation.

With the show now behind him, Dex could concentrate on what was really foremost in his mind: defining his plan to go after Snake Wilson. The drive back to River City gave him several hours alone to think about a plan and consider any problems he might encounter. He considered and rejected several ideas before deciding on one that he thought could be executed if he didn't get killed in the process. He wanted Snake to be arrested and sent away for the rest of his miserable life, but only after he had personally had the pleasure of kicking the crap out of him.

If Morgan found out what he was doing, Dex would be the one who was locked in a cell. Morgan himself was no closer to making an arrest than when he first started, and Snake was still running around creating mayhem. It might not be Morgan's fault, but Dex understood why the mayor and district attorney were losing patience with his lack of success.

Dex respected Morgan, but he had completely lost confidence in the procedures that handicapped law enforcement officers. Why hadn't they been able to catch a guy with a room-temperature IQ? Dex thought they were too busy following the rules of their job to do their job. He didn't have to abide by the ridiculous rules that gave an unfair advantage to criminals. He felt it would be more pragmatic to do it his way and beg forgiveness from Morgan after Snake was either behind bars or dead.

Snake had to be hiding somewhere in the mountains. It was the only explanation for how he could suddenly appear, commit one of his criminal acts, and quickly disappear. Throughout history the mountains had always provided refuge for people fleeing from the authorities. Dex knew the mountains as well as Snake and certainly better than Morgan. He also knew it would be both foolhardy and unproductive to go after Snake while he was in the mountains. The success of any plan would depend on being able to trick or flush him out onto neutral ground.

Dex was sure Rufus and Elroy were the answer; he just hadn't yet figured out the question. The premise of his plan was that he knew they were lying; it was a genetic fault inherent in the Wilson DNA. It was inconceivable that they didn't know how to contact Snake, and he couldn't believe that Morgan was willing to accept their word at face value. They were all career criminals, and Dex was going to find some way to exploit their activities and force Rufus and Elroy to lead him to their demented brother.

However, before he started chasing criminals, Dex wanted to get some advice from an old friend who was a former policeman and now a private investigator.

Chapter 46

Lundy Sloan was the owner of Sloan Investigations. He was also the only employee. Dex heard his friend answer the phone as he approached his open office door.

"Good morning, Sloan Investigations. Yes, Mrs. Gregory, I still have him under surveillance. No, I haven't found any evidence that he is seeing another woman. Yes, I will keep you posted on what I find out." Lundy hung up the phone, and Dex heard him talking to himself. "Damn, I hate divorce work."

Lundy had only been in business for a year but had already discovered why he didn't have a lot of competition: there wasn't much need for private investigators in River City. He hated undercover divorce work, but he had to do it to survive. No one was ever happy in a divorce case. The suspicious wife always wanted to shoot the messenger who told her about her philandering husband. And the cheating husband wanted to kill the wife's investigator. Lundy had learned to live with the abuse, as long as the clients could afford his hourly rate, but he didn't have to like doing it. He was sitting at his desk smoking a particularly foul-smelling cigar when Dex walked in the open door.

"Good Lord, Lundy, did you set the place on fire?" Dex was waving the smoke away from his face as he stood in front of his friend's battered desk.

"Well if I had known a celebrity was going to drop in, I would have taken a bath and had the office deodorized. It's about time you came to see the one who sacrificed his body blocking oversized goons just so you could look like a hero."

"Yeah, and I've still got cleat marks on my body from all the linebackers you didn't block."

"Dex, how are you? Have they caught the guy that shot you? I always thought some jealous husband would get you. Is that really what happened?"

"No Lundy, there isn't a jealous husband involved, and they haven't caught the idiot that shot me. I'm sure you know better than I do that the police in this town aren't world-class crime solvers, present company excluded."

"No offense taken. I'm not a cop anymore and didn't like the job very much when I was one. Of course there are also days when I don't like this job very much. By the way, I've seen your girlfriend on television. She's too good looking to be stuck with you, but if she's cheating on you, I'm the guy to catch her at it."

Dex laughed and said, "No, Lundy, I don't want you to check up on Marie; I just want to pick your brain. Is there any charge for that?"

He grinned and said, "Not unless I have to leave the office."

"Lundy, Snake Wilson is the idiot that shot me. Do you remember him from high school?"

"Yeah, and I also remember you kicking his ass in front of school one day."

"Well, believe it or not, he apparently is still harboring a grudge about that."

"Is he also the one who kidnapped your girlfriend and killed Hoagie?"

"We think so, but the police only have enough evidence to hang him for shooting me. The problem is that no one has been able to find him. He's got two worthless older brothers who have never worked a day in their lives. They've got to be doing something illegal to support their families, and Snake is probably mixed up in it too."

"Okay, what have you got in mind."

"I'm going to find out if they are drug dealers, thieves, or whatever and threaten to expose them if they don't lead me to Snake."

"Why do you think you can locate him when the police haven't been able to find him?"

"Because they are so hamstrung by procedures that they can't get away with what I just suggested. I need for you to help me figure out how to execute my plan. We fought a lot of battles together on the field, and I've always known I could depend on you to have my back."

"Thanks for your confidence, Dex. I don't get to hear a lot of that in my job, but let me start coaching you by calling a great play. Stay the hell out of this, and let the police do their job."

"I'd be delighted to stay out of it if I had any confidence that the police could catch him. The detective in charge is a good man, but he is so caught up by the Mickey Mouse rules that he can't do anything."

"Dex, if the police don't follow the rules, a bleeding-heart judge will just pat the criminal on the head and put him right back out on the street to sin again. Do you know where Snake's brothers live?"

"No, but I'm sure I can find out somehow."

"I am not going to tell you what to do because I don't want to feel so guilty that I have to take time off from work to attend your funeral."

"Yeah, yeah, I hear you. I don't want you to tell me what to do, but if you have any suggestion on how I can avoid being the guest of honor at a funeral, I would appreciate it."

"Dex, if I was doing it, I'd follow one of the brothers until I found out what he's doing that's illegal. You should document whatever it is with photographs if possible. Then I would follow him until I caught him in a very public place and confront him. Now listen closely, Dex. I would make sure it was a place where he couldn't just shoot me and walk away. I'd tell him what I had discovered about his illegal activities and offer proof, if you have it. For self-protection I'd tell him I have proof of his activities in a sealed envelope and I've instructed someone holding the envelope to immediately turn it over to the police if anything happened to me or anyone connected to me. If you can make him believe that, and he still swears he doesn't know where Snake is hiding, he's probably telling the truth. Now that's what I would do, but again, I'm not making any recommendations to you."

"Okay, I've got it. I appreciate you telling me what you would do. I would have never thought about the envelope. I promise not to tell anyone that we discussed this, and I also acknowledge that you are recommending that I let the police handle it."

"Dex, I do still think you should let the police handle it, because you are playing with fire when you start fooling around with career criminals. They'll squash you like a gnat if you aren't careful."

"Thanks, Lundy. I appreciate your advice. I don't have a death wish, so I'm definitely going to be careful."

Chapter 47

Although he knew the consequences, Dex changed his mind about not telling Marie. What he planned to do was for both of them, and she deserved to know what he was doing. He knew there would be an argument as soon as he told her, but he was determined that her anger or tears were not going to change his mind. She wanted Snake caught as much as he did, she just didn't want him in harm's way. She was in jeopardy as long as this lunatic was free, and he was tired of constantly worrying about her safety.

Dex knew that telling Marie might be the most hazardous part of the operation, so he chose to tell her in a busy downtown restaurant while they were having lunch. His reasoning was that Marie was a cultured woman who wouldn't create a scene in front of a lot of people. He was dead wrong. She blew her stack, and there wasn't a soul in the restaurant who didn't know he had done something to really infuriate his luncheon date.

She jumped to her feet so fast that her chair almost overturned, and her face flushed a blotchy red color. She was trembling with anger when she stuck her finger in his face and said, "You are as crazy as he is. He killed Hoagie and almost killed you, and now you want to give him another chance? You know he's insane and unpredictable, and you still sit there and calmly tell me you are going to try to track him down in the mountains." She was practically screaming, and everyone in the restaurant stopped eating to look at them. To her credit, she stopped just short of profanity.

"Marie, I'm tired of waiting on someone else to solve our problems with him. Morgan is a good cop, but he's so bogged down with legal restrictions that he can't do what it's going to take to catch him. I've got to go after him myself, and I had hoped you would understand."

"Dex, you knew dang well that—"

He stopped her by saying, "Marie, let's talk about this outside."

Dex quickly paid the check and followed Marie as she stalked out of the restaurant ready to continue the argument. Every eye in the restaurant was on them when they left the restaurant.

Marie was standing on the sidewalk with her hands on her hips ready to confront him, but Dex spoke first. "Most of those people in there know us, and they heard everything you said."

"I don't care what they heard. If they heard about your stupid plan, they would agree that you're out of your mind."

He grinned and said, "Well, it probably wouldn't be a good idea to come back here for a while."

"Don't try to make a joke out of this, Dex. This is serious, and you're treating it like there's no other option. You're pretty arrogant to even think you can find Snake when half the cops in Tennessee haven't been able to find him. He can't stay hidden forever, and when he comes out of hiding, Morgan will catch him."

While she was talking, he took her arm and was trying to steer her toward his car.

"Okay, Marie, you've made your point. I only told you because I thought it would be unfair not to do so. You're right; I didn't expect you to agree with me. I know you're upset, but I'll never forgive you if you tell Morgan or do anything else to stop me. I know you don't want to hear it, but I'm doing this for—"

Marie interrupted him. "Don't you even dare say you're doing this for me. You're the one he wants to kill, and you're going to be dumb enough to make it easier for him to do it."

"Just calm down a minute and let me make one point and then you can yell at me until you get hoarse. You've got to know that we are never going to be able to live a normal life until Snake is caught. I can't sit idle any longer and depend on the police to protect us. That is not the way either one of us wants to live."

"Dex, I've told you time and again to quit worrying about me, and—" Dex stopped Marie in midsentence with a glare that reminded her that she wasn't supposed to offer an opinion until he had finished making his point.

"Marie, Snake's brothers are lying to the police. They know where he's hiding, and I'm going to find a way to get them to give him up. They are as mean and dishonest as he is, but they're a lot smarter."

"But if they're as mean—" Dex's stare stopped her again.

"None of the Wilson brothers have ever had a job, and they sure didn't inherit any money. They have to be doing something illegal. I'm going to find out what it is and threaten to expose them if they don't tell me how to find Snake. Everything I've learned about them suggests they would sacrifice their mother if it would save their butts. They are probably also embarrassed by Snake's stupidity."

Marie was overcome with a sense of dread because she knew that Dex had already made up his mind, but she wasn't ready to give up if there was any chance to talk him out of what she thought of as a suicide pact with the devil.

"Okay, Dex, are you through now?" He nodded and she continued. "First of all, I love you for being concerned about me, but if you are really concerned about me, you should think about what I would do if something happened to you. I'm against the whole idea of you playing cop, but I doubt that it makes any difference. You seem to have already made up your mind."

"Marie I don't have a death wish, and I'm not going to take any more chances than I have to. I just can't go on any longer looking over my shoulder and worrying about you day and night."

Marie sat at her desk the remainder of the day but couldn't concentrate on the paperwork. All she could think about was the danger to which Dex was exposing himself. Snake was completely without a conscience and would lash out at anyone who crossed him. No one could predict how that idiot would react to anything. His reactions were animalistic, except most animals were far less aggressive and more predictable.

Chapter 48

It was dark, and Dex had been sitting in his car a block away from Rufus's mobile home since early in the afternoon. When he checked earlier, Rufus's pickup truck was parked in front of the mobile home on a dead-end road. From his vantage point, Dex could see the truck if it passed by, and so far it had not come up the road where he was parked.

Dex was about ready to give up for the night when he saw approaching headlights. He identified the truck as it passed and waited for it to get several hundred yards away before pulling out with his headlights off. He drove without lights for several blocks until Rufus turned onto a main highway headed away from River City. Dex switched on his lights and merged into traffic, keeping several cars between him and Wilson. On the outskirts of the city, Wilson pulled into the parking lot of a convenience store and another man got out of a parked car and into his truck. Dex had never seen the other Wilson brother, but he said to himself, "I bet that's brother Elroy."

Rufus left the parking lot and continued straight ahead for a couple of miles and then veered right onto a secondary highway. There was less traffic on this road, but fortunately another car turned off the main highway between him and Wilson. He continued following the pickup truck for another few miles until Wilson slowed and made a sharp left turn onto a dirt road leading up the mountain. When Dex purposely drove past the dirt road, he could see the taillights of the pickup truck disappearing up the mountain.

He waited for a few minutes before doubling back to the spot where Wilson had turned onto the old logging road. He and Hoagie had hiked to the top of this mountain when they were in high school, and he knew that it was uninhabited. He assumed that whatever the Wilson brothers were involved in was probably taking place somewhere on this remote mountain, but only a fool would go up there after them at night.

Dex parked about four hundred yards up the highway in an area that would allow him to see the truck if it came back down the mountain. He had been sitting there for less than an hour when he saw a red Ford Explorer also turn onto the logging road. He ran through the possibilities in his mind. Mountain men often staged disgusting chicken or dog fights to wager on the winners. But those events drew large crowds of rednecks, and he had only seen two vehicles go up the mountain. And he didn't think they were making moonshine. They wouldn't risk having a new Explorer and a relatively new pickup truck confiscated by federal agents. Bootleggers preferred older cars that could be abandoned without much loss.

Dex waited for another hour, but there was no further traffic on the logging road. He figured that even if the two vehicles came back down the mountain, there was nothing he could do, so he decided to leave for the night. If he had waited another hour, he would have seen only Rufus's pickup come down with not two but three men in the cab. The bed was filled with bright red parts from the Ford Explorer.

Dex figured that whatever the Wilson brothers were doing on the mountain, they weren't doing it until after dark. He got up at sunrise the next morning and headed for the mountain. He didn't notice anything unusual in his trip up the old logging road until he reached the summit.

He parked his car and walked around the cleared area. There had been a recent heavy rain, and he was initially confused by the proliferation of tire tracks. Then he walked over to the precipice and looked down several hundred feet to the base of the cliff. It was obliterated with the rusted hulls of automobiles piled on top of each other. The riddle was solved. Dex had heard about chop shop operations, but this was the first time he had ever seen where the work was actually done.

So this was what Rufus and Elroy were doing to support themselves. He now had the leverage he needed to get them to talk, but the tricky and dangerous part was how to use it without getting killed in the process. Although he was going to have to be very careful, Dex was fairly certain he could make them realize it was in their best interest to cooperate. But if he let one of them get the drop on him, he was a dead man.

Chapter 49

Two hours after he discovered the chop shop, Dex was again parked where he could see the dead-end road where Rufus's mobile home was located. He anticipated a long wait before Rufus emerged, but he got lucky. He had only been there about thirty minutes when he saw him pass by in his pickup.

He let the pickup get several hundred yards down the road before pulling out to follow it. Rufus drove straight to a Wal-Mart store and parked near the entrance. Dex parked and followed him into the store. He panicked when he momentarily lost him in the crowd but soon spotted him standing in front of a car battery display. There were probably ten or twelve people in a position to see the display.

Dex thought to himself, *It's now or never*, and walked up and stood within two feet of the oldest Wilson brother.

"Rufus, you don't know me, but I'm Dex Martin and I've got a message for you."

"You be that football guy."

"That's right, and you are Snake's brother. Your brother tried to kill me, and he did kill my best friend. I need to find him, and you're going to help me."

"Git outen my face fore ye git hurt."

"You better listen to me if you don't want to spend a long time in the state prison. I know about your chop shop on the mountain, and I've got pictures to prove it. They are being held in a sealed envelope with instructions to turn the envelope over to the police if anything happens to me or anyone connected to me."

"I's ain't know what you'se talkin' at."

"Yeah, you do, and you better pay attention. I know you lied to the cops about not knowing how to contact Snake, and if you stick by that story, the envelope will be delivered to the cops within an hour."

Rufus thought for a few moments before saying, "I ain't know whar he be."

"This is your last chance before I walk away and tell the one holding that envelope to deliver it. I don't give a damn about your auto theft business, so I'm not going to report it to the police unless you refuse to tell me how to find Snake."

Rufus stared at Dex with a murderous scowl, moved up beside him, and whispered in his ear, "Boy, ifen you tell the cops, you ain't gonna live long nuf to see me hind bars."

From no more than six inches away, Dex stared directly into Rufus's face and said in a controlled voice, "If the situation was reversed, what do you think Snake would do? Are you going to tell me or not?"

Rufus knew the answer to that question, but he wasn't going to give Dex the satisfaction of an answer. "I's gotta talk to Elroy. Weuns git back and talk atter dat."

Dex replied, "No, this is a onetime offer. I'm going to find him with or without your help, but if you walk out the door of this store without telling me where he is, I'm calling the police from the store phone."

Rufus couldn't control the angry contortions of his face. He was flushed and breathing heavily because he knew he was trapped. He didn't doubt that Dex would follow through on his threat, and he knew that a jury would find him guilty and send him away for a long time. He glared at Dex for several minutes, and Dex glared back at the lifetime criminal.

Finally Rufus said, "I ain't know whar he's at. I ain't talked at him in two weeks."

"That's not good enough. You're lying and I know it."

"I ain't lying. I ain't got no notion whar he's at. Atter he left outa Mama's house, ain't nary a one of us knows whar he's been staying."

"You just said you had talked to him, so you must know how to contact him."

"I has a cell phone numer, but that be all I know. It's writ down on paper in my pocket."

Now thoroughly frustrated, Rufus fumbled with his wallet and pulled out a folded piece of worn paper with a number scrawled on it.

Dex took the number and said, "This better be on the level, or you haven't heard the last of me. Don't warn Snake, and if I were you I wouldn't even tell Elroy about our little conversation. I've told you I'm not going to tell the police anything, and I won't tell Snake how I found him unless you try to warn him. Also, remember the sealed letter that will go to the police if anything happens to me or anyone close to me."

Rufus nodded and Dex walked away leaving him looking helpless and still standing in front of the battery display. From his car in the parking lot, Dex called his friend Lundy.

"Lundy, I got Snake's cell phone number from Rufus without getting killed. Now I've got to figure out how to use it."

"What happened?"

"I'll tell you all about it later, but do you have any way to trace a cell phone number?"

"Dex, it would be easy to find out who the phone is registered to, but that's not going to do you any good because I'll bet you it will be either stolen or registered under a phony name. I've still got some friends on the police force, so let me see what I can find out. Give me the number."

Several hours later Dex got a call from Lundy. "Dex, forget I told you how I got this information because it's illegal, but it may help you. We had a woman place a call to the cell phone number, and when it was answered by a male voice, she simply apologized and said she had a wrong number. Using technology I don't understand, and you don't want to know about, we identified approximately where the cell phone was located when it was answered. I've got a map with a quarter-mile-wide circle drawn on it. The phone was somewhere inside that circle when it was answered. Interestingly, most of the circle is on the side of the mountain where there are no houses."

Dex picked up the map at Lundy's office.

"Have you got access to a pistol?" Lundy asked when he saw Dex. "You need some kind of protection before you confront him."

"I've got a shotgun that I use for dove and rabbit hunting."

Lundy laughed and said, "You can't walk around carrying a shotgun. You need a pistol that you can carry in a holster or in your belt."

"There's a pistol at my grandmother's that belonged to my dad, but I've never shot it. I'll have to slip it out of the house or Gigi will go crazy."

As he was talking Dex remembered that this was the day Gigi met with her mission group at the church. He went by the house and took the pistol out of the closet and stopped by a store and bought a box of shells. Then he drove to the circled area and parked while he studied the map. It was an upscale neighborhood with expensive homes sitting on large, manicured lots.

From the back of these lots the mountain rose steeply to a height of several thousand feet. The homes didn't look like the type of places where Snake would be welcome, so Dex was fairly certain he was hiding somewhere on the mountain portion of the circle. He also reasoned that Snake would have to have some kind of shelter from the weather and would not be brazen enough to set up a tent where it could be easily discovered.

From those facts it didn't take Dex long to surmise that Snake was probably hiding in a cave. He was not very familiar with this section of the mountain, but he knew the entire mountain was honeycombed with caves of various sizes. Some had large openings and were well charted and regularly explored by spelunkers, but others were obscure and had never been mapped or even discovered. These were the types of caves that he and Hoagie had sought in their boyhood adventures.

Dex knew that even if he found the cave in which Snake was hiding, it would be suicide to go in after him. He would have the advantage of being familiar with the cave and could wait for an intruder to come to him. It would be more logical to catch Snake coming out of the woods.

The road ended a block beyond the houses, but in the other direction the area was well developed. There was a large shopping center only two blocks away. Snake had to have an automobile, and the closest place to park it without drawing attention was probably at the shopping center.

After surveying the terrain, Dex decided that it would be too risky for Snake to move around in this neighborhood in the daytime. He apparently stayed holed up until after dark and then walked out to wherever he had his car parked. Dex made the decision to go back late that afternoon and position himself somewhere between the mountain and the shopping center. Dex hoped to catch Snake walking toward his car.

Chapter 50

At twilight Dex was in place, partially concealed behind a row of hedges. The .38-caliber pistol was stuck in his belt at the small of his back. He purposely left his shirt hanging over his belt so it would conceal the pistol.

He was excited because it was finally time to take action. He was nervous, not from fright but from anticipation. It reminded him of a college teammate who had habitually wet his pants just before kickoff in every game. The emotion that caused his teammate to embarrass himself now gripped Dex. He hadn't lost control of his bladder, but adrenalin was coursing through his body with the rush of a springtime flood. He was ready to put an end to this nightmare.

He was finally in position to execute the plan that everyone had told him he was crazy to undertake. Lundy, the only professional he had consulted, had strongly advised him not to attempt to catch Snake by himself. Marie was still furious with him. Actually, she was probably wavering between anger and fear for his safety.

He understood they had his best interest at heart, but he rationalized that sometimes common sense has to take a backseat when one is faced with a crisis. How else could one explain a fireman rushing into a burning building, or a father diving into a torrent of rushing water to save a drowning child? If he didn't do this, no one else was going to and there might never be a better opportunity. Tonight was the night, and he was going for it.

As it began to get dark, Dex was concerned about whether or not the ambient light in the area would be enough to allow him to identify Snake if he walked by or crossed the street toward the shopping center. He also wondered what he would do if he caught Snake. He had borrowed a set of handcuffs from Lundy and had a small roll of duct tape in his pocket, but his plan hadn't gone beyond the actual capture. He hated Snake so much that if he did catch him, he questioned whether he would be able to pull back before he killed him.

Dex had never before thought he was capable of taking the life of another human, but then he didn't think of Snake in human terms. He was afraid that if he was ever face to face with the one who killed Hoagie and chained, Marie he might actually kill him with his bare hands. He didn't doubt that he had the physical ability to kill Snake. The question with which he was struggling was whether or not he had the self-control not to kill him. Until the opportunity arose, he would never know the answer.

While he was thinking through all these things, Dex saw movement out of the corner of his eye. He turned and saw someone emerge from between two houses on the mountain side of the street. The individual turned toward the shopping center but stayed on the side of the street across from the hedges where Dex was hiding.

He could tell that it was a man, but he was still seventy-five to one hundred yards away. As he got closer, Dex thought he recognized the ungainly gait he remembered from high school, but he couldn't be sure. He didn't think the light was going to be bright enough to let him positively identify the man unless he could get closer.

When the man was directly across the street, Dex stepped out from behind the hedges and started walking toward him. When the man saw him, he immediately stopped in his tracks. Dex took several more steps forward, and although he still couldn't clearly see his face, he said, "Snake, I want to talk to you."

Snake pulled a pistol from his coat pocket and pointed it in Dex's direction. Dex dove back behind the hedges just as the shot was fired. When it wasn't followed immediately by a second shot, he peeked over the top of the hedges and saw Snake running back in the direction from which he had appeared.

Dex pulled the pistol from his waist and immediately started chasing him. Snake was a hundred yards ahead of Dex when he turned and fired another shot toward him. This time Dex returned fire. He knew he couldn't hit him at that distance, but he wanted Snake to know that he was also armed. He really didn't want to shoot him. He would prefer for Snake to either rot in jail for the rest of his life or be executed by the state.

Snake ducked between two houses while Dex was still fifty to seventy-five yards behind him but quickly closing the gap. Dex was just running between the houses when he saw Snake disappear through the gate of a solid wooden fence into the woods. Now he had to make a critical decision: should he follow him into the thick underbrush and take a chance on getting ambushed, or should he call in the cops? Dex decided not to do either of those things. He slipped through the gate, but rather than follow Snake, he sat down just inside the fence. He was well concealed and planned to wait on daylight before pursuing him. It was going to be a long night.

After his nerves finally settled down, Dex leaned back against the fence and actually slept fitfully for a few hours. He was wide awake by 4:00 a.m., but he waited for daylight. At 7:00 a.m. he decided it was light enough to begin his search. He was pretty sure that Snake's lair, probably a cave, was somewhere nearby. He also thought that Snake would continue to stay in hiding until after nightfall.

Dex started slowly moving through the underbrush with the pistol in his hand. He searched for over an hour before he finally saw an opening in the earth between two boulders. The underbrush around the opening was bent and broken, and he knew that this had to be Snake's hiding place. It was less than two hundred yards from the gate through which Snake had disappeared the previous night. Dex backed well away from the opening and used his cell phone to call Lundy.

"Lundy, I've got Snake trapped in a cave on the mountain. I surprised him on the street and we exchanged some gun shots, but no one was hit. He ran back to the mountain, and I waited until daylight and then found his cave. The problem is I don't know how to get him out. If I go in there, he can ambush me before I ever see him. Do you have any suggestions?"

"You mean other than my initial suggestion that you let the police handle it?"

"Come on, Lundy. I need to figure out something before one of us kills the other one."

"What the police use to empty out a house is a tear gas grenade, and I still have three or four of them from when I was on the force."

"How do they work?"

"Some are made to be launched from a weapon, but the ones I have don't look like a regular hand grenade; rather than exploding into shrapnel, they are filled with tear gas. If you throw a couple of those babies into an enclosed area like a cave, I guarantee you it will flush out a grizzly bear if he's in there."

"Will you give me two of them?"

"I'll give them to you, but you will get me locked up and I will lose my license if you tell anyone where you got them."

"If I get caught with them, I'll swear I bought them from someone on the street."

Dex asked Lundy to bring the grenades and meet him on the street near the shopping center in thirty minutes. They met and Lundy handed him a sack containing the grenades. Before driving away, he spent a few minutes telling Dex how to use them and what to expect after they exploded in the cave.

Dex picked out a spot to hide behind one of the boulders near the cave entrance. He took the two grenades and slipped up to a point beside the cave entrance. He pulled the pin and threw the first grenade as far back in the cave as possible. Before the first one exploded, he threw the second one in behind it. He quickly moved back behind the rock and waited.

Almost instantaneously hundreds of bats came streaming through the opening. Not long after that he heard uncontrollable coughing and saw Snake crawling out of the small opening. He was on his knees rubbing his eyes with both hands and coughing at the same time. He was only wearing a T-shirt, and the pistol was nowhere in sight.

Dex moved out in the open, holding the pistol in front of him and said, "I hope that stuff causes permanent blindness, you bastard."

Snake looked toward the sound of his voice, but probably couldn't see him clearly because of the tears pouring out of his eyes. "Martin, you be a dead man."

"If you don't shut up and do what I tell you, that hole in the ground is going to be your final resting place. I'd love to shoot you right between the eyes for what you did to Hoagie and Marie."

"I ain't done nuttin to 'em."

"Get up and start walking toward that gate you've been using."

Snake could see well enough to see the pistol Dex was pointing toward him. He struggled to his feet, and while still coughing and rubbing his eyes, he started making his way through the thick underbrush toward the gate.

They had only gone about twenty-five yards when Dex got his foot tangled in a honeysuckle vine and fell. He dropped the pistol to catch himself, and when he tried to get back on his feet, he got even more tangled in the thick vines. Snake started running through the brush as soon as he saw Dex fall. Dex couldn't immediately locate the black pistol in the heavy dark vines and saw that Snake was getting away. He got to his feet and started chasing him. He went through the gate about twenty feet behind Snake but caught up to him about halfway across the lawn behind the houses. He left his feet and executed a perfect open field tackle on the lanky felon.

Snake came up swinging, but his fighting skills hadn't improved since that schoolyard fight so many years before. Dex easily overpowered him and ended up sitting on his chest beating his face to a pulp. When Snake stopped fighting back, he realized that he was unconscious. With all of his willpower, Dex stopped pounding him.

Snake's face was a bloody mess, and he was still unconscious when Dex stood up and pulled his cell phone out of his pocket. He dialed Detective Morgan.

"Morgan, I've captured Snake Wilson. He's unconscious and lying on the ground at my feet right now."

"Don't tell me you've killed him?"

"No, he isn't dead, but he needs an ambulance."

Dex gave Morgan directions, and the detective said he could be there in fifteen minutes. He also said he would notify the city police and call an ambulance. Snake was still unconscious, and he folded up like an accordion when Dex lifted him by his belt. He dragged him all the way to the street with his head bumping along the ground. He could have carried him, but Dex didn't think Snake deserved the extra effort. Snake was still only semiconscious when Morgan and the ambulance arrived, just ahead of two city police cars. One eye was already swollen completely closed and he had several cuts on his face. From the distorted appearance of his long nose, Dex assumed it was broken. Snake was loaded into the ambulance, and one of the city cops rode in the ambulance with him.

After the ambulance left, Morgan turned to Dex and asked, "Do I want to know how you found him?"

"No, you really don't want to know. Just assume that I came onto some information that wasn't available to you. I didn't have time to contact you, so I went after him myself to keep him from getting away."

Morgan smiled and said, "Dex, is that really what happened?"

"No, but it's close enough to the truth to keep me from being charged with perjury."

The city cop asked him a few question and then said, "We'll have to get a detailed statement from you tomorrow. Can you come by the station tomorrow morning about ten?"

Dex agreed to meet him the following morning, and when he got in his car, the first thing he did was call Marie.

"Don't ask me any questions, but meet me at your apartment. I'll be there in fifteen minutes."

He disconnected the call before she could question him. He drove directly to her apartment, but she had arrived before him. When she opened the door and saw he was covered in blood, the anger that had been building since they last talked immediately melted.

Her nursing instinct kicked in. She pulled him into the room and started an initial triage procedure. He said over and over, "It's not my blood." Most of it was not his, but the knuckles on both hands were raw and still oozing blood.

"Marie, I got him. He's in the hospital and under arrest."

"Thank God he's been caught and you didn't get killed."

As she dressed the abrasions on his hands and cleaned the splattered blood off his face and arms, Dex told her the story of how he had finally captured Snake. He winced each time she touched his right hand, and she told him he might have fractured it and would need to have it X-rayed. After she finished bandaging his hands, they held each other for a long time. They had been worried for so long that they didn't even know how to act or what to do now that it was apparently all over.

"Marie, maybe now we can begin to live a normal life. I'm sorry for everything you've had to go through because of me. If it takes forever, I swear I'm going to make it up to you."

"Oh, Dex, you don't owe me anything but to love me. I was just so scared when I thought about you going after Snake; I was sick to my stomach all night. Please don't ever take a chance like that again because I need you in one piece."

Chapter 51

S nake was released from the hospital the next morning. The media either anticipated his release or got a tip from someone on the staff about when he would be transferred from the hospital to the jail. They were camped out waiting for the opportunity for photos or maybe even an answer to a shouted question. Overnight, the news had leaked out that Snake had taken a terrible beating from Dex and his face was really messed up. When he was rolled out in a wheelchair, he was handcuffed and had leg irons. While Snake was being transferred to the waiting police car, the photographers got several shots of his swollen and lacerated face. Both eyes were almost swollen shut.

Photos of Snake's face appeared on the front page of the newspaper that evening, and a film clip of him leaving the hospital provided the lead story for the local telecast. In the film clip, a TV reporter was heard yelling a question at Snake while he was surrounded by police officers.

"Why did you kill Hogan and kidnap Ms. Murphy?"

The policeman pushing the wheelchair tried to turn Snake away from the reporter, but he yelled back over his shoulder. "I ain't kilt Hoagie, and I ain't took Marie. The cops done got the wrong man."

The newspaper that day raised the first questions about his guilt. The reporter wrote that the police claimed to have conclusive evidence that Snake had been the one who shot Dex, but an unnamed source in the department had admitted that the evidence was only circumstantial that he had committed the other crimes. It was also reported that Snake continued to insist he was innocent of the murder and abduction. Dex and the police were sure he was lying, but they didn't yet have the proof to back up their assumption.

Dex turned down an offer from a national magazine for a story on the ordeal. He did, however, talk to the local newspaper and television stations. He was well aware that the police were not at all happy with him because he had not only gone after Snake with no authority to do so, but he had also made them look incompetent. He needed to make amends.

In the several interviews he carefully complimented the police and especially praised the untiring efforts of county homicide detective Lester Morgan. He explained that he just happened to come across some information that was not available to the police and he had to act quickly to prevent Snake from escaping. He refused to reveal the source or the nature of the information that led to the capture.

In each interview the reporters questioned Dex about Snake's motive. Every time the question was raised, he gave the same answer: "Mr. Wilson and I had an altercation in high school. Apparently he has never gotten over a schoolboy fight that I had forgotten about long ago. I want to emphasize that neither Mr. Hogan, who was killed, or Ms. Murphy, who was abducted, were his intended targets. He simply used them as a way to get to me. That's a burden that I'll have to carry with me for the rest of my life."

When one of the reporters remarked about the condition of Snake's face, Dex took the opportunity to say, "Yeah, he looked pretty bad. I hope they have a lot of EaseFast at the jail. He needs some really fast pain relief."

Surprisingly, the television station left the remark in the broadcast, which forced them to then have to explain the relationship between Dex and EaseFast.

Snake was arraigned two days later. The arraignment was announced on TV and in the newspaper, so the curious local citizens turned out in droves to pack the courtroom for the arraignment. The murder and mayhem allegedly committed by Buford "Snake" Wilson was River City's most widely covered news event of the decade.

Dex and Marie had not planned to attend the arraignment, but the prosecutor asked them to be there. He thought the psychological shock of Snake seeing them together might provoke an outburst that could potentially help the prosecution. Although courtroom seats could technically not be reserved, the prosecutor had two of his office workers sit on the front row until Dex and Marie arrived and then surrender their seats to them.

Snake, in leg irons and an orange prison jumpsuit, shuffled into court led by a deputy. His hands were manacled behind his back. He was met at the defense table by a young, court-appointed attorney with a "Why me?" look on his face.

Just before he sat down, Snake saw Dex and Marie sitting in the first row, smiling at him. Most people would have the intelligence to realize they were being baited and would at least try to mask their raw emotions, but Snake wasn't smart enough to conceal anything. His bruised and battered face contorted into an animalistic snarl. His intense hatred of the couple was clearly evident to everyone in the room, including his young attorney, who was powerless to prevent Snake's reaction. He launched into a diatribe that contained enough admissions to convict him on the spot.

"I ain't bout quit with youens. I ain't gonna miss agin. You'ens is both deader'n hell iffen I's get outta here."

Two deputies finally forced the enraged defendant into his seat. His attorney whispered in his ear, "If you don't shut up, the judge will gag you. I can't defend you when you threaten to kill two people in front of a room full of witnesses."

The prosecutor was sitting at the adjacent table trying unsuccessfully to suppress a smile. His tactic had worked beautifully. He had notified the court reporter to be ready because he expected an outburst from the defendant, and he wanted a transcript of exactly what was said even before the court convened.

The defense attorney and the deputies managed to get Snake partially settled down by the time the presiding judge entered the chamber. His attorney warned him not to say anything else and not to turn around until the arraignment was over.

The charges were read to the court. Snake was charged with capital murder in the first degree, aggravated kidnapping, attempted murder, and grand theft auto. They had discovered that the car he had been driving was stolen in addition to the Lexus he had wrecked.

When the judge asked for a plea, Snake stood silently. His attorney said, "Mr. Wilson pleads not guilty, your honor."

"Well, that's interesting, Mr. Levi, but I would like to hear a plea from your client after the disturbance I understand he caused in my courtroom."

When a nudge in his side elicited no response, the attorney whispered in his ear, and Snake said, "I's ain't kilt nobody, but I wish I's had kilt Dex Martin."

Bail was denied and the trial was set to begin in two months. Snake was led from the courtroom, but not before he turned, glared at Dex and Marie, and said, "You'ens don't ferget what I tole you."

The threat sounded ominous coming from this manacled creep, but with the evidence against him, there was little chance he would ever again be free to carry out his threat. Marie knew she would have to see him again when she testified, but she was going to enjoy helping to convict the animal that killed her friend and almost killed Dex.

Marie and Dex walked out of the courtroom hand in hand, feeling safer than they had at any time since their ordeal with this madman had begun. They were now ready to put it all behind them and get on with their life together.

The reporters were waiting at the courthouse steps, but this time the couple declined an interview. Dex said, "Guys, this story is over as far as we're concerned, and we will not be making any further comments to the media. We appreciate you staying involved in the story until Wilson was captured. Your diligence helped keep the pressure on him and no doubt contributed to his final capture. Thank you very much."

As they walked away, Marie smiled and said, "I thought you weren't going to make a statement. I think you miss the spotlight already." Dex started to pat her on the butt and then realized the reporters were still watching.

Chapter 52

In the first few weeks after Snake's capture and arraignment, Dex was like a recovering heart attack victim. He kept waiting for the next event.

Dex and Marie's relationship had unfurled on the River City stage like a star-crossed Shakespearean tragedy. It had begun with Dex's career-ending injury and desperate search for a new life outside athletics. As soon as that crisis had passed, they almost immediately faced the tragedy of Hoagie's murder and the agony of Marie's captivity. Then just when they thought their troubles couldn't possibly get worse, Dex was shot and almost killed.

That this many tragedies could happen to one couple was almost unimaginable. But if one was searching for a silver lining in the dark cloud, perhaps it would be that things couldn't possibly ever again be as bad as what they had already endured. If their love survived this kind of rocky beginning, it could probably survive any curve ball that life might later toss their way.

Marie's nursing business had benefitted from all the publicity, and she had gotten behind on her paperwork. She told Dex that she was going to have to work overtime for several days to get caught up. For the next few days she arrived at the office early, ate lunch and dinner at her desk, only left for scheduled appointments, and didn't close the office before midnight. On the third day of her exhausting self-imposed schedule, Marie had been sitting at her desk so long that the words on the computer screen were beginning to blur. She had dozed off twice with her fingers still on the keyboard. When her eyes popped open moments later, there was a jumble of letters stretching across the page. That was the final sign that she had been there too long.

Marie turned off the computer, stood up for the first time in two hours, picked up her purse, and left the office. Her apartment was only a few minutes away, but she had driven today although she often walked to work if she had no out-of-office appointments for the day. Dex was watching a late football game on television so she knew that he would still be awake at midnight. She hit his speed-dial number on her cell phone during the short drive home and was still talking to him when she parked at her apartment. She had the phone to her ear when she stepped out of the car and saw Dr. Bill Bishop standing a few feet away.

She whispered into the phone, "Dex, Bill Bishop is here outside my apartment, and he's got a pistol."

Bishop said, "Turn off the cell phone, Marie."

She made the motion as if she was turning off the phone but wisely didn't do so.

"Bill, what are you doing with a gun, and what do you want?"

"I just want to talk to you, and you won't sit still long enough if I don't have some way to force you to listen to me."

"So talk; I'm listening."

"No, we're not going to talk here. You were probably talking to that damn Dex, and he'll no doubt be here in a few minutes."

"Well, I'm not getting into a car with you, so you'll just have to shoot me."

"Marie, don't make this more difficult than it has to be; just get in the car. I don't want to hurt you. I just want you to come to your senses before your silly schoolgirl crush leads you into the mistake of your life with a do-nothing jock."

Dex was still listening to her conversation with Bishop since she had not disconnected the call. He grabbed the pistol and the box of shells as he ran out the door to his car. He realized Marie was trying to stall Bishop to give him time to get there. He could be at her apartment in less than ten minutes.

Dex knew that Bishop didn't realize that Marie had not disconnected the cell phone call, so he tried not to make any noise that might alert him. He pressed his phone tight against his chest to block the sound as he opened and closed the car door and started the motor.

"Marie, we can take your car and you can drive, but if you don't get in it right now, I'm going to be forced to hit you in the head again."

"Again? You mean you were the one who knocked me out and killed Hoagie?"

"I didn't intend to kill him; it was an accident. I was just trying to get him out of the way."

"No, Bill, an accident is when something unexpected happens. You deliberately hit him in the head, and that's called murder."

"I told you, I didn't mean to do it."

Marie sarcastically replied, "Well, I'm sure it would be okay with his mother as long as you didn't intend to do it."

Bishop raised the pistol over his head as if he was going to strike her with it, and Marie said, "Okay, I'll drive my car, but we're not going out of the city limits, and I'm not going to go inside any building with you. You kept me locked up in the cabin for days, and I'd rather you just shoot me now than to chain me up again."

They both got in Marie's car with her behind the wheel. She laid the cell phone in her lap.

Bishop said, "I had no choice but to keep you in the cabin. You were hysterical, yelling, and cursing at me. I wasn't going to try to talk to you until you calmed down. You are getting mixed up with someone who doesn't deserve you and could never support you the way I can. I just wanted to make you understand that."

The cell phone was still in Marie's lap, and Bishop was not paying any attention to it. Dex was now in his car, speeding toward the apartment.

Marie asked, "Where do you want me to go?"

"I don't care, just drive around town while we talk."

"Okay. I'm going to take Andrews Parkway downtown, turn north onto Battleground, and at the dead end I'll double back down Main Street. That should give you plenty of time to say whatever it is you want to say."

Surprisingly, Bishop didn't pick up on the way she so carefully detailed the route she planned to follow. Dex understood why she was doing it and immediately turned right and cut diagonally across town. From the directions Marie had given, he knew that he would have time to intercept them on Battleground.

Dex reached the intersection of Battleground and Oak Street and waited at the intersection until Marie's car passed. The pause gave him the opportunity to load the pistol and cram his pockets full of shells. When her car passed through the intersection, he slowly pulled out and started following about one hundred yards behind it. When Marie turned onto Main, he took a chance and flashed his lights twice. He figured it would get her attention in the rearview mirror and not be noticed by Bishop, who was sitting in the passenger's seat.

Unfortunately, Bishop was turned toward Marie and saw the flashing lights. He glanced quickly at Marie and saw her looking in the rearview mirror.

He said, "What was that?"

"What are you talking about?"

"You know what I'm talking about. I saw you looking at the flashing lights. That's your boyfriend, isn't it?"

"I don't know what you're talking about."

"Yes, you do, and if you don't speed up and lose him, both of you are going to be sorry."

Marie was worried about Dex; she had no way of knowing that he was also armed. She increased her speed, and Bishop told her to get out of town and onto a highway. She turned north onto the highway leading to the next town, and he told her to speed up to about seventy miles per hour. She saw Dex also make the turn and continue to follow them.

Bishop had removed his seat belt and turned in the seat so he could watch the car following them. They were outside the city now, and Marie suddenly stepped on the brakes and swerved off the road into a sage field. The bump crossing the shallow ditch between the road and field caused Bishop to bang his head on the roof and drop the pistol in the floorboard. As soon as the car stopped, Marie bolted out the door and within a few steps was running at full speed.

When Bishop regained his equilibrium, he located the pistol in the floorboard and started after her. In the meantime, Dex had stopped and was getting out of his car. To distract Bishop and give Marie more time to get away, he fired a round toward him. Bishop was running after Marie, but he turned and shot back in the general direction of Dex's car. A half-moon was the only light available so there wasn't much danger in either of their shots doing any damage.

Dex could still see Marie running in the distance, and he was afraid to shoot again for fear of hitting her. Bishop was about twenty yards behind her when Dex saw her stumble and fall. Bishop was on her before she had a chance to get to her feet again. They both disappeared below the top of the four-foot-high sage.

Dex couldn't shoot for fear of hitting Marie, and if he got any closer he would be an easy target for Bishop. He yelled, "Are you okay, Marie?"

"I'm okay, but—"

Whatever she was about to say was garbled. Bishop had obviously put his hand over her mouth.

"Martin, I've got a gun to her head. I don't want to hurt her, but I will if you don't stand up and drop your gun right now."

"How do I know you won't shoot me and her as soon as I'm unarmed?"

"I don't want to hurt Marie, and I don't have a problem with you as long as you stay out of the way and don't try to keep us from leaving."

Dex thought about the dark and how Bishop was so far away; the chance of getting shot if he stood up was pretty slim. He decided to do it while he tried to figure out some way to end the stand-off.

"Okay, Bishop, I'm going to stand up and drop the pistol."

He slowly stood and dropped the pistol at his feet. He wouldn't have been surprised if Bishop had taken a wild shot in his direction. Fortunately, Bishop did not fire his pistol.

Bishop said, "We're going to get up now, but remember that I'm still holding the pistol to her head. Don't try anything funny if you don't want her hurt."

Dex saw them stand up, and they were not as far away as he had estimated. It was dark but he could see enough by moonlight to see that Bishop had his left arm around Marie's shoulder and was pressing the pistol against her head with his right hand and arm. They started walking slowly toward Dex. They had to pass him to get back to the cars. If they continued on their present path, when they passed Dex, Marie would be between him and Bishop.

Bishop said, "I'm going to have to borrow your car. Marie's is probably bogged down in this field. Give me your keys."

"I don't have the keys. They're probably still in the car. Bishop, why can't we just work something out? Marie obviously doesn't want to go with you, so why don't you just take my car and go? You could be a long way from here before we could walk to get help."

"Marie doesn't know what she wants. She's got a silly schoolgirl crush on you. As soon as she gets out from under your influence, she'll realize what a mistake she was about to make. I'm not leaving here without her, so just shut up and stay out of the way."

Bishop was leading Marie around Dex, making sure there was about a ten-foot separation as they passed him. Marie hadn't said anything during their verbal exchange, but she was afraid Dex was going to try to be a hero.

"Dex, don't do anything. He's crazy enough to shoot you. Just let us go and maybe he'll come to his senses and release me."

Dex didn't see any way to stop Bishop without endangering Marie, so he let them walk past him and on toward his car on the road. Marie's car was in the field only about twenty yards from where Dex was standing, but he didn't know if it could be moved out of the field.

Dex watched as Marie and Bishop got into his car. Marie was in the driver's seat, and she made a U-turn and headed back toward River City. It was also toward the Georgia state line. Dex figured Bishop intended to pass through the city and on to Georgia where he was more familiar with the area.

As soon as they started his car, Dex picked up his pistol and ran to where Marie's car was sitting in the field. He found the keys still in the ignition and held his breath as he started the car and put it in gear. Fortunately it wasn't stuck. It started moving forward, but he wasn't sure if he could get up enough speed to jump the shallow ditch and get back on the highway. Then he spotted an entrance on his left that tractors obviously used to get in and out of the field. He took that exit onto the highway and turned in the direction Bishop had taken.

Dex floored it and was quickly traveling well above the posted speed limit. In a few minutes he saw the tail lights of their car in the distance. He was steadily catching up when he suddenly remembered that his car was almost out of gas. He had thought he was going to run out while he was following them out of town. He knew they were not going to get very far before running out of gas, so he slowed down and was content to follow them as long as he could still see their tail lights.

Bishop and Marie were just inside the city limits when the car drifted to a stop. As Dex was getting closer, he saw Bishop get out of the car and walk around to the driver's side. He pulled Marie out and they started walking away from the car. Dex stopped about half a block behind the car and got out. The area was well lit with streetlights, and he was sure they had seen him.

Bishop was carrying the pistol down at his side, probably so a passerby would not notice it. Dex suddenly saw Marie pivot her body and slam her elbow back into Bishop's face. He dropped to his knees, and Marie started running toward Dex. Bishop was dazed and it took him a moment to realize what had happened. Marie was now barefooted and running full speed but was caught in the open, halfway between Dex and Bishop. Dex couldn't shoot toward Bishop without taking a chance of hitting Marie.

Dex yelled, "Run to your right," just as Bishop fired his pistol. Marie wasn't hit, and Dex heard the bullet hit something metal behind him. He didn't know if Bishop was trying to hit him or Marie, but he quickly fired two rounds directly at Bishop.

Marie reached Dex, and he yelled, "Take cover, Marie." She continued by him as she ran toward where Dex had left her car.

Dex saw Bishop stumble and knew he'd been hit, but he was back on his knees and shooting again in Dex's direction. Dex was in the open so Bishop wasn't a very good shot. Dex ran to the side of the road and knelt behind a telephone pole. He took time to aim carefully, and when he fired this time, Bishop straightened up and then fell forward on his face. When he didn't move for several minutes, Dex stood and walked slowly up to where he was laying in the street. He knelt beside him and felt for a pulse. There wasn't one.

Marie ran to where he was standing over Bishop's body and said, "I found my cell phone in the car and called 9-1-1. The police should be here in a minute."

"Marie, are you okay?"

"I'm fine, Dex. You weren't hit, were you?"

He shook his head and they began to hear sirens coming from both directions. Two police cars arrived at about the same time. Both cops got out of their cruisers and knelt behind the doors. One of them yelled for him to put the pistol down. Dex did as he was told and raised his hands over his head. The officers walked to him with their guns drawn and pointed at him.

"Officer, my name is Dex Martin, and this is Marie Murphy. I hope you've read the newspaper lately and know what has been happening to us. The man I just shot is Dr. Bill Bishop. He killed my friend and abducted Marie. He took her again tonight and was holding her at gunpoint while he tried to kill me."

"Martin, I know who you are and all about what has been happening, but I need to see some identification from both of you. Remove your wallet with your left hand and pass it to me."

Marie said, "Officer, my purse is in my car. That's it parked in the middle of the street."

The officers checked both of their identifications and then holstered their pistols. An ambulance arrived, Bishop's body was placed in it, and it left the scene.

One of the officers said, "We're going to need complete statements from both of you. Please follow us to the station and we can get started. We'll have the area canvassed by a crime scene unit."

Dex said, "May I call Detective Lester Morgan of the county police and have him meet us at the station? He's the one who has been investigating the murder and abduction. I've got his number stored in my cell phone."

The officer agreed and Dex called Morgan and briefly told him what had happened. Morgan said he would meet them at the station. They spent several hours talking with the city police, and Morgan was there to support everything they said about what had happened in the past.

Chapter 53

Over the next few months things returned to normal, or at least as normal as possible for individuals who had reluctantly been in the public spotlight for months. Dex and Marie were recognized everywhere they went and had grown accustomed to the stares and whispers. They had reached the point where they were no longer offended by personal questions posed by strangers. They understood that people thought they knew them just because they had followed their story so closely in the media.

Marie's business continued to grow exponentially. She no longer handled patients herself but still tried to spend some time each week visiting with a few. She regularly visited the nursing homes to check on patients and evaluate the facilities for future patient referrals. The reputable nursing homes welcomed her visits and regularly sought her opinion on elder care.

Marie knew she received more credit than she was due but was happy with the way the publicity had helped her business. She was now established as a local authority on eldercare, and the media regularly quoted her on the subject. She was also overwhelmed with local speaking engagements.

Dex's career was also going well. EaseFast was now firmly established in the marketplace, and he had received a bonus and substantial salary increase. His travel schedule eased off considerably after the initial sales blitz and he was able to spend more time with Marie in River City.

Marie testified in the fraud trial of Norton and McPherson. They were both convicted and confined to the state prison. A date had been set for Snake's trial, and Dex and Marie were both scheduled to testify.

Marie was told she would be the key witness, but Dex could only testify to the possible motive related to their schoolyard fight and his role in Snake's capture. He didn't recall anything about being shot until he woke up in the hospital after surgery. The prosecution had dropped the first-degree murder and kidnapping charges against Snake, but he was still charged with attempted murder and auto theft. He had escaped an almost-certain death decree when it was discovered that Dr. Bill Bishop had murdered Hoagie and abducted Marie.

The district attorney was planning to run for congress and didn't want to take a chance in the high-profile case against Snake. He did what DA's with political ambitions often do: he copped out and let Snake plead guilty to lesser charges in exchange for a shorter sentence. He would still spend many years behind bars for shooting Dex.

Dex didn't get a vote on Snake's fate, but his primary goal had always been to prevent him from having any chance to hurt Marie. He had exacted his personal revenge by beating him to within an inch of his worthless life. He was content that Snake would be locked away for years and that Marie was finally safe.

Dex thought it was time for a special celebration.

"Marie, let's host a party this weekend. This will be a good chance for me to spend some of my first bonus. I'm going to spring for a celebration at the Harbor Light. We can invite your mother and father, Gigi, Coach and Mrs. Delaney, and Jim and Andrea. What do you think?"

Marie was counting the people on her fingers. "Dex, counting us, that's nine people. How much of that bonus do you want to spend?"

"I don't care if we blow it all. This is an occasion that we have waited a long time to celebrate."

Dex and Marie invited all of their guests to meet in the restaurant bar before dinner. As the guests arrived, Dex introduced those who had not met.

Jim Mitchell offered a toast. "Our lives were blessed the day we met Dex and Marie. They both mean so much to us, and we are happy that their long ordeal is finally over. Let's drink to their future happiness together."

After they were seated, Dex ordered wine and the group talked for a long time before ordering their entrees. Five waiters brought the covered plates to their table. The last waiter in line set his plate in front of Marie. The domes were lifted from the plates one at a time, and Marie's was the last one to be raised. When the waiter lifted it, there was no entrée. Sitting in the middle of her plate was an opened velvet box with a sparkling diamond engagement ring.

The collective gasps were loud enough for patrons at other tables to look around. When Marie finally took her eyes off the ring, Dex was on one knee beside her.

"Marie, you're the love of my life, and I can't imagine spending the next fifty years without you by my side. Will you marry me?"

When she said yes, tears started to slide down her cheeks and the entire restaurant erupted in applause. A photographer appeared from somewhere and flashes illuminated the group at the table.

Marie stood, pulled Dex up beside her, and said again, "Yes, yes, yes." She smothered his face with kisses as they embraced. When the embrace lasted for what was probably much longer than was appropriate, the people started applauding again. The excitement of the moment made Marie forget their happiness was being shared with a restaurant full of strangers. It was the first time Dex ever saw her blush.

Dex had been planning to propose for a long time, but he wanted to make it a very special occasion. He told everyone at the table that he had wanted their families and best friends to share this special occasion with them.

He had been looking at rings for weeks but made the final selection only a few hours before the dinner. He had driven to the restaurant directly from the jewelry shop, dropped off the ring, and told the manager what he wanted to do. The manager set it up and even arranged for the photographer.

Everyone at the table was standing now. Gigi and Marie's mother were embracing, and Andrea grabbed Marie as soon as Dex turned her loose. Jim Mitchell ordered a bottle of champagne, and they all drank another toast.

On the way home after the party, Dex watched Marie out of the corner of his eye. She was holding up her left hand and twisting it slowly so the headlights of the car behind them reflected off her new engagement ring. He watched her for a few minutes before she noticed him looking and smiled at him. He couldn't believe that he was going to be lucky enough to spend the rest of his life with her.

Marie was silent for a few minutes, and her expression was the one she always had when she was in deep thought. She finally said something that made him almost run off the road. "Dex, as soon as we are married I want to start making babies right away."

"Whoa, where did that come from?" There had never been any discussions about babies; children had never even crossed his mind.

"Marie, you did say babies, as in plural. Meaning more than one?"

"Actually I was thinking about four." She was smiling as she snuggled up next to him and kissed him on the cheek.